# MIRROR, MIRROR

Verity had only to look in the mirror to see how foolish her romantic dreams of Lord Sherington were.

Her modest dress and slight figure could not compete with the gorgeous garb and flame-haired sensuality of the woman who had been pointed out as Sherington's current mistress.

Her humble position in her sister's household was a world below that of her sister's social butterfly of a daughter, who had so skillfully set her cap and was working her wiles to hook the catch of the marriage mart.

But what use was the truth that the mirror told when she looked into Sherington's mocking eyes—knowing, as everyone did, that the wife he would choose would be a beauty fresh from the schoolroom. . . .

# FALLEN ANGEL

*by*

*Charlotte Louise Dolan*

A SIGNET BOOK

SIGNET
Published by the Penguin Group
Penguin Books USA Inc., 375 Hudson Street,
New York, New York 10014, U.S.A.
Penguin Books Ltd, 27 Wrights Lane,
London W8 5TZ, England
Penguin Books Australia Ltd, Ringwood,
Victoria, Australia
Penguin Books Canada Ltd, 10 Alcorn Avenue,
Toronto, Ontario, Canada M4V 3B2
Penguin Books (N.Z.) Ltd, 182–190 Wairau Road,
Auckland 10, New Zealand

Penguin Books Ltd, Registered Offices:
Harmondsworth, Middlesex, England

First published by Signet, an imprint of New American Library,
a division of Penguin Books USA Inc.

First Printing, February, 1993
10  9  8  7  6  5  4  3  2  1

This book is dedicated to my agent,
Ruth Cohen,
who had faith in me
through all the years I was
learning to write.

# 1

ON A COLD, drizzly morning in mid-December, Gabriel Rainsford, Lord Sherington, was comfortably ensconced in the study of his London residence. Rereading the latest correspondence from his agent in Calcutta, he considered the merits of investing in additional property in India.

His ruminations on the potential benefits of outright purchase versus long-term lease were interrupted by Kirkson, his butler, who entered the library and informed him that Lady Ottillia Cudmore wished to speak with him.

Mildly surprised to hear that his aunt was calling at such an unfashionable hour, Gabriel said, "Put her in the rose salon, and tell her I shall join her as soon as possible." Then his thoughts returned to his business affairs in India, which were complicated enough to demand his complete attention.

Three-quarters of an hour later, he entered the rose salon to find his aunt positively seething with indignation. Since that was her normal condition whenever she was near him, he did not bother to apologize for making her wait.

"Would you like some brandy, Aunt Cudmore?" he asked politely, pouring himself a stout measure, then moving to lean negligently against the mantel.

"Certainly not," she snapped. "In the first place I do not indulge in strong spirits, and in the second place I did not come here to socialize." Her more than ample bosom was heaving with emotion, and the long, underslung Rainsford jaw was jutting out even farther than

7

usual, making her resemble nothing so much as a pugnacious bulldog.

"Forgive me, Aunt, but I am still at a loss as to why you are here."

"I have come," she said, making a grotesque effort to smile at him, "to offer you my assistance."

"I was not aware that I stood in need of your assistance," he replied.

"Well, you certainly cannot be expected to handle everything that must be done. Why, Christmas is only a week away, and it would appear that you have not even sent out the invitations yet. I suppose you have assumed that all the relatives know who is to come for a week and who for a full month, but it is still only good manners to send out proper invitations. They must be written out in good copperplate, too, you know, because if a thing is to be done at all it must be done properly."

"Are you sure you do not touch strong spirits, Aunt Cudmore? You seem remarkably bosky to me. Since I entered this room, not a word you have uttered makes the slightest sense."

"I am talking about Christmas at Sherington Close," his aunt said, giving him a withering glare. "I am here to help you make plans for the holidays, for despite your lack of proper education, you must know that entertaining upward of fifty people is not a matter to be undertaken lightly."

"Indeed, Aunt, I do not plan to undertake it at all."

"I do not follow your meaning," she said, her expression one of total bewilderment, whether real or feigned he could not determine. Not that it mattered to him one way or another; his mind was already made up.

"Then I shall speak more plainly. I do not intend to invite fifty relatives to spend Christmas at Sherington Close, nor do I intend to invite ten, nor even one. In short, you may all of you make other plans for the holidays."

"But—but—but, this is preposterous!" she said, struggling to her feet. "You know perfectly well that it is a custom of long standing for all the Rainsford family to spend Christmas at Sherington Close. How dare you even consider breaking with tradition! It is not to be thought of!"

Gabriel was completely unmoved by her histrionics. "Now that is patently false. The entire family has not always gathered at Sherington Close. Need I remind you that I am one of the family—indeed, due to circumstances beyond my father's control, I am now head of the family. And I have not spent Christmas at Sherington Close since I was eight and my father sent me off to sea."

His aunt came nearer and glared up at him. "You are *not* one of the family, and my brother, the late earl, was not your father."

For the first time she captured his interest. "Pray explain yourself, madam."

"Your mother played my brother false, and you are the result of her adulterous liaison. Heaven only knows who your father was, because so abandoned was she to virtue, I doubt she even knew which of her lovers fathered her son."

If she expected to see him taken aback or even cast into despair by her words—and indeed her expression indicated she thought she had dealt him a mortal blow— she was doomed to be severely disappointed. "That no doubt explains why I was not blessed with the Rainsford jaw," was all he said, and the amusement in his voice only served to increase her rage.

"As dark as you are, I should not be at all surprised if her lover was some groom or a common seaman on shore leave," his aunt said. "Your mother had not a shred of good taste when it came to such matters."

"Ah," he said, raising his eyebrows in mock astonishment, as if a great light had suddenly dawned, "so that is why she accepted your brother's offer. Indeed, I have always wondered why she chose to marry into such a havey-cavey family, but if she had remarkably bad taste in men that would explain it."

His aunt—or rather, his legal father's sister—was turning an alarming shade of red, quite like a boiler being stoked with too much wood. "You are nothing more than a bastard," she screeched up at him, "and you have no moral right to call yourself Lord Sherington."

Feeling not the least bit insulted, he smiled down at her, which only made her face redden even more. "But under the laws of England," he pointed out, "I am the seventh Earl of Sherington, and setting aside questions of morality, I am the legal owner of Sherington Close, and there is nothing you can do or say to alter that, even if you yourself had been an eyewitness to my mother's adultery and were willing to appear before the court and describe my conception in explicit detail."

"You, sirrah," she said, waving a finger in his face, "are no gentleman to speak so to a lady. I cannot think where you learned your manners."

"Why, at sea, Aunt Cudmore, at sea. On board ship one has no time for pretty compliments and clever dissembling, which is what passes for manners ashore. You must keep in mind that I did not attend Eton and Oxford like my brother did. And in the merchant marines, the penalty for failing to learn a lesson properly is a watery grave."

For a moment his aunt was silent, glaring up at him. Then she spoke slowly and distinctly, emphasizing every word as if she were uttering a curse. "It is downright wicked that you are still alive and your brother is in his grave. He would have spared no expense entertaining the entire family this Christmas, whereas you are completely heartless—no, your heart is as black as Lucifer's, and so you should have been named, for you are the devil's spawn. I cannot think what my brother was about to allow your mother to name you Gabriel, for there is nothing saintly or angelic about your character. You are arrogant, rude, and selfish beyond measure, and I am amazed that you are accepted by the *ton*."

"Have you forgotten that due to my own efforts I am also disgustingly rich? I have found that money can make the most execrable manners tolerable, even among the *ton*."

"Bah! You are nothing more than an adventurer—a pirate—a *tradesman*." She said the last word with absolute loathing.

"How short your memory is, Aunt Cudmore. Must I keep reminding you that I am also the seventh Earl of Sherington? You will find that such an old and respected title allows even the highest stickler to overlook the fact that I am in trade."

She was gathering herself for another attack when reinforcements arrived in the person of Phillip Rainsford, Gabriel's cousin and legal heir. There could be no doubt as to Phillip's paternity, because although he had not inherited the title, he *had* inherited the Rainsford jaw in full measure.

"Before you likewise attempt to convince me that it is my moral duty to entertain the entire Rainsford clan at Sherington Close this Christmas, let me tell you that my mind is quite made up," Gabriel said as soon as the butler left them alone.

Gabriel's words were not without effect, but with visible effort, Phillip managed to maintain a surprising degree of equanimity.

"You need not bait me, cousin. I should not presume to dictate to you whom you should or should not invite for the holidays," he said with no real conviction. "I have other, more important matters to discuss with you."

"Indeed," Gabriel said, "I am all aflutter to know what has driven you to the desperate extreme of seeking me out before noon."

His voice trembling with barely suppressed emotion, Phillip said, "I have just heard the most preposterous rumor—you will doubtless laugh when you hear it." He paused, but when Gabriel merely waited silently, he continued. "It is being bruited about London that you have not yet paid off the mortgages on Sherington Close. Astonishing, is it not, what petty-minded people will say?"

Lady Ottillia gave a shriek and fell backward onto the settee. "No, no, even you would not be such a villain!"

Phillip hurried to her side and began patting her hand. "Rest assured, Aunt, it is without doubt all a scurrilous lie. Whatever his faults, I am sure my cousin is mindful of his duty to the name of Rainsford, and besides, everyone knows he is a veritable nabob. Really, I cannot think why I even listened to the rumors in the first place."

Looking at the pair of them, Gabriel felt no small measure of satisfaction that he was not related to either of them by blood. No matter what future pleasures life might bring him, his aunt's revelations would make this day remain golden in his memory forever.

"You *have* redeemed the mortgages, have you not?" Phillip asked point-blank.

Two pairs of eyes stared at him with ill-concealed hostility. After a short but tense silence, Gabriel said quite calmly, "Actually, I have not yet gotten around to it."

Phillip started to say something, but Gabriel forestalled him. "Nor do I intend to pay them off so long as you are my heir. I see no reason to spend my hard-earned brass to increase your future holdings."

"But—but, this is unthinkable!" Phillip said, the color draining from his face. "You cannot be serious."

"You will find I do not lie about such things," Gabriel said. "Nor can I be persuaded to change my mind. Until and unless I marry and have a son, I shall not pay off the mortgages."

His aunt abruptly found her voice. "You, marry? That is totally preposterous. No lady with a shred of decency about her would accept a mongrel like you for a husband, no matter how rich you are."

"Now, there you have confirmed what I have long believed," Gabriel said with a smile. "Since all the well-bred women I have met in London are throwing themselves at my feet, I can only assume that despite their titles and their lineages, which are for the most part impeccable, they are all courtesans at heart."

"You are the most insulting, most obnoxious, most repugnant man it has ever been my misfortune to meet," Lady Ottillia said vehemently. "And I shall pray every day that you may die without a son, because the title must and shall revert to a true Rainsford."

"Come along, dearest Aunt," Phillip said. "It is clear that we are wasting our time talking to such an underbred oaf."

Clutching his arm, Lady Ottillia allowed him to escort her out of the room. Gabriel could hear her out in the corridor tearfully complaining, "You must do something,

Phillip. He does not mean to allow the family to use Sherington Close during the holidays. It will not seem a proper Christmas if we cannot celebrate it together."

Returning to his study, Gabriel found himself unable to pay proper attention to the business at hand. Lady Ottillia's earlier revelations about his parentage kept distracting him and interfering with his concentration. Finally he laid aside the balance sheet he was inspecting and allowed himself to consider what he had learned about his ancestry.

As a child, discovering he was a bastard—even if the laws of England declared him to be the legal offspring of his mother's husband—would doubtless have caused him great mental anguish, which would have made it even more difficult to endure the unremitting physical misery he had suffered during those early years on board ship.

But now that he was an adult, he found it mattered not at all who his father had been, or the number of lovers his mother had admitted to her bed. Scandal, whether old or new, had no power over him, as his aunt would soon discover if she attempted to besmear his reputation.

It was clear from her rage that she had thought it within her power to coerce him into obeying her dictates regarding the affairs of the Rainsford family at large, but so far as he was concerned the past had no bearing on the present or the future.

She would soon discover, as so many people had learned to their own regret, that no one in England—or indeed in all the civilized world—possessed any power to bend his will or indeed to change him in any way.

The jeweler in St. James Street was obviously accustomed to dealing with gentlemen and their ladybirds. Entering the shop at four o'clock that afternoon, Gabriel looked around, but did not see his current mistress, Mrs. Eleanor Lowndes, among the customers.

A most entrancing widow of only six-and-twenty years, she had flaming red hair, a voluptuous figure, and was in general not a woman easily overlooked, no matter what social setting she found herself in. She tended, rather, to draw attention toward herself—fascination on the part of any man in her vicinity, and jealousy on the part of any woman.

Before he could inquire about her, an elegantly dressed clerk approached him, bowed, and informed him in a discreet undertone that a lady was waiting for him in a small private room.

Gabriel did not find her sitting all alone. Besides being attended to by the owner himself, she was enjoying the warm companionship of various and assorted diamond bracelets, emerald pendants, amethyst pins, and ruby brooches.

"Oh, you must forgive me, Gabriel, my love, but I could not wait to begin choosing my present."

He bent down to kiss her cheek, and his nostrils were assailed by her musky scent, which brought back vivid memories of making love to her in the little house in Somers Town that he had leased for their assignations.

Impatient to be done with the tiresome business of buying her a present so that they could retire to that selfsame house, Gabriel picked up a bracelet and after a cursory inspection, dangled it before her eyes.

Heavy and encrusted with diamonds, it would cost him a packet, but on the other hand, it was designed to delight the heart of even the most rapacious female.

Except, apparently, the lovely widow, who was now looking at it with a tiny frown. "Gabriel, dearest," she said, standing up and resting her hands on his chest, "you must know how madly I love you, and you are so clever to remember how fond I am of diamonds." She swayed closer until she was pressing herself against him in a way that caused the jeweler to cough and then turn his head discreetly away.

"But what I would really like for Christmas, my love," Eleanor said, gazing up at him with coaxing eyes, "is for you to put a ring on this little finger." Pouting prettily, she kissed the third finger of her left hand and then pressed it against his lips.

All his desire to dally with her for an hour or two in that little house in Somers Town left him.

"In the long run, my sweet, I am sure I shall find the diamonds a better bargain." Signaling the jeweler, he quickly wrote out a bank draft for the bracelet and left, ignoring the widow's belated attempts to recover the ground she had lost.

The hack he had hired was waiting for him, and he gave the driver instructions to take him to his house in Grosvenor Square. Settling back against the somewhat grimy squabs, he considered what should be done about the widow Lowndes.

This was not the first time she had hinted that she wished to be his wife, nor had he ever deluded himself into thinking she would be content to remain his mistress forever, no matter how satisfying their arrangement might be to both of them.

But at this point, the benefits of continuing the liaison still outweighed the disadvantages. If he replaced Eleanor with someone new, that new mistress—be she lady or opera dancer—would undoubtedly also try to entice him into marrying her.

Since that was the case, it was less effort simply to allow the present arrangement to continue until the widow began to bore him in bed as much as she already did out of bed.

Gabriel's servants, which he had inherited with the house on Grosvenor Square, apparently shared Lady Ottillia's opinion as to his duties as head of the Rainsford family. Upon his return from the jeweler's, they set in motion a campaign to instill in him the proper measure of Christmas spirit, with the obvious purpose being to persuade him to fall in with his aunt's plans.

Taking his hat, Kirkson casually mentioned that life was enriched by traditions. "For it is traditions that separate us from the lower beasts of the field, m'lord."

Without bothering to inquire just what traditions Kirkson had in mind, Gabriel mounted the stairs to his room, where Fitch, his valet, was waiting to help him change for dinner. It soon became obvious that turning Gabriel out in proper style was only incidental to Fitch's main purpose.

Instead of being respectfully silent while Gabriel was concentrating on tying his neckcloth, the valet waxed eloquent in praise of life in the country with its opportunities for hunting and merrymaking, concluding with, "I think you must agree, m'lord, that there is nothing quite as satisfying as bringing in a Yule log and burning it in the fireplace at Sherington Close."

Gabriel did not agree, but he felt no obligation to enumerate the activities that he found more stimulating and satisfying than watching an oversized piece of wood burn.

Much to his disgust, he discovered that the entire household had apparently been recruited by his aunt. On his way down to the dining room, every housemaid Gabriel passed—and there seemed to be an inordinate number of them lurking about—was humming a Christmas carol.

To add to his irritation, no sooner was Gabriel seated in solitary splendor at the dining table than Kirkson informed him the cook wished to consult with him as soon as possible about the size of the plum pudding that would be needed for Christmas Day.

"I believe that I have had a surfeit of Christmas cheer, Kirkson. You may inform the rest of the servants that they are to cease and desist, because I shall not change my mind."

All innocence, the butler protested, "But, my lord, I have no idea what you are talking about."

"Then I shall explain," Gabriel said. "The next person who mentions Sherington Close or who alludes to tradition or who says or does anything that might conceivably serve to remind me that Christmas is approaching, will be turned off without a character. Do I make myself clear?"

"Quite clear, my lord," Kirkson said, but although his words were properly subservient, the look he gave Gabriel was not.

With every passing day the rooms at Brooke's were becoming more sparsely occupied. Given sufficient days,

Gabriel decided the next afternoon, the club might actually become a pleasant place to spend a few hours.

At the moment, however, there were still too many members present, specifically my Lords Marwood and Ibbetson, who pounced on Gabriel the moment he walked through the door.

"Ah, my dear Sherington," Marwood began with hearty joviality in his voice, "just the man I have been wishing to see. I was meeting with Perceval the other day, and he asked me as a personal favor to do my best to persuade you to take your seat in the House of Lords this coming year. We can always use another staunch Whig of your caliber, don't you know."

"Well, you may tell Mr. Perceval that you have followed your orders," Gabriel said smoothly.

"Then we can expect to see you in Parliament soon?" Marwood asked, a look of growing delight on his face.

"On the contrary, I think it is highly unlikely that I shall be there this year, but you have certainly done all you can do to persuade me," Gabriel replied.

Marwood's face became extremely red, but before he had a chance to say anything further, Gabriel adroitly sidestepped him, only to find his way blocked by Ibbetson, a short, pudgy man whose aspirations inclined more toward dandyism than toward political power.

"Now, now, Marwood," Ibbetson said cheerfully, "can't you see Sherington and I ain't interested in listening to a flock of old windbags drone on and on. We've got better things to do with our time."

Mentally Gabriel lifted an eyebrow at the use of the word "we." Although since his return to England he had encountered Ibbetson at half a dozen social events around London, they were at most nodding acquaintances, and not at all close friends.

In truth, there were but few men Gabriel called friend, and none of them were at the moment residing in England. Here in London, however, there was an unfortunate overabundance of toadeaters, sycophants, and bootlickers who sought out his company virtually every time he set foot outside his own house, and who appeared overcome with delight whenever he deigned to snub them or even when he insulted them quite rudely.

His lack of friends did not disturb him in the slightest, and as for the others who sought to ingratiate themselves, their attempts to manipulate him inevitably worked to his advantage rather than to their own.

He strongly doubted that he could benefit from an association with Ibbetson. But on the other hand, on such a gray day when he had no other pressing business, it might prove amusing to discover what ulterior motive was lurking behind Ibbetson's smile, which was every bit as false as Marwood's joviality.

"What did you have in mind?" Gabriel asked, making no particular effort to be genial.

"Thought you might like to play a hand or two of piquet," Ibbetson said gamely, although Gabriel could see that his cool attitude was making the man more and more uncomfortable.

"Pshaw!" Marwood said rudely, attempting to elbow Ibbetson aside. "Sherington is no more a gamester than he is a politician. I have no idea why he bothered to join the club in the first place since he does not care for deep play."

Seeing an opportunity to deflate the overly pompous Marwood, who although not old, could definitely be described as a boring windbag, Gabriel said, "I shall be delighted to play a game of piquet with you."

"Told you so," Ibbetson said with a smirk, and Marwood turned on his heel and stalked away, his displeasure clearly written on his face.

"I must warn you that I have had little experience with this game," Gabriel said quite mendaciously. If Ibbetson thought him a plump pigeon to pluck, he would find to his sorrow that he had chosen the wrong mark.

"Never you worry," Ibbetson said, the light of victory already gleaming in his eyes. "This will be just a friendly little game." He led the way to a small table at the opposite side of the room from where half a dozen other members were playing faro, and then signaled a waiter to bring them a fresh deck of cards.

Gabriel played cautiously at first, not wanting to give

his opponent any advantage, but oddly enough, Ibbetson was discarding erratically and overlooking even the most obvious opportunities to increase his score.

Could the man possibly be that inept a gambler? Given the high stakes he had suggested they play for, if Ibbetson were in truth so little skilled with cards, he would doubtless have been locked up in debtor's prison long ago.

Out of sheer perversity, Gabriel began to let his own game slide, but for every poor choice of discards he made, Ibbetson countered with a worse one. Gabriel won the first game easily, but he still had no idea why Ibbetson was trying so desperately to lose.

It was not until halfway through the third game that Ibbetson revealed the true reason he had wanted Gabriel to win money off him. In a burst of false bonhomie, the little man said, "Do you know, Sherington, I have just had the most marvelous idea. We are having such a good time here, why don't you come along to Ibbetson Hall with me for the holidays? I'm not having a large party down—just a few close friends. I'll make sure you enjoy the company. Bound to be more convivial than spending a few weeks with your relatives. No offense, but they're a stiff-rumped bunch of sourpusses, as you've undoubtedly discovered for yourself."

Gabriel had indeed discovered that, but at the mention of relatives it occurred to him that Ibbetson was also bound to have a relative or two lurking about at Ibbetson Hall. Casting his mind back to the stories he had heard since his return to England, he remembered someone saying that Ibbetson was cursed with not one, but four daughters of marriageable age. And if the gossip was correct, all four were roly-poly little butterballs like their father.

Which meant that Ibbetson was undoubtedly attempting to lure Gabriel into a matrimonial trap by allowing him to think that he would be able to win vast sums at cards if he would but spend a few jovial weeks at Ibbetson Hall.

"My dear Ibbetson," Gabriel drawled, "if only you had asked me last week. But I am afraid I have already made my plans, and as much as your kind invitation tempts me, I fear I really cannot see any way they can be canceled at this late date. But please extend my regrets to your lovely wife and daughters."

Ibbetson looked morosely down at his cards. "Didn't think it would work, but m'wife insisted I try. Told me you'd not been in England long enough to have heard about m'daughters."

"I heard," Gabriel said simply.

"Was sure you must have," Ibbetson said. "They're good girls, you know. Just a trifle on the plumpish side. They'll not be best pleased when I show up without you."

He looked up expectantly, as if hoping Gabriel might still change his mind—might willingly offer himself as a sacrifice.

"As much as I pity your plight, I fear I have not a single altruistic bone in my body," Gabriel said, and Ibbetson looked even glummer.

The game altered after that, and not with any great subtlety. Ibbetson's discards became well thought out, and his play was smooth and skillful.

Unfortunately for him, he was not quite the expert Gabriel was, and at the end of the third game, Ibbetson could not completely hide his disgruntlement that Gabriel had managed to take the bait and still avoid the trap.

# 2

ALTHOUGH OUTWARDLY obeying Gabriel's orders not to mention Christmas, the servants were quick to show their disapproval of him for refusing to fall in with his aunt's wishes. His dinner that evening was burned, and when he retired for the night, he discovered the fire in his bedroom had—inadvertently, or so the maid claimed—been allowed to go out.

In the merchant marines he had learned early on to endure worse hardships than charred meat and chilly quarters, so he chose not to make an issue of it, since that was obviously the purpose of the servants' machinations.

But the next morning he reached the end of his patience when Fitch, his valet, attempted to assist him in pulling on a boot whose mirrorlike shine was marred by a large and conspicuous smudge from someone's thumb.

Such deliberate provocation—such studied insolence—could not go unremarked, else a full-blown mutiny would surely result. "You appear to have forgotten who pays your salary," Gabriel said mildly, staring at the offending boot.

His valet immediately affected great concern. "Ecod, how did that happen? It must have been one of the footmen, m'lord. If you'll give the boots to me, I'll have them repolished at once."

Gabriel was not at all taken in by the conspicuous show of regret. "For today I shall wear another pair, and as for tomorrow, either my household is properly run, or I shall be hiring a new complement of servants."

His voice was not raised in anger, but apparently Fitch

believed him capable of doing just that, for the skinny
little man became quite apologetic.

"It is j-just that some of the servants are disappointed
that they will be spending Chr—that is to say, that they
will remain in London for the rest of this month,
m'lord," the valet stammered out. "It is n-natural
enough that they should feel some resentment, and you
should not hold it against them."

"If any of them are dissatisfied working for me, they
are welcome to go into service with my aunt," Gabriel
said, and Fitch's face became as white as the belly of a
dead fish.

It would appear that Gabriel's suspicions were correct:
Lady Ottillia obviously had a finger in this current epi-
demic of domestic disobedience—something he would
need to keep in mind, he decided while Fitch was helping
him into his jacket. It did not sit at all well with him to
employ servants who felt they owed their loyalty to another person.

He was considering whether it might not be wise to
fire the lot of them, when one of the footmen brought
him a heavily scented note. Breaking the seal, Gabriel
unfolded the two pages and began to peruse their
contents.

It was a tearful—if one could judge by the blotches
nearly obliterating some of the words—apology from Eleanor Lowndes, who missed him quite, quite, *quite*
dreadfully. The diamond bracelet was so *beautiful*, and
such a *generous* present, she assured him, and she would
treasure it forever.

The letter continued in much the same vein, but somehow by the back side of the first sheet, the apology became less abject and more reproachful. The reproof was
quite gentle and cleverly disguised, but Gabriel was
adept at reading between the lines, and he knew when
he was being scolded.

With a violent oath, Gabriel crumpled the letter and
threw it into the fire. Cousin Phillip had little to worry
about, did he but know it. Eventually he would inherit
the title and all the numerous estates that went with it,
because as much as Gabriel would have liked to cut his

cousin out of the succession, he could not stomach the thought of being married to any woman.

A female was all sweetness and charm, wanting nothing more than to please the man in her life. Until, that is, she thought he was totally ensnared—hopelessly, blindly in love with her—at which time she immediately became determined to mold him into the man she actually wished him to be.

Women were born manipulators, and infatuation was their chief weapon. In England, in Macao, in India, in the Americas—everywhere he had traveled, he had seen too many men made miserable by the women they married. Ibbetson was a case in point. Clearly living under the cat's paw, the poor man was apparently also browbeaten by his daughters.

Despite his intention to remain in London for the entire holiday season, Gabriel now abruptly changed his mind. He was thoroughly sick of being pestered by people who all wanted something from him. A little solitude would be more than welcome.

Retiring to his study, he soon located the list of his estates that his solicitor had prepared for him. The most remote property he owned appeared to be in Northumberland, not far from the Scottish border. It should do very nicely for his purposes.

Sending for Fitch, Gabriel ordered him to begin packing.

"Then we are to go to Sherington Close after all, my lord? How delightful. I feel I can say with certainty that the other servants will likewise be pleased to learn that you have changed your mind."

"If you continue in my service, which at this time is not a foregone conclusion, you will discover that I rarely change my mind," Gabriel said dispassionately. "Although my destination is no concern of yours, I will tell you that I am going north, and I have decided to travel by Mail. Pack sufficient clothing to last me for three weeks."

"You are not taking your own carriage?" Fitch asked, unable to conceal his astonishment. "But my lord, surely you will wish to reconsider—only think how inconvenient that will be for all of us."

Really, it was beyond belief the fools and dolts Gabriel was expected to put up with. "You mistake my meaning. I am not taking my carriages or my valet or my groom or my coachman or indeed any of my servants. I am leaving you all in London where you can stuff yourselves with plum pudding and sing nauseating carols until you are hoarse. And now if you have no more impertinent questions, perhaps you might be persuaded to bestir yourself a bit. I intend to leave this evening, and I shall be most displeased if you delay my departure by so much as a day."

"Gor blimey," Fitch said, all his proper English diction deserting him, " 'e's gone and lost 'is wits."

"That is quite possible," Gabriel replied, "but if you do not set about your business quickly, you will soon discover that you have lost your job."

Since it was an unscheduled stop, the stagecoach halted only long enough for Verity Jolliffe to climb out and the guard to throw down both her bags. Then the coachman cracked his whip, and the horses leaped forward, leaving her alone in front of the Crown and Thistle.

Mr. Noke, the landlord, did not come out to meet her, nor were there any hostlers bustling about, which was most odd. It was almost as if the inn were abandoned, but that was clearly ridiculous.

Seeking an explanation, Verity carried her bags through the gate leading into the yard, then stopped in dismay. Where formerly there had been a neat stable housing half a dozen horses, there were now only charred beams and blackened stones. Smoke was still curling up from the ruins, indicating that the fire had been quite recent.

Hearing footsteps behind her, Verity set her bags down and turned to see Mr. Noke approaching. He looked ten years older than when she had seen him a year ago, which was not to be wondered at considering the disaster that had befallen him.

"So it's you, Miss Jolliffe."

"Oh, Mr. Noke, I am so sorry you have suffered such a tragic loss."

The landlord shrugged. " 'Tis not the first time we've had a setback, and doubtless it won't be the last."

."But your horses—" Verity did not want to think about the poor beasts suffering such a painful death.

"Thank the Lord we didn't lose a one, although they got their hides singed good and proper. Tom Hesketh's putting them up in his barn, but I'm afraid none of them will be in any condition to wear a harness or saddle for a week or two, which won't help you get home. And it's sorry I am to tell you that there's nothing left of the gig you were wanting to hire but a worthless pile of twisted iron."

For the first time since she had seen the smoldering ruins of the stable, Verity realized fully how this disaster would affect her. How could she possibly get home for Christmas now?

Oh, if only she could have left London even a day or two earlier! But her sister, who had been totally opposed to this journey, had thought up one task after another that Verity absolutely had to finish before she could be allowed to indulge herself and her own selfish wishes by callously and wickedly abandoning the people who depended upon her.

It was only on the last possible day that Verity had simply packed her bags, bidden her sister good-bye, and taken a hackney to the staging inn.

Now, with regret in her heart and a lump in her throat, she asked, "Is there not someone else in the village who might have a vehicle I could hire? Even a pony or a dogcart would be adequate for my needs since it is only a little over six miles to Oakwood Manor."

Even before the landlord answered, Verity knew from his downcast expression that she was out of luck.

"I am sure you could if this was just an ordinary week. But tomorrow being Christmas and all, so many folks have gone visiting, I doubt there is a single vehicle left in the entire village, nor is there a riding horse to be found. No, the only way you'll be getting home is to go back to Belford, where doubtless you can find a gig for hire."

Verity did not bother to point out since she was not known in Belford, it might be difficult to persuade anyone to trust her with a horse and gig. But she would worry about that problem later. First there was a more pressing obstacle to overcome. "And how do you suggest I travel to Belford?"

The landlord scratched his head. "Now there's another thorny problem. I suppose there's nothing to be done but wait until the next southbound stage comes through and hope we can flag it down."

"And when will that be?" Verity asked, heartsick at the thought of missing Christmas with her family.

"Monday," Mr. Noke said. "Northbound on Saturdays and Wednesdays, and southbound on Mondays and Thursdays."

Verity's heart sank. "But that means I shall miss celebrating Christmas with my family. I suppose the only thing to do is simply leave my bags here with you and walk home."

"Indeed and that you shall not do," Mr. Noke said, looking quite fierce. "I'll not have you risking your life on such a foolhardy venture, for I've no wish to discover your frozen body lying in some thicket come spring."

"Surely there is no danger of that," Verity protested. "The road is well marked, and the weather is unseasonably warm, and—"

"And a fog can roll in from the North Sea without warning," the landlord pointed out, "and no matter how balmy the day starts out, the temperature can drop abruptly, and then where would you be? And have you considered what will happen if you twist an ankle or wrench your knee? The road from here to your father's house is little traveled, so it is unlikely anyone would chance to find you. No, I'll not let you risk your life and health, not even to get home for Christmas. But you're welcome to stay here for as long as you need. My wife will be happy to have some company, since our daughter went off with her husband last week to spend the holidays with his people."

No matter how much she might have wished to contradict him, Verity knew the landlord was correct. Only a fool put his faith in the constancy of the weather in Northumberland. She was about to accept—with great reluctance, to be sure—Mr. Noke's invitation to spend Christmas Day with him and his wife, when behind her she heard a sound that could only be the jangle of harness and bit.

Glancing around, she was astonished to discover, standing patiently in the far corner of the courtyard, a splendid team of chestnuts who were hitched to a black chaise whose wheels were picked out in scarlet. For a moment she thought they must surely be an illusion brought on by wishful thinking on her part, but when she rubbed a hand across her eyes and looked again, the elegant equipage had not vanished.

"But how is this, Mr. Noke? You told me there was no vehicle available here."

"Here it may be, but I'm sorry to say it's not available," he said gruffly. "It belongs to a London gentleman, who only stopped for a bite to eat."

"Do you suppose he is going toward Belford?"

Mr. Noke shook his head. "He has just come from there and is traveling west." He paused, and when Verity looked at him questioningly, he did not meet her eyes. Finally, staring fixedly at the ground, he said, "From what I understand, he will be going right past Oakwood Manor."

"Then perhaps he might be willing to take me along," Verity said, her spirits rising for the first time since she had arrived at the Crown and Thistle.

Mr. Noke shuffled his feet and again looked everywhere but at her. "He does not strike me as the kind of man to be doing favors for strangers, and I could not be so presumptuous as to ask him."

Even while they were speaking, the London gentleman appeared in the doorway of the Crown and Thistle. About six feet tall with dark hair, he had broad shoulders made to appear even wider by the many-caped driving coat he wore. He was indeed a most intimidating figure, and Verity could well understand why the landlord was so reluctant to approach him.

It was not only his size, but something about his expression, or perhaps his bearing, that made it obvious to her that he was a man accustomed to having his own way. Nothing about his appearance gave the slightest indication that someone could persuade him to do anything that he did not choose to do.

On the other hand, there was no harm in trying. If there was the slightest possibility that she could get home for Christmas, Verity was prepared to be most presumptuous. After all, the worst the London gentleman could do would be to tell her no, and even if he snapped and snarled at her—which from the frown creasing his forehead he seemed likely to do—even then, she would be no worse off than she was now.

Pausing in the doorway of the village inn, Gabriel could detect on the breeze not only the odor of wood smoke, but also the tangy smell of the sea, which lay only a mile or so to the east. For a brief moment he longed to feel a deck rising and falling beneath his feet, to hear again the creak of the masts, to feel once more the sting of salt spray on his cheeks.

But in reality, December was not an auspicious time of the year for sailing on the North Sea, and Gabriel pushed such nostalgic thoughts out of his head and looked around for the landlord so he could pay his shot and be on his way across the Kyloe hills to his estate, which lay on the River Till near Crookham.

The landlord was only a few yards away, and standing beside him was a woman, who was staring intently back at Gabriel. He had never seen her before, but dressed as she was for traveling, with a serviceable bonnet and gray cloak, and given the disastrous state of the landlord's stables, it was not hard for Gabriel to surmise where her interest in him lay.

Could he not escape importunate people even here in such a godforsaken village as this?

It was typical of his recent luck that the stranded traveler was a woman. In her efforts to persuade him to assist her on her journey, she would doubtless drag out her whole bag of feminine tricks. First the fluttering eyelashes and the bashful smile, then if that failed to turn him up sweet, she would try sighs, tears, and a piteously trembling chin.

He did not think he could stomach another such farce.

He flipped the landlord a gold coin, which that man caught with practiced dexterity. Then acting as if he had not noticed the stranger, Gabriel strode over to his carriage and climbed in, but the woman was not to be put off so easily.

"Excuse me, sir, but I understand you are traveling west. I am stranded here with no means of getting a message to my family, and I would greatly appreciate it if you could take me as far as Oakwood Manor, which is only a little more than a mile beyond Barmoor."

Scowling in a way that reduced most supplicants for his favor to quivering wrecks, Gabriel looked down at the woman. She was neither young nor old, and quite plain.

He felt mild surprise that she was not smiling coyly up at him, nor was she flirting boldly. Instead she met his gaze squarely and said, "It is quite important to me that I get home for Christmas."

"But I fear it matters little to me where you spend the holidays," Gabriel said curtly, picking up his whip.

Undeterred by his deliberate rudeness, she tried again. "I am quite prepared to pay you the amount that I had intended to spend for the hire of Mr. Noke's gig."

Gabriel was about to tell her how little he needed her money, but something about her straightforward manner stopped him. If she had batted her eyelashes at him once, or if a single tear had trickled down her cheek, he would have driven away without a qualm. Instead, he said tersely, "Climb in."

He regretted the words as soon as they were out of his mouth, but it was too late to alter anything, because the woman instantly did his bidding, and no sooner was she seated beside him, than the landlord tossed her baggage in behind her.

Had he taken leave of his senses? Apparently so, because now he would have to endure the vapid chattering of a female for an hour or two.

In this she also surprised him. After they had gone a mile along the road, he himself broke the silence by asking her name.

"Verity Jolliffe," she replied without elaboration.

"Well, Miss Jolliffe," he said, "allow me to tell you that you are a remarkably foolish woman." His tone was sarcastic, and his words provocative, but apparently the lady was not easily miffed.

"In what way?" she replied calmly, tilting her head so she could see his face.

Her hair, he noted absently, was a mousy brown, and her eyes were gray. All in all, a most unprepossessing female. "Has your mother never warned you that it is unsafe to accept rides with strange men?"

With a smile tugging at the corners of her mouth, she answered him. "But, my dear sir, I am six-and-twenty and so plain no man would look at me twice. I am quite past the age where I need to worry about being compromised."

Her appalling naivety angered him. "Are you so ignorant of the world, then, that you do not realize there are dangerous men who will not hesitate to assault an unprotected woman whether she is young or old, beautiful or ugly?" He scowled down at her, but again she refused to act suitably chastised.

"Are you one of those dangerous men?" she inquired, her voice still calm.

"No, I am not!" he barked out. "But you had no way of knowing that when you climbed into my carriage."

After a short silence, she said meekly, "Indeed, sir, you are right. I shall make it a point in the future not to accept invitations from strange men."

"If you will recall," he said, "I did not issue any invitations." He regretted the words as soon as he uttered them. They sounded petty and vindictive even to his own ears.

"Then I shall endeavor not to accost strange men from now on," she said meekly.

Unfortunately, her head was now tipped down and her

bonnet concealed her face, so he could not tell if she planned to heed his admonitions or if she was merely being sarcastic.

They drove another mile up into the hills without speaking, then he asked, "So what are you doing traveling alone?"

"I am going to spend Christmas with my family," she said, as if that explained everything.

"And who is your family?"

"My parents are Sir Sidney and Lady Jolliffe of Oakwood Manor. My brother Francis also lives with them. He is married and has three children."

Gabriel waited, fully expecting her to elaborate in great detail just how she and her family were connected to all the most important families in Northumberland, but she remained silent. It would seem that she was not cut from the same cloth as the vast majority of women.

Or was she perhaps slow-witted, that she did not utilize the opportunity to brag about her connections?

"And is that your entire family?" he prompted, giving her a second chance to drag out her pedigree.

"I also have a sister, with whom I live in London. She is married to a baron, who is very active in politics. Have you perhaps heard of Lord Wasteney?"

"No, I have not. Do you know, Miss Jolliffe, I am becoming quite exasperated at the effort it is taking to drag information out of you. Do you suppose you might be a bit more forthcoming?"

Again those clear gray eyes looked up at him. "But what is it you wish to know?"

"Tell me the story of your life," he snapped out.

"There is really little to tell," she replied. "I have led quite a humdrum existence until now."

"I shall be the judge of that."

"Well, Francis was fifteen and my sister Petronella was seventeen when I was born, and according to my governess, I was rather a surprise for my parents. My sister married before I was out of leading strings, so I did not really come to know her well until I had a Season in London. Do you wish to know about my years as a child? They were in no way remarkable."

"I believe we can skip ahead to the Season you mentioned," Gabriel said.

She hesitated, then said, "Do you know, I am not at all sure it will be any more interesting. My sister presented me at court, and my father paid for me to have a Season, but I did not take. Because I am so very plain with no vivacity to speak of, my father saw little point in wasting his blunt giving me a second Season, especially when my sister offered me a place in her household."

With effort Gabriel resisted the impulse to tell her that her life was in truth every bit as boring as she had warned him it was.

"And now, sir, might I know a little about you? I am afraid I do not even know your name."

"Sherington," he said curtly. When he did not elaborate, she lapsed into silence.

The bracken-covered moors and fells around them became more bleak and bare, and the higher the road climbed, the more snow lay in the ditches and hollows, out of reach of the feeble rays of the winter sun.

But when they attained the crest of a particularly tall hill and Gabriel looked beyond to the distant horizon, he discovered in himself a surprising affinity for this desolate land, which had a stark beauty all its own.

"Tell me about Northumberland, Miss Jolliffe," he ordered, not bothering to disguise his command with polite phrases.

"Well, to the south lies Hadrian's Wall, which was built by the Romans, and here in the north there are any number of castles and castle ruins—"

"I have no interest in stones, no matter how ancient or how cleverly they have been piled on top of each other," he said, putting an end to that topic of conversation.

After a moment's thought, she tried again. "I have heard that the salmon fishing is quite good in the River Tweed, but"—she added quickly before he could interrupt again—"perhaps not in December."

Tilting her head, she looked up at him inquiringly, but he merely waited silently, leaving the burden of the conversation with her.

"Do you hunt?" she asked finally.

"No," he said flatly, then added, "it has always seemed a singularly pointless pursuit compared to managing an import and export business."

"Then since you are in trade, I suppose I need not tell you that there is a strong coal mining industry along the coast?"

"Indeed, Miss Jolliffe, I am not such a lackwit that I do not understand what the expression 'carrying coals to Newcastle' means."

There was an even longer pause, then Miss Jolliffe made another effort. "Have you ever had any particular interest in sheep?"

Any number of sarcastic replies popped into his head, but mindful of the tedium of the miles which still lay before them, Gabriel said merely, "I do not believe that I have actually, up until this time, spared a thought for sheep, either individually or collectively."

With a sigh of relief, which brought a reluctant smile to Gabriel's lips, his companion began to discourse knowledgeably on the subject of sheep raising and the wool industry. She was surprisingly well-informed and could answer every question he put to her, and by the time he turned his team down the lane leading to Oakwood Manor, he felt himself quite thoroughly prepared to discuss such matters with his bailiff.

Assuming, of course, that his estate, about which he as yet knew nothing except the yearly income, actually included a sheep or two.

Miss Jolliffe's excitement grew more obvious with each turn of the wheels, and when her father's house came into view in the distance, she leaned forward, as if her eagerness were so great she would have preferred to jump out of the carriage and run ahead of the horses.

What would it be like, he wondered, to spend Christmas in the bosom of a loving family? It was an experience he would never have, since his own relatives would never accept him. Not that he cared tuppence about them either.

But then a little voice in the back of his mind asked how much of Miss Jolliffe's excitement was caused by

eagerness to see her family, and how much was triumph
that she was bringing home a peer of the realm to parade
before them all.

But Miss Jolliffe, as was apparently normal for her,
did not do the expected. No sooner did he pull his team
to a halt beside the front door, than she said, "You will
doubtless not wish to keep your horses standing, so I can
manage from here."

Something in her tone of voice and the way she turned
her head made him suspect that she was deliberately trying to get rid of him, which made him equally determined
not to vanish politely on cue. Without needing to rack
his brain unduly, he surmised that she was having second
thoughts about the wisdom of accepting rides from
strange men, and did not wish her parents to know that
she had behaved in such an unladylike manner.

Well, Miss Jolliffe, he thought with a smile, now it is
time to pay the piper. "On the contrary," he said, "my
horses could well use an hour or two of rest if it would
not be too much trouble."

The dismay in her eyes made it quite clear that he had
judged her correctly, but she was not brave enough to
utter any objections.

# 3

CLIMBING OUT of the chaise, Gabriel tied the reins to a hitching post, by which time Miss Jolliffe had climbed down unassisted. Without a word to him, she rapped on the oaken door with the lion's head knocker. When no one appeared, Gabriel banged it with considerably more force.

The butler, when he finally deigned to open the door, looked at the two of them disdainfully. "Oh, so it's you. I'll thank you not to pound on the door with such violence in the future."

Sidling past him into the house, Miss Jolliffe said timidly, "If you please, Hagart, send word to the stables that Mr. Sherington's horses need to be tended to."

Hagart drew himself up stiffly and said, "Indeed, I'll do no such thing. It is not my responsibility to go traipsing out to the stables on your behest. If you wish to speak to a groom, then go out there yourself."

Gabriel was amused by Miss Jolliffe's assumption that Sherington was his family name rather than his title, but he found nothing funny about the way the butler had responded to her request, which had been quite reasonable. Were all the servants in England as insolent as his own? Gabriel would not have suspected such a thing was possible.

He had been told by numerous people that he could be quite intimidating. He saw no reason to doubt that it was a fair observation, because one black scowl from him, and the butler at once lost his air of pompous self-importance and seemed to shrink in upon himself.

"On the other hand, Miss Jolliffe," the man said,

cringing away from Gabriel as if trying to ward off a blow, "you are doubtless chilled from your journey, so it might be better if you joined your family in the drawing room, and I'll just see to the gentleman's horses myself." Making a wide circle around Gabriel, he hurried out, closing the door behind him.

Again without waiting for any assistance, Miss Jolliffe removed her cloak and bonnet and laid them on a chair.

"Do you know, someone should give you lessons in the proper way for a lady to behave," Gabriel said, his tone sarcastic.

"Oh dear, I am so sorry," she said. "May I take your coat and hat?" She moved toward him, but with a scowl he forestalled her.

"It is not a matter for you to assist me, but you should have waited for me to assist you. You are making it very difficult for me to play the role of gentleman." Removing his coat, he tossed it carelessly on another chair, then laid his top hat down on a small table.

"Well, I suppose I could always put my cloak back on again," she said, tipping her head to one side as if she were actually considering doing just that. He could see a sparkle of mischief in her eyes, and although it was gone in an instant, he was not taken in by her meek manner.

He had noticed at the Crown and Thistle that she was on the tall side for a woman, and now, without the enveloping folds of her cloak, he saw that she was also quite skinny. Mentally he compared her lack of curves to his mistress's well-endowed figure, and he could easily understand why Miss Jolliffe "had not taken." Most men, himself included, preferred more abundant charms.

But his staring was beginning to discompose her, so he offered her his arm. "Shall we join your family?" he asked.

Although she was obviously reluctant to meet her fate, she rested her hand on his arm and together they mounted the stairs to the first floor, where she led the way to the drawing room.

The proportions of the chamber were bad, with the ceiling far too low for the size of the room, and the furnishings had a heaviness about them that completely negated the innate beauty of the woods and fabrics from which they had been fashioned.

Doubtless Sir Sidney and his wife harbored the mistaken opinion that their manor house pronounced to all the world that here dwelt a prosperous, substantial family, worthy of inclusion in the highest ranks of society, but the word which came to Gabriel's mind when he studied the room and its occupants was *sullen*.

The entire family was gathered for tea—at least everyone Miss Jolliffe had previously described to him seemed to be present. The older couple sitting rigidly side by side on a massive upholstered couch were undoubtedly her parents, and the rather paunchy, middle-aged dandy holding a quizzing glass up to his eye was no doubt the heir apparent. The woman with frown lines already etched between her eyes and three children of assorted ages and sexes seated on stools at her feet would, of course, be the sister-in-law.

It took Gabriel only a single glance around the room to realize that he had once again misinterpreted Miss Jolliffe's motives. Her reluctance to invite him in had not been caused by a desire to save herself from a proper scolding, but rather she had obviously been trying to spare him this unpleasant meeting with her relatives, who appeared to be even more surly and oafish than his own.

"I cannot believe my eyes," her brother said, his sneer becoming more pronounced. "We expected you weeks ago, and here you have waited until the very last minute."

"Really, Verity, it is most inconsiderate of you not to have come in time to help," his wife added in a shrill voice that grated on Gabriel's nerves. "After I have slaved away getting everything ready for Christmas, you appear on our doorstep when all the work is done. It is too much, I tell you."

At the first pause in the conversation—if one could call the steady stream of recriminations directed at her a conversation—Miss Jolliffe introduced him to her family, again referring to him as Mr. Sherington, rather than Lord Sherington.

"Never heard of you," her father growled, and after Gabriel had been thus dismissed, none of the adults exhibited any further interest in him.

Instead they began bickering among themselves as to which of them was most inconvenienced by the tardiness of Miss Jolliffe's visit. Only the three children remained mum, staring at him as if he were some kind of freak displayed at a street market in Rangoon. Their faces, even at their young ages, were already beginning to show the same repulsiveness as their elders, and there arose in Gabriel's mind an image of the greasy broth made from maggoty beef that he had often been forced to eat on board ship.

Miss Jolliffe appeared unruffled by her family's diatribe, and she murmured conciliatory phrases while pouring herself and Gabriel some tea.

He was not sure why he felt compelled to speak up in the end. Perhaps it was simply because as plain as she was, Miss Jolliffe did not appear to belong in this ugly room. Or perhaps he wished to have an opportunity to quiz her as to why she was so determined to reach home in time for Christmas, when home meant nothing but rejection. Or more likely it was some misguided feeling of pity that caused him to speak out, deliberately raising his voice loud enough to momentarily halt the others' conversation.

"When do you mean to return to London, Miss Jolliffe? It may well be convenient for you to drive back with me to catch the stage in Belford."

"Oh, I could not ask you to put yourself to so much trouble," she began.

Her father interrupted before Gabriel could press his invitation. "But you care little how much inconvenience you put me to, is that it, daughter? Well, I'll not be hitching up my horses to drive you just because you're too missish to accept this gentleman's offer. If you want to be so niffy-naffy in your ways, you can *walk* to Belford for all I care."

"I had thought to return on January ninth," Verity said softly, and this time it was her mother who reprimanded her.

"You'll go when this gentleman finds it convenient, and I'll brook no arguments," the old woman said tartly.

Feeling the need for some fresh air and solitude, Gabriel stood up and said, "January ninth will be fine for me. And now if you will excuse me, I need to continue my journey. The days are short this time of year, and I wish to reach my destination before nightfall."

No one made any effort to detain him longer, but when Miss Jolliffe started to rise from her seat to show him out, her father told her crossly that she was not dismissed, and she obediently sank back down in her chair, casting Gabriel a look of apology that he did not feel was necessary to acknowledge.

Deliberately leaving the door partly ajar behind him, Gabriel paused in the corridor and listened with idle curiosity to the questions being asked about him—questions about his business and his familial connections that Miss Jolliffe was quite unable to answer in a way that her relatives found the least bit satisfactory.

He soon abandoned his listening post and descended the stairs. If he had harbored any doubts about his decision not to entertain his relatives at Sherington Close, he was now completely convinced that coming north had been the right course.

Just so would his relatives have engaged in bickering among themselves, alternating with casting venomous remarks in his direction.

Miss Jolliffe, he decided while the butler obsequiously helped him on with his driving coat and then respectfully handed over his top hat, was proving after all to be a fool, despite her knowledge of sheep raising in Northumberland.

By the time dinner was over, Verity had managed to cajole her family into a somewhat better mood, although she rather suspected her meek responses to their complaints were not the sole reason for their grudging acceptance of her presence in their midst.

More than likely her mother and sister-in-law had bethought themselves of several household chores that had not yet been done—tasks they could now assign to Verity.

As soon as her mother rose from the table, signaling that it was time for the ladies to leave the men to their port, Verity excused herself on the grounds that she still had her unpacking to do. Instead of going to her bedroom, however, she slipped up the back stairs to the small room under the eaves where her grandmother had spent her declining years.

The sparsely furnished room with its sloping ceiling and single tiny window had changed little in the five years since her grandmother had died. Her parents did not need it for the servants, and it was too mean a room to offer to a guest.

Wrapping a threadbare woolen shawl around her shoulders, Verity seated herself in her grandmother's rocking chair, seeking the comfort she usually found from being surrounded by her grandmother's possessions.

But after only a few minutes, she stood up, walked to the window, and looked out across the moonlit fells. With her forehead against the cold glass, she admitted to herself that it was not her grandmother's loving embrace she was missing the most at this moment.

Straining her eyes as if she might somehow see beyond the distant horizon, she thought about Mr. Sherington and wondered where he was and what he might be doing.

He had been right to warn her about strangers, but he had been wrong when he said he was not dangerous.

Although she had believed him completely when he said he was no threat to her person, she rather feared he was going to be a threat to her heart.

At odd moments during his stay in Northumberland, Gabriel found himself thinking about Miss Jolliffe and wondering what she was doing. Was she perhaps at this moment being chastised by her mother or browbeaten by her sister-in-law? Criticized by her father or belittled by her brother? Or was she merely being forced to look after those three repulsive children?

By the time the New Year arrived, he actually felt a slight impatience to see her again—to discover for himself how she was surviving in the loving bosom of her family—and he almost sent her a message setting forward their departure date. But then the weather improved, and his attention turned to other activities.

On the morning of the ninth of January, Gabriel arose quite early, and having the previous day instructed his servants—who unlike his London household were remarkably deferential to his wishes, perhaps because none of the previous earls had deigned to come this far north—he set forth on his journey just as the sun was peeking over the horizon.

Since he had likewise had the forethought to send Miss Jolliffe word that he meant to pick her up quite early, he was reasonably sure that he could avoid furthering his acquaintance with the other members of the Jolliffe household. Still, he derived some amusement on the short trip to Sir Sidney's residence by imagining how impatiently Miss Jolliffe must be awaiting his arrival.

He fully expected her to be in a foul humor after two weeks with her relatives—doubtless by this time she was wishing them all in Jericho—and he resolved to treat her with forbearance. After all, he had enjoyed an agreeable holiday, while she had . . . ? Again he wondered what she might have been forced to endure, but he was sure she would soon be regaling him with a detailed account of all that she had suffered.

With a feeling of anticipation, he reined in his team in front of the manor, which was dark and still in the early morning light, and which offered no indication that anyone was stirring inside.

Deliberately disregarding the butler's admonition to rap gently, Gabriel banged the door knocker loudly enough to wake every occupant of the house, and before the last echo died away, the door was opened by Miss Jolliffe herself.

Clutching her portmanteau, she emerged from the house and pulled the door firmly shut behind her.

"Did you not bring two bags with you?" he asked, handing her up into the carriage and tossing her portmanteau in on top of his own. "I have no wish to turn back a mile or two down the road because you have discovered you have forgotten half of your things."

"Indeed no," she replied, displaying the same serenity of spirit she'd had when he'd left her two weeks previous. "The other portmanteau was filled with presents for my family."

Beginning to feel a trifle irked by her unflagging good humor, he asked rather nastily, "And did your family not reciprocate in full measure? Did they not load you down with presents to take back with you?"

Turning to gaze earnestly up at him, she said, "No, but then I was not expecting to receive anything."

Her calm acceptance of this injustice angered him. Had she no backbone at all? Why did she not stand up to her relatives? Why did she meekly tolerate their criticism, which he was sure was unjustified.

"You are a fool to try to buy their love," he snapped out.

"I did not intend for the presents to be bribes," she said without raising her voice. "Christmas is a time for giving gifts to the ones we love."

He was amazed—nay, he was astounded. "You love them? That is preposterous! No one could love such narrow-minded, selfish, self-centered bores. If I had relatives like yours, I would avoid them like the plague. As a matter of fact, I do have relatives just as obnoxious as yours, and I make every effort to be where they are not."

"But I still love them, despite what you say, because they are my family."

"Bah! I had not thought you a complete fool, Miss Jolliffe, but it appears I was wrong."

So harsh was his voice, he expected her to lapse into silence, but instead she explained, "If I cease to love them simply because they are imperfect or because they do not love me back, then I do not hurt them, but only myself."

Unable to follow her convoluted and obviously faulty line of reasoning, he found himself asking, "How so?"

"Do you not see? It is really quite simple. If I stop loving them, then I become diminished as a person."

The time had obviously come again for him to open her eyes to reality. "If you think you will change them by your example, you delude yourself totally, Miss Jolliffe. No matter how many times you meekly turn the other cheek, all you will ever get for your efforts is more bruises."

At his words, her eyes did open—but only in astonishment. "You misunderstand completely. I have no expectation or indeed any intention of changing them. It is not true love when one seeks to change another person."

With that Gabriel found himself in complete agreement. Where he differed from Miss Jolliffe was in believing that there was no such thing as true love in the world. Love, in his experience, was invariably selfish and demanding.

But he did believe in luck, both good and bad. And he had to acknowledge that it was possible that he could have, through sheer good fortune, met the one female who would enable him to cut his cousin out of the line of succession.

Looking at her with renewed interest, Gabriel began to evaluate her potential as a possible wife.

Beginning with her physical appearance, there was no denying that she was quite plain, with mousy brown hair, nondescript eyes, and no figure to speak of. Not at all the attributes one looked for in a mistress, but greatly to be desired in a wife. After all, he felt no inclination to follow in his father's footsteps and end up with a son whose paternity was in doubt. Since Miss Jolliffe was not likely to inflame any man's passion, that was a definite point in her favor.

On the other hand, although she possessed no particular beauty of face or form, she was not at all an antidote. Moreover, she was neatly dressed and from what he had seen, fastidious about her person, so he should have no trouble consummating the marriage. Another point in her favor.

Although of gentle birth, which was a definite requirement for any wife of his, she was not so highly connected that she would fail to be appreciative of the great honor he would be bestowing upon her by making her the Countess of Sherington.

In addition, if one excepted her peculiar ideas about love, her understanding was above average for a female. Gabriel had, over the years, noticed that intelligent men who married beautiful ninnies frequently sired offspring who were notable lackwits, and he had no intention of falling into that trap.

Since a man must unfortunately expect to spend some time in his wife's company on occasion, it was likewise in Miss Jolliffe's favor that she did not drive him to distraction by chattering. Yet when called upon to do so, she was able to converse easily on a variety of topics. Moreover, if she had any of the normal, thoroughly aggravating, feminine wiles, she had yet to display them.

Another woman with so many desirable attributes would be difficult, yet probably not impossible to find. But where could he find another female who would not try her best to change him, and who would not demand that he love her in return?

If he married Miss Jolliffe, he could continue the life he was accustomed to leading without having her fall into a jealous tantrum because he spent more time at his clubs or with his mistress than with her. And if he decided to leave her at Sherington Close and set forth on a journey, she would neither complain that he was abandoning her nor berate him when he decided to return.

Yes, on this trip north, his luck had definitely been in. With only a slight effort on his part, he could acquire a proper loving wife, and in due course an heir.

All he had to do was make Miss Jolliffe fall in love with him, which given his way with women, should be the easiest thing in the world to do.

Verity was quite sick with the intensity of her feelings for the moody and irascible gentleman seated beside her in the carriage. She had hardly been able to get him out of her mind since the moment she had first laid eyes on him. He was like a hero in one of Mrs. Radcliffe's novels, come to life.

No, that was not correct—he was more like one of the

villains. Unfortunately for her peace of mind, she had always found herself more in sympathy with the villains than with the heroes, who in comparison were such a namby-pamby lot.

Although Mr. Sherington was not precisely handsome, he was quite the most compelling, most forceful man she had ever met. She could not envision him bending his will to suit another man . . . but on the other hand, she could not picture a woman passing him by without a second glance.

Undoubtedly he had a mistress—perhaps even more than one. What woman could look at him without wanting him? And if he wanted her, what woman could deny him her favors?

Verity had only to look at his hands, presently encased in supple driving gloves, to want to feel them touching her. Just remembering the way the muscles of his arms had rippled inside his perfectly fitting jacket made her want to be clasped in his embrace. Feeling the heat emanating from his body made her want to risk being burned, and the curve of his lips was so enticing, she wondered what his kisses would taste like.

Most dangerous of all, whenever she looked into his eyes, she saw a hunger there that she longed to assuage— a need in him that she felt an answering need to satisfy.

But that was patently ridiculous. She had to be imagining things. Sneaking a peek at him now out of the corner of her eye, she found it difficult to believe that such a man could lack for anything.

Equally impossible was her longing to be with him every waking minute, and yet she could not deny that she did hunger after him.

No matter how improbable—how absurd for a spinster like her, who had resigned herself years ago to being on the shelf—she wanted to be with him at night also. She even—and she felt her face grow warm thinking such improper thoughts—wanted to give herself to him with no reservations, no holding back.

But of course such a man as Mr. Sherington could have no interest in her. If only she were beautiful and alluring and adept at flirting—if only she were a dashing widow with a slightly unsavory reputation, then maybe he would set her up in a little house in Somers Town and give her carte blanche.

She knew all about such things, because like a quiet little mouse, she often sat in the corner of the drawing room doing her needlework, so inconspicuous that sometimes her sister, Petronella, and her sister's best friend, Harriet Coupland, forgot she was even there. On such occasions, the two older women gossiped about things no unmarried miss should be allowed to hear, even if the young lady in question was not so young anymore.

But none of their gossip had given Verity an inkling of an idea that love could feel this way. Listening to their chatter, Verity had never understood why a young lady of respectable birth would wish to elope with a man whose station in life was not equal to her own, or how a married woman could risk home and family by having an adulterous affair.

But now, knowing she would soon be saying good-bye to Mr. Sherington, perhaps never to see him again, Verity regretted more than ever before in her life that she was a plain spinster of advancing years.

The sensible, responsible part of her mind persisted in pointing out that it was illogical even to dream that Mr. Sherington would ever make her an offer, honorable or dishonorable.

But the wild part of herself, which she had never before suspected she possessed, was ready to sacrifice everything to be in his arms. Despite her upbringing, which had been in all ways respectable, if Mr. Sherington turned to her and offered her carte blanche, she would accept with alacrity, even though she knew full well that taking such a drastic step would mean the total destruction of her life . . . and more than likely the eternal damnation of her immortal soul.

While she was staring at him hungrily, he turned and smiled at her, and she realized it was already too late—she had become unchaste and wanton in her thoughts. Even if he never touched her, she had already lost her soul.

\*     \*     \*

Accustomed as he was to making quick decisions in his commercial dealings, Gabriel saw no reason to procrastinate in this case, which was, when all was said and done, strictly a business venture rather than an affair of the heart.

He therefore began his campaign to win her affection by inquiring solicitously, "Are you warm enough, Miss Jolliffe? Do you perhaps wish to stop at the Crown and Thorn for a bit of refreshment?"

"No, thank you. I do not want to risk missing the stage, for the next southbound one does not come through Belford for another three days."

So much for planning things thoroughly. Already he was faced with his first obstacle. Naturally enough, he wished to be private with Miss Jolliffe so that he might begin wooing her.

Since they would be together only another hour or two, his opportunity to establish himself firmly in her affection was severely limited, and he could not solve the problem by simply continuing on in a hired post-chaise.

While there was no particular problem with being unchaperoned on a back road in Northumberland, it was quite another matter for Miss Jolliffe to travel the length of the Great North Road in his company. And the closer they got to London, the greater the risk that they would be seen by someone with a wagging tongue.

He could, of course, hire a maid to lend them a degree of propriety, but it would still look suspicious should anyone chance to recognize him. And despite his own notoriety he did not wish his future wife's reputation to be tarnished in the slightest degree.

Besides, the maid would be bound to chatter, which he was not prepared to tolerate.

But still, he balked at the idea of putting Miss Jolliffe on the stage while he went by mail coach. She had already proven to be disastrously naive about the world. Left to her own devices, who knew what strange man might accost her, and with what potentially catastrophic results?

Nor would traveling separately do anything to advance

his cause, which meant it made far more sense for him to accompany her on the stage.

On the other hand, could he stomach traveling at a snail's pace in a poorly sprung coach operated by a second-rate stage company? The prospect held no appeal. Therefore the only remaining option was for both of them to travel by mail.

To be sure, Miss Jolliffe's name was not on the waybill, but in Gabriel's opinion that was not an insurmountable obstacle. He had never yet encountered an impediment that he could not remove by the lavish application of money, and since he never traveled without sufficient funds, the matter was as good as settled.

Smiling congenially and keeping his voice as pleasant as possible in order to keep his companion from becoming skeptical about his motives, while at the same time wishing he had not been quite so quick to lecture her about the dangers of accepting rides from total strangers, Gabriel informed her of his decision.

"Since you are, in a manner of speaking, presently under my protection, Miss Jolliffe, I fear I cannot in good conscience allow you to travel unescorted back to London. I shall therefore make it my responsibility to secure a place for you on the Mail, and to ensure against idle speculation about our relationship, which might be detrimental to your reputation, I have decided that it would be best to tell people that you are my sister."

# 4

VERITY COULD NOT help but notice the exact instant Mr.
Sherington's smile became spurious and his tone of voice
patently false. Over the years her relatives had manipu-
lated her on too many occasions for her suspicions not
be instantly aroused.

She sneaked a glance at him now out of the corner of
her eye, and there was no way she could pretend that
his present behavior did not positively reek of duplicity.

Whereas up to this moment he had displayed a strong
tendency to scowl at her for the slightest offense, real
or imagined, and had, when he was not ignoring her
completely, spoken to her quite frankly and even rudely,
now he was obviously doing his best to turn her up sweet.

What was not so obvious was his true purpose. What
could this man possibly want from her?

Although she could not begin to fathom his motives—
other than to be sure that he was not merely playing the
role of knight errant—she had to admit to herself that it
did not matter; whatever he was trying to obtain from
her she would give him gladly.

"I should not wish to be a bother," she said, wondering if she were not perhaps letting her imagination run
away with her. No doubt he was merely being polite,
and would jump at the chance to continue on his way
without the encumbrance of a stranger like herself.

"I doubt you will be any trouble," he said. "On the
contrary, I am quite certain having you to talk to will
keep the trip from becoming tedious."

He smiled at her in a most engaging manner, which

only served to increase her suspicions rather than to dispel them.

There was, Verity soon learned, a vast difference between traveling alone on the stage and going by mail, especially when one had a forceful gentleman along to smooth the way. Without so much as raising his voice, Mr. Sherington somehow contrived to have their food brought to them first whenever they stopped at a posting house, and this despite the grumblings and complainings of the other passengers.

It was also a novel experience to travel through the night, rather than stopping when the sun set.

"You should try to sleep," his voice came quietly out of the darkness beside her. "You will be more comfortable if you lean against my shoulder."

Sleep? She hesitated, unable to believe that she would be able to sleep a wink if she were touching him.

"Come now, sister, do as you are bid," he said. "We would not wish you to arrive at our mother's house in an exhausted condition."

Verity hoped no one else had heard the laughter lurking behind his sober words. Fearing what he might say or do if she did not comply with his wishes, she leaned her head against his shoulder.

Immediately his arm came around her, and she started to jerk away—from surprise only, not because it was unpleasant in the slightest.

"Don't fidget," he ordered, "else I shall let you risk being cast to the floor when we hit an especially large bump."

She did her best to relax, but being held in his arms was even more intensely exciting than she had envisioned, and sleep eluded her while the carriage raced through the night.

Someone was speaking in such a loud voice that Verity was awakened from a pleasant dream about her grandmother, only to discover she was no longer leaning against Mr. Sherington's shoulder, but was actually sitting directly on his lap.

"I say sister or no sister, it is highly improper conduct," the voice continued indignantly.

Horrified to find herself behaving in such a wanton manner, Verity wasted no time in resuming her proper place on the seat beside Mr. Sherington, but the woman who had spoken, a parson's widow on her way back to London after visiting her daughter in Edinburgh, did not make any attempt to conceal her displeasure.

"Scandalous is what I call it. To behave so in public. What is the world coming to?"

Stung by the criticism, even though it was completely justified, Verity turned helplessly to Mr. Sherington, who opened one eye to peer at her. In response to her unspoken plea, he opened both eyes, and scowled at the woman sitting across from Verity.

With a last angry mutter, the woman averted her gaze from the two of them and stared pointedly out the window.

It took much longer for Verity's heart to subside to a normal rate, and she resolved to stay awake for the rest of the journey.

Unfortunately, her mind kept returning to those few moments when she had been on Mr. Sherington's lap. What must be his opinion of her now? That she should repay his kindness by . . . by . . .

Her face grew hot at the thought of what she had done. And even hotter when she realized how much she wanted to climb back onto his lap and wrap her arms around his neck and kiss him full on the mouth.

But then her heart plummeted when she looked out the window and realized it would not be long before they reached London, where Mr. Sherington's self-appointed responsibility for her safety and well-being would end.

"I cannot believe you were so lost to propriety as to travel the length of England with a total stranger," Petronella whispered to Verity. Then she smiled at Mr. Sherington, who was sitting across from them.

"He was most helpful," Verity started to explain.

"You must get rid of him at once, before Ralph comes home," her sister hissed in her ear. "More tea, Mr.

Sherington," she said in a louder voice. "At once, do you understand me?" she repeated in a whisper to Verity.

Not at once, Verity decided. No matter how her sister fussed—and she could only be grateful her sister had better manners than the rest of their family and so was able to conceal her displeasure—Verity was determined to postpone saying good-bye to Mr. Sherington for as long as possible.

So she ignored her sister's repeated admonitions and offered their visitor more tea cakes. From the look in his eye, it was obvious to her that he knew precisely how welcome he was not, but he was even more adept at dissembling than was her sister.

There was a sound of footsteps in the hall, and Petronella rose with alacrity. "That is doubtless my husband," she explained, then hurried out.

"Somehow I have the impression that your sister does not approve of me," Mr. Sherington murmured, sending Verity another of his lethal smiles.

"Why do you say that?" Verity asked, smiling back at him as calmly as if her heart were not racing madly in her breast.

"Perhaps it is the daggers she has been shooting at me," he replied. "Or perhaps it is because the tea she poured for me is stone cold."

Before Verity could reply, the door was thrust open and Ralph, Lord Wasteney, entered the room, obviously intent upon ejecting the unwelcome visitor in person.

Instead he stopped so quickly that his wife crashed into him, almost knocking him to the floor. Keeping his balance with difficulty, he goggled at Mr. Sherington. There was no other possible way to describe it—his eyes positively bulged out of his head.

Before Verity could recover from her astonishment at such unusual behavior, her brother-in-law hurried across the room and bowed deeply. "Sherington, this is an honor. I had not heard you were back in London. Welcome to my humble abode." Turning to his wife, he beckoned her forward. "My dear, you should have warned me *Lord* Sherington was coming to visit."

Petronella recovered nicely and immediately rang for

a pot of fresh tea, but Verity sat as if turned to stone. Even she had heard of Gabriel Rainsford, Lord Sherington, the darling of London society ever since his return from abroad at the beginning of the Little Season.

His was one of the oldest and most respected titles in the land, and as if that were not enough, he was as rich as Croesus, or so people said in the most reverent tones.

Ralph had filled many a dinner hour waxing eloquent in praise of his lordship, at the same time bewailing the fact that the nabob held himself aloof, refusing to take his seat in the House of Lords and turning down almost every social invitation extended to him.

And she had called him *Mr.* Sherington. And had sat on his lap! And had dared to dream about kissing him.

Feeling totally, abjectly, dismally miserable, Verity looked at him, wishing there were some way she could apologize to him in private, but Lord Sherington did not so much as glance in her direction. How he must despise her!

"We are so grateful you have taken such good care of our little sister," Petronella said in a cloyingly sweet voice. "You must allow us to show our appreciation—to reciprocate in some small measure. London is so sparse of company, perhaps you would be pleased to take pot-luck with us this evening? We will just be dining *en famille*, but you are more than welcome to join us. Shall we say eight?"

"Thank you, I accept your kind hospitality," Lord Sherington said, rising to his feet. "And now if you will excuse me, I have pressing business matters to attend to."

With Verity trailing along behind, Lord and Lady Wasteney escorted their guest out. No sooner had the front door shut behind him, than they began to make their plans.

"Otterwall," Petronella commanded, "send a footman to fetch Antoinette home. Of all the days for her to decide to spend the night with a friend, I am sure she could not have picked a worse time."

"And send all the rest of the footmen to find Bevis and Cedric," Ralph added, rubbing his hands together.

"Whatever are you doing?" Verity asked in dismay. "Surely you do not mean to make such blatant use of a guest in this house after you have offered him your hospitality?"

"You are talking utter rubbish," her brother-in-law snapped out, eyeing her crossly. "It is clearly my duty to further my nephews' careers."

"And I should find myself quite unable to hold up my head in society if I did not make a push to capture Lord Sherington for my daughter. Really, Verity, you are being much too particular. Instead of criticizing your elders, you had best bestir yourself, for we have not a moment to lose. I am counting on you to speak to Cook at once. Plan something especially tasty for his lordship—but no, we must not make it look as if we went to any extra effort. But on the other hand, we would not wish to insult him by offering him mutton. Oh dear, such a dilemma, I vow I do not know how we shall manage in such a short time. But you are a clever puss, and I am sure you will come up with just the thing."

"Mutton will be fine," Verity said despondently, even while she allowed her sister to push her in the direction of the back stairs, "since it is highly unlikely that Lord Sherington will ever set foot in this house again."

"Well, of course he will come back. He accepted, did he not? Did you not hear him say he was most pleased by our kind invitation? Oh, Ralph, do you suppose you can persuade him to take his seat in the House of Lords? What a feather in your cap that would be. Helping your nephews' careers is all very well and good, but you must not neglect your own." Taking her husband's arm, she drew him up the stairs, and Verity could hear them discussing the possible ramifications of this evening's visit until they were out of earshot.

Left alone, Verity realized it did not matter how many family members her sister collected. As she had tried unsuccessfully to point out to Petronella, Lord Sherington had doubtless accepted the invitation only as a convenient way of removing himself from their company with a minimum of fuss and bother. After all, if he had declined, Petronella and Ralph would doubtless have been most persistent in their attempts to persuade him.

But once having made good his escape from such a household, there was no chance Lord Sherington would voluntarily return. More than likely, he would simply send a polite note around with one of his footmen, saying that something unexpected had come up.

And if any of them tried to make use of the acquaintanceship, as slight as it was, doubtless he would end the matter ruthlessly by giving them the cut direct.

Descending to the kitchens, Verity realized she already missed his lordship so terribly that it seemed almost as if her life, as dismal and boring as it had been in the past, was now well and truly unendurable.

No one she met in the future could possibly begin to compare with Lord Sherington. Her only regret was that she had so very few memories of him, which must of necessity suffice for the rest of her days upon this earth.

One advantage of expecting such exalted company for dinner was that Ralph had ordered the fire built up in the drawing room, and for the first time during any of the Januaries that Verity had lived in her brother-in-law's house, she was warm enough that her arms were not covered with gooseflesh.

She was not, however, especially comfortable standing there waiting for the others to join her. Since Lord Sherington had not sent a note around canceling the engagement, Verity was one minute trembling with excitement thinking that he might actually appear, and the next minute falling into total despair, convinced that she would never see him again.

When Otterwall announced Lord Sherington, Verity could still not quite believe that her traveling companion had truly returned, not even when he crossed to where she was standing and bowed politely.

"May I say that I am indeed delighted to see that the journey today has not unduly fatigued you," he said. "I was half expecting to be told that you were lying down in your room, prostrate with exhaustion."

His words were in all ways correct, but again Verity

had the feeling that he had some ulterior motive behind
his polished manners. Without stopping to think, she
blurted out, "Why have you come here, my lord?" Then
realizing how rude she had just been, she hurried to
explain, "I mean, I know that my sister invited you to
dine with us, but I cannot understand why you
accepted."

"Should I have declined? Is your cook notorious for
producing inedible dinners? Does your brother-in-law
keep an inferior cellar?" His eyes narrowed. "Or is it
perhaps that my reputation has proceeded me, and I am
no longer welcome now that you know my full identity?"

Without any roundaboutation, Verity looked him
straight in the eye and said, "You told me yourself that
if you had relatives like mine, you would avoid them like
the plague. Yet now you seem to be going out of your
way to surround yourself with them."

"Surround myself?" he asked. "You exaggerate, Miss
Jolliffe. Your sister and brother-in-law are scarcely sufficient in number to surround me."

"But my niece, Antoinette, who is to be presented this
Season, is to dine with us also, as well as my brother-in-
law's two nephews, Bevis and Cedric Wasteney."

"Even so, that is not an impossible number to contend
with," he said, not looking the least bit put out. "But
you are still looking worried. Having offered you my
protection—in a manner of speaking—on the journey
back to London, do you now feel obliged to reciprocate
by protecting me from your relatives?"

Verity's thoughts, which had been confused for the last
several hours, finally settled, and she realized what it
was that she was afraid of. "I am well aware, as I am
sure you are also, that people in the higher levels of
society delight in making sport of others—that sometimes
they cultivate a friendship only so that they can later
relate amusing stories to their cronies."

"I assure you," he said, "that I never tell stories,
amusing or otherwise."

The smile he gave her was seductive . . . but also every
bit as false as any she had ever seen in London society.
Before she could question him further, however, she

heard voices in the hallway and knew that their few moments of privacy were at an end.

Quickly and efficiently shunted aside by her sister, Verity soon grew quite fed up with her relatives. Not only was Antoinette flirting far too boldly for a young lady not yet out, but even Petronella was batting her eyelashes at Lord Sherington as if she were not a good eight or ten years his senior.

Paying no attention to the antics of his wife and daughter, Ralph was attempting to discover his lordship's opinion on various political issues, and to add to the confusion, Bevis and Cedric were trying to interest him in investing in a horse currently running at Newmarket.

Somehow through it all Lord Sherington managed to remain polite and make the correct responses without committing himself to anything, but Verity felt her own frustration mounting with every passing minute.

Retiring to her customary chair in the corner, she wished she could make all these chattering people vanish, leaving her alone with Lord Sherington.

Just when she thought she could not stand it another minute, Otterwall announced that dinner was served.

Standing up, she heard Lord Sherington say, "Since it is potluck, I am sure there is no need to stand on ceremony."

Then before she realized his intention, he was beside her, offering her his arm.

"Oh, but my lord, we had thought—" Petronella began to simper, but Verity wasted no time.

Quickly, before her sister could intervene, Verity laid her hand on Lord Sherington's arm. Unless her sister wished to make a spectacle of herself by physically separating the two of them, Lord Sherington was now Verity's dinner partner.

Unaware of the drama that had just taken place under his nose, Ralph offered his wife his arm and led the way into the dining room.

The meal had been superbly prepared, but closer acquaintance did not make Miss Jolliffe's relatives any more palatable, Gabriel decided by the time the ladies withdrew, leaving the gentlemen to their port.

Offending Miss Jolliffe's relatives was hardly the way to make her fall in love with him, but he decided to do his best to keep the contact between the Wasteneys and himself to a minimum during the courtship. And after the wedding he would have no compunction about cutting the connection quickly and ruthlessly.

Luckily, it should only take a sennight, or perhaps a fortnight, for Miss Jolliffe to fall in love with him. Unfortunately, this single evening already seemed to have been dragging on for an entire week. He could only pray that none of the females in the household were musically inclined.

His wish was only halfway granted. Joining the ladies, he skillfully secured a seat for himself and Miss Jolliffe on a small settee, leaving no room for a third party to join them.

Thwarted in that respect, the baroness prevailed upon her daughter to play a tune for them on the piano. As entertainment, it fell far short of the mark, and as punishment for his failure to accommodate his hostess's wishes, it was much too severe.

"Do you sing?" he murmured to Miss Jolliffe, keeping his voice low enough that the others would not be able to hear above the music.

Glancing up at him, she replied quietly, "I am afraid I am not musically inclined, my lord."

"I suspect, Miss Jolliffe, that you are not being completely honest with me."

"No, I assure you, I neither sing nor play on an instrument."

"But from the slightly glazed look about your eyes, I am inclined to believe that your ear is good enough to recognize the difference between good music and what we are hearing at present."

With a smile tugging at the corner of her mouth, she said, "I must confess, I do prefer to hear the pianoforte played more . . . gently."

"I would appreciate it, Miss Jolliffe, if in the future you would be honest with me."

Stricken, she looked up at him. "I had not meant—"
Her voice faltered, then sitting up a little straighter she
met his gaze as squarely as she had at the Crown and
Thistle in Northumberland. "I promise I shall never lie
to you again."

Strangely enough, he believed her. Such an odd person
she was—and obviously it was not her looks alone that
made her a total misfit in London society. He could well
understand why other men had not had the wits to recognize her sterling qualities, and any last doubts he may
have had that he made the right choice for his wife
vanished.

"And you must promise never again, under any circumstances whatsoever, to allow your niece to play the
piano in my presence," he added in an undertone.

"She also sings," Miss Jolliffe pointed out, this time
making no effort to hide her amusement.

"On key?" Gabriel asked, wondering what further tor-
tures he had let himself in for.

"No," she replied quite candidly, "but Antoinette does
her best to make up in volume what she lacks in pitch.
Fortunately, as you pointed out before dinner, I do owe
you something for your assistance in Northumberland, so
I shall contrive somehow to cancel future performances."

"If you do, you will earn my undying devotion," he
said lightly.

Gabriel perused the invitations that had accumulated
during his absence. The Season might still be months
away, and London might be almost devoid of company,
but even so there were an adequate number of activities
for the socially minded to engage in: Poetry readings,
musical evenings, improving lectures, political dinners—
the ingenuity of London hostesses was impressive.

Unfortunately, having met Lord Wasteney in person,
Gabriel knew there was little chance that the baron, despite the name-dropping he had engaged in the previous
evening when they were sitting over their port, had received any of these same invitations.

Which meant Gabriel would have to exert himself to
an unaccustomed degree today and call upon some of

the more socially prominent matrons—those without marriageable daughters, to be sure. A few hints dropped in the proper ears, and the word would soon spread that the elusive Lord Sherington might be persuaded to put in an appearance if certain close friends of his were likewise issued invitations.

Selecting a half-dozen gilt-edged cards, he cast the others aside and rang for his carriage. To alleviate some of the boredom, since making morning calls was not his chosen way to spend an afternoon, he made a bet with himself as to how quickly the news would spread.

When the fourth hostess managed within the first three minutes of his visit to mention casually that she and Lady Wasteney had been schoolgirls together, he decided that he did not need to visit the last two ladies on his list.

Halfway home a further thought occurred to him, and he ordered his coachman to proceed to the Wasteneys' residence. He arrived on the heels of the lackey wearing Lord Finzel's livery, who handed over a gilt-edged invitation to the butler, who admitted Gabriel to the drawing room, where Miss Jolliffe was sitting with her sister.

Lady Wasteney accepted the invitation from the butler's hand with open astonishment, and even Gabriel found it somewhat astounding, since Lady Finzel's had been the last name on his list, and he had not even called upon her that day.

Seating himself beside Miss Jolliffe, he said, "I wish to thank you both for the pleasant evening last night."

The baroness did not immediately reply, and turning to her, he saw she was caught in a most unfortunate dilemma.

She could not quite manage to hide her curiosity to know the contents of the invitation, but on the other hand, she could not be so rude as to read her mail while entertaining a caller. Her eyes kept darting from him to the missive lying on the little table beside her, and as a result her conversation was most disjointed.

As amusing as it was to observe, Gabriel had no wish to spend the rest of the afternoon watching her dither. "I see you have also received an invitation to attend Lady Finzel's musical evening today. I have heard that she has engaged the services of that new Italian soprano everyone is talking about."

At his words, Lady Wasteney snatched up the missive and broke the seal. Unfolding it, she glanced quickly at the contents, then laid it aside. "We have not yet decided if we shall attend, for in general my husband finds such events boring." She smiled suggestively at Gabriel and batted her eyes.

Only a fool would have missed such a blatant hint, and Gabriel was no fool. "Then you must allow me to escort you," he said promptly.

"Oh, you are too kind, my lord," Petronella simpered, "but I should not wish to put you to any inconvenience on my behalf."

"It will be no trouble. I shall be delighted to act as escort for you ladies this evening."

Verity should have been happy at the reappearance of Lord Sherington in her life. After lying awake for hours the night before remembering every look he had given her, every word he had spoken to her, she should have been delighted that he was to accompany them to the party.

But one thing she knew she could count on—her sister would see to it that she, not Verity, was the one hanging on to Lord Sherington's arm this evening.

"It is settled then," Lord Sherington said, rising to his feet. "I shall pick you ladies up at eight this evening. And now, Miss Jolliffe, might I prevail upon you to drive out with me?"

"But it is too chill outside," Petronella said immediately. "It will be so much more cozy for us all to stay inside by the fire, and besides, I am expecting Antoinette to return from her shopping at any minute."

"I shall fetch my cloak," Verity said, ignoring her sister's objections and hurrying from the room.

Her hands were trembling so much she had difficulty tying the strings of her bonnet, but still she was ready to go by the time Otterwall had helped Lord Sherington with his greatcoat and top hat.

The day was damp, and there was a sharp wind out of the northwest that cut to the bone, but sitting beside

Lord Sherington in his carriage, Verity was so happy just being with him, it seemed as if an intense warmth were radiating out from her heart to every limb of her body.

But just as they were about to go through the gate into Hyde Park, he began to swear softly under his breath.

# 5

"MY LORD?" Verity asked, wondering why Lord Sherington's mood had changed so suddenly and without any warning.

"Why did you not tell me you were becoming chilled?" he asked, scowling down at her.

She opened her mouth to reply, but her teeth began to chatter too much for her to speak, and she was forced to clamp them tightly together.

"All females are cork-brained idiots," he muttered under his breath, but instead of turning the horses around and taking her back to her sister's house, which she fully expected him to do, he sent the pair trotting briskly along in the direction of Oxford Street.

Halting the carriage in front of Nicholay's Fur and Feather Manufactory, which had on display a beautiful sea-green cloak, he said curtly, "Come inside, and we shall see how that cloak in the window will suit you. It appears to be lined with fur, which will at least stop the wind."

"Oh, but I am sure it will be much too expensive. I could not possibly afford such an elegant cloak," Verity said, even while she gazed with envious eyes at the beautiful garment.

"You needn't worry about the cost. I have every intention of paying for it," he said, climbing down and reaching up to assist her.

Pulling back, she said, "You may buy whatever you wish, of course, but I am afraid it would be most improper for me to accept such an expensive present from you, my lord."

For a moment he looked so angry she rather thought he intended to drag her bodily out of the carriage and force her to do as he bid, but apparently upon further consideration, he saw the wisdom of her words.

He did not, however, allow her objections to deflect him from his chosen course of action. "Then I shall give you the money, and *you* shall go in and buy the cloak, Miss Jolliffe."

"Which is no less improper, my lord," she felt obliged to point out even though she was sure he was well aware of the rules of society.

"But much more discreet, which is all that matters in such instances."

Still she hesitated, and finally in exasperation he said, "I am not a patient man, Miss Jolliffe, and I dislike being crossed. You would do well to keep that in mind."

Knowing in her heart that what she was doing was morally wrong, Verity nevertheless allowed him to help her out of the carriage. He tucked a leather pouch heavy with coins in her hand, gave her a shove, and with great trepidation, she entered the shop, which was heavenly warm.

There was but one customer, a rather stout woman who appeared from her dress to be the wife of a prosperous merchant. She was keeping both clerks busy fetching out ostrich plumes of assorted colors for her inspection.

Verity tried several times to catch the attention of one of the young men, but they had apparently decided she was not rich enough to afford anything in their shop, and after a single glance in her direction, they rather pointedly ignored her.

After about five minutes, the door of the shop was thrust open, allowing a gust of very cold air to enter and with it a most irate Lord Sherington.

The elder of the two clerks immediately rushed to his side and asked if he could be of any assistance, but Lord Sherington merely scowled and pointed out crossly that another customer was ahead of him.

Looking around, the clerk's glance fell on Verity, but again he dismissed her. "I am sure the lady is not in any particular hurry, my lord," he began. "Might I show you some fine beaver pelts we received only last week—"

His voice more chilling than the wind outside, Lord Sherington said, "I have no wish to be waited on out of turn."

The other clerk and the merchant's wife gaped in astonishment, then the senior clerk hurried over to Verity, and demanded impatiently to know how he could help her.

"I should like to try on the green cloak in the window," she said.

"That is one of our most expensive items," the clerk said, looking down his nose at her.

Knowing Lord Sherington was there to back her up, even though he was pretending an interest in some driving gloves lying on the counter, Verity felt bold enough to say, "If you do not wish to show me the cloak, perhaps you could inform the owner of this shop that I wish to speak to him? I feel sure he will be interested in learning how his customers are being treated."

With ill grace and making no particular effort to hide his continuing displeasure, the clerk finally did as she had bid him and fetched the cloak out of the window, reluctantly spreading it out on the counter for her inspection.

The woolen outer fabric was so soft, it was even more delightful to touch than to look at, and the pelts lining it were so beautifully matched, they appeared to be seamless. "I shall take it," Verity said, refusing to think about what a truly shocking thing she was doing.

Paying for it with some of the coins Lord Sherington had given her, she instructed the clerk, who was now showing her all the respect a most valued customer might require, to wrap her old cloak up in a bundle. Then settling her new cloak about her shoulders, she left the shop without a backward glance and strolled unhurriedly down the street until she could not be easily seen by anyone curious enough about her identity to be spying on her from the shop window.

Less than a minute later Lord Sherington emerged empty-handed, climbed into his carriage, and drove the few yards to where she was waiting for him to pick her up.

"Are you warm enough now?" he inquired once she was settled beside him again.

"Quite warm, my lord," she said, trying to suppress an attack of the giggles. Shopping with Lord Sherington was not at all the tedious chore that running errands for her sister was.

Gabriel looked down into her laughing eyes, and for a brief moment he had an urge to kiss Miss Jolliffe.

Unaware of the direction his thoughts were taking him, she thanked him quite prettily for the present. She did not, however, tell him she loved him, the way his mistresses had always done after he gave them expensive presents. To be sure, a cloak, even if it was lined with fur, was not in the same category as a diamond bracelet.

Unaccountably irritated with her, he brushed off her attempts to thank him all over again. "I have no wish for you to catch a chill that will keep you housebound for weeks," he said curtly, signaling to his horses to proceed.

She said nothing during the drive back to her sister's residence, and when they arrived, she seemed almost reluctant to enter the house.

Remembering that he was supposed to be courting her, he solicitously inquired as to what was troubling her.

"Nothing, really. Only that I shall have a great deal of difficulty convincing my sister that I have saved enough from my quarterly allowance to pay for this cloak. She is certain to ask me how I came by it, you know."

Impatiently he said, "Do not be such a nodcock. Your sister will cause you no difficulties. If you cannot think of a plausible lie, you may count on it that Lady Wasteney can find a way to avoid noticing that you did not return wearing the same cloak you set out in."

Miss Jolliffe still looked guilty, which made him feel as if he had corrupted an innocent. Which he had done, of course—first by forcing her to accept an expensive present from a man not related to her, and then by encouraging her to lie.

Not having her scruples, however, he did not feel any

great remorse. His aunt had said he should have been
named after Lucifer, the fallen angel, and perhaps she
was right, because it mattered not to him what stories
Miss Jolliffe fabricated for others, so long as she kept
her promise not to lie to him.

But now that he thought of such things, he hoped she
was smart enough to realize that if she accepted so much
as a posy from another man, he would not be responsible
for his actions.

"As a general rule," he informed her, "I prefer to
drive out earlier in the day when there are fewer people
about. Therefore I shall pick you up at nine tomorrow."

"Very well," was all she said, and rather belatedly it
occurred to him that he was supposed to be catering to
her every whim, rather than expecting her to automati-
cally fall in with his wishes.

"I do beg your pardon," he said, "I did not think to
ask if nine o'clock is too early for you. Would you prefer
to drive out at a more customary hour, such as four?"

There was clearly no understanding women, because
instead of looking pleased at such a show of consideration, she seemed to withdraw from him, even while she
assured him that since she usually rose at seven, it would
be no trouble at all for her to be ready by nine.

Entering the house, Verity decided that there was no
understanding men. After such a pleasant drive, during
which Lord Sherington had been as casual with her as
he had been in Northumberland, he had once again,
without any warning whatsoever, changed before her
very eyes into a virtual stranger.

She could not put into words precisely what he was
doing, but she could tell immediately when he began to—
to playact, was the only way she could think to explain it.
The look in his eyes, the tone of his voice, his whole
manner changed. And when that happened, he reminded
her quite forcibly of Bevis and Cedric when they were
trying to sweet-talk her into loaning them a little money
to tide them over until the end of the quarter.

Lost in her thoughts, she slowly climbed the stairs to
her room, only to be waylaid in the corridor by her sister,

who followed her into her bedroom and demanded to hear every word of the conversation that Verity had had with Lord Sherington.

"Did he speak of this evening? Did he ask you where Antoinette was? Really, I shall have to speak to that girl. She is never here when she is wanted. I am sure he invited you to go for a drive only to show her that she may not count on his attentions."

Verity had no desire whatsoever to share her memories with her sister, so she concocted an innocuous conversation about the weather and a pair of horses that Lord Sherington was thinking of buying.

"Oh, if only Bevis and Cedric could have been here. They are such good judges of horseflesh." Suddenly Petronella's eyes narrowed, and she stared at the cloak Verity had just laid across the bed next to the parcel containing her old cloak. Anyone seeing the two items side by side would be bound to jump to the conclusion that Verity had just purchased a very expensive cloak . . . or that someone had bought it for her as a present. And given the amount of money Verity had spent on Christmas presents, added to the fact that she had left with Lord Sherington and returned with him, there could really be no doubt in her sister's mind as to how the cloak had come into her possession.

Frowning, Petronella opened her mouth as if to say something, but then she snapped it shut again. Shortly thereafter, she made an excuse to leave the room.

It would appear that Lord Sherington was correct, Verity thought sadly, picking up the cloak he had given her and hugging it to her for comfort. Her sister was obviously willing to bend any rule, even to allow Verity to step so far out of bounds that they would all be shunned by society forever if the truth were ever known.

And all because her sister wanted to use Lord Sherington to gain entreé into a higher level of society than she was accustomed to mingling with.

But who was Verity to cast the first stone? She herself was certainly not without sin. Moreover, it was rapidly being borne in upon her that the first step down the road to depravity was seldom the last.

Having essentially acted out a lie in that little shop in Oxford Street, and then having lied by omission to her sister, it was clear to Verity that her own conscience was becoming daily more flexible and accommodating.

And having admitted to herself that she would accept a dishonorable proposal from Lord Sherington, if offered, how could she draw the line at accepting any further presents from him, no matter how expensive or inappropriate? If the truth were known, she rather suspected she could refuse him nothing he wanted to give her . . . or take from her.

Unfortunately, instead of feeling properly repentant, all she could think about was seeing him that evening and once again in the morning at nine. And something about the way he had said that he generally preferred to drive out earlier in the day—did that mean?—could she assume?—that he intended to make a habit of taking her with him?

"But their names are not even on the invitation," Verity protested. "And—"

"Pish tosh, that is of no importance. Do you really think Lady Finzel will refuse to admit us all when Lord Sherington is one of our party? She would not be so reckless," Petronella said with a self-satisfied chuckle.

"But—"

"Enough," Petronella said firmly. "I wish to hear no more of this matter. Antoinette and Bevis and Cedric are accompanying us this evening, and that is that. If you do not wish to go with us, then that is, of course, for you to decide."

The look in her eye made it obvious what response she desired, but Verity was not about to give up an evening with Lord Sherington, even if all she could do was look at him from a distance.

And given Petronella's determination, Verity would be lucky to come close enough to Lord Sherington to touch the hem of his coat.

Gabriel deliberately arrived early at the Wasteney residence, expecting to have an opportunity for a private word with Miss Jolliffe before she and her sister were ready to depart.

Instead of a private tête-à-tête, however, he again found himself positively surrounded by Wasteneys of one sort or another. There was nothing he could do about Lord and Lady Wasteney, to be sure, but he had no intention of dragging along a schoolgirl who was not yet out and two horse-mad young men whose names were not even on the invitation.

His own consequence was great enough that he could have led a veritable regiment of uninvited guests into Lord Finzel's house, but that would not help him accomplish his purpose, which was to spend some time with Miss Jolliffe so that he could make her fall in love with him.

He was about to reduce the party by three, when it abruptly occurred to him that as unlovable as they might seem to him, Miss Jolliffe loved this motley assortment of people. Following that thought to its logical conclusion, it was quite possible that the way to her heart was through her family.

As much as it pained him—and he was quite sure they were capable of pushing tediousness to new heights—he would somehow contrive to be nice to each and every one of them. He drew the line, however, at transporting all seven of the party to Lord Finzel's house in his carriage, even though Bevis and Cedric readily volunteered to sit outside on the coachman's box.

Splitting up the party, even for the short drive, resulted in a good half hour of discussion as to who would ride in Lord Wasteney's carriage—Lady Wasteney's suggestion was that Miss Jolliffe should do so, but Gabriel squashed that idea as soon as it was presented.

When it was finally determined that the ladies should ride with him and the gentlemen in Lord Wasteney's carriage, there followed, of course, another half hour's delay while Lord Wasteney's horses were harnessed and the carriage brought round, because no one had remembered to send word to the stables that transportation would be needed.

Gabriel, however, was up to the occasion. While they

were waiting, he allowed Lord Wasteney to instruct him
on the intricacies of government finances, which Lord
Wasteney did not understand in the slightest. Gabriel
also showered compliments on Lady Wasteney and soon
had her cooing at him and calling him a dear boy. He
even allowed the two young men—and he could never
remember which one was Bevis and which one was Cedric—
to describe for him their exploits on the hunting field.

The only time he slipped up was when Miss Wasteney
was irritating him so much by fluttering her eyelashes at
him and rapping him on the arm with her fan that he
was unable to resist the temptation of giving her a set-
down. "Do you have something in your eye, Miss
Wasteney?" he asked.

Far from being discomposed, the chit immediately giggled, rapped him on the arm with her fan, and batted her
eyelashes at him. Females were all so totally predictable.

Except, of course, for Miss Jolliffe, who was sitting
meekly in the corner with her needlework, watching the
farce with interest. And with approval? He could not tell
from her face, but surely she must admire his fortitude,
his valor, his truly incredible patience.

With difficulty he stifled a yawn.

The evening passed much as Verity had expected it to.
The Italian soprano was quite talented, the guest list
quite rarified, and Lord Sherington even managed, at an
odd moment now and again, to escape from her relatives
long enough to bring her a glass of punch or to introduce
her to one or another person of note.

But for Verity the best parts of the evening were the
beginning and the end, when she was sitting beside Lord
Sherington in his carriage. Even though her sister and
her niece were occupying the opposite seat, both of them
chattering a mile a minute, Verity found quiet pleasure
simply in being so close to his lordship.

Without the morning's drive to look forward to, of
course, her mood would have been vastly different, but
she could be patient a few more hours. For now it was
enough just to be aware of his shoulder almost touching
hers, of his knee almost bumping hers. . . .

All too soon, the carriage turned onto Curzon Street and stopped in front of their residence. In his usual efficient way, Lord Sherington somehow managed to arrange things so that the Wasteneys entered the house first, giving her a few all-too brief moments alone with him on the stoop.

"Thank you so much for a lovely evening," she said, smiling up at him.

"I am pleased you enjoyed it," he replied with easy charm.

"I am very grateful that you were so kind to my relatives. It has been such a treat for them."

To her astonishment, Lord Sherington's smile vanished, to be replaced by a scowl—which was actually too weak a word to describe the look of rage on his face. Then as if too angry to speak, he turned away without even saying good-bye and left her standing alone on the stoop, unable to think what she had done or said that had offended him.

She wanted to run after his carriage—to catch up with him and demand an explanation for his strange behavior. But before she could take a step, she realized too late what had angered him, and indeed she could not blame him in the slightest. In truth, the fault rested entirely upon her shoulders.

It was her family who had pushed him to this point— her relatives who had fawned on him, clung to his side, assaulted him with their demands. All five of them had, in addition, shamelessly and blatantly used Lord Sherington to advance their own positions in society.

Although it had not been Verity's idea for them all to tag along, clearly she had not made an adequate effort to prevent them from acting in such a crass manner, quite like the most encroaching mushrooms.

It must have seemed the crowning blow when she had actually thanked Lord Sherington for allowing her relatives to impose upon him to such an unconscionable degree.

Shivering from the cold, she entered the house and reluctantly climbed the stairs to her room. Huddled in her bed that night, she lay awake while the clock on the mantel ticked away the minutes and the hours. She had learned years ago to keep her tears in her heart, but she could not stop her thoughts from going around and around in an endless circle.

If only she could reverse time . . . if only she could have a second chance . . . if only she had not been so foolish as to lose Lord Sherington's regard forever . . . if only she had tried harder to prevent her sister from dragging everyone along . . . if only . . .

Gratitude! After all his noble efforts this evening, all that wretched female felt was gratitude! Miss Jolliffe was supposed to have told him she loved him!

Gabriel paced back and forth in his study, so overwrought he could not sit still even for a minute.

Gratitude, bah! What did she think he was, a philanthropist? There wasn't an altruistic bone in his body, as anyone in London could have informed her.

Why did she think he had wasted an entire evening being nice to her relatives? Because he enjoyed torturing himself? Because he was a kind person?

Gratitude? If he had the silly girl here now, he would be hard put not to wring her neck.

The devil take her gratitude. He had accomplished nothing by allowing her relatives to hang on his sleeve, so the devil take them also.

Would he come? Verity paced the hallway, stopping every few minutes to check the clock, which seemed to be broken, so slowly did the hands move.

Would he remember that they were to drive out this morning, or was he still angry at her for what she had done? He had every right to break their engagement, and no obligation to send her a note canceling their drive, but she could not keep from hoping.

Please, she prayed, biting her lower lip to keep from crying, let him come. I cannot bear to lose him now. I know I cannot expect to hold his attentions for long, but this is too soon. I love him so much, I shall surely die of a broken heart if he abandons me. Please, let him come—please!

*    *    *

By the time he pulled his phaeton to a stop in front of the Wasteney residence at precisely nine o'clock, Gabriel's temper had cooled somewhat. He was still angry enough at the failure of his efforts the previous evening, however, that he decided if any of Miss Jolliffe's family wished to invite themselves along on this morning's expedition, he would not hesitate to be rude.

Bad manners were not necessary, however, because Miss Jolliffe herself opened the door for him, already cloaked and bonneted and looking quite bright-eyed and well-rested. The remnants of his irritability made him inquire after her relatives.

"Oh, none of them arise before noon," she replied, following him to the carriage.

"Then why do you get up so early, or have you perhaps been less than honest with me?"

She looked up at him and in the early morning light he could see that her eyes were not actually gray, but gray-green, without the slightest fleck of yellow. "Oh, no, I really do get up at seven every day. Someone must supervise the servants, you see, or they become quite lazy and shiftless."

"There are times, Miss Jolliffe," he said, picking her up by the waist and virtually tossing her into his carriage, "when you make me so angry, I am tempted to strike you."

She did not offer a word in her own defense, which only reminded him of her habit of sitting alone in the corner of the drawing room, and that in turn only made him that much angrier. "How can you allow your sister to use you like a drudge? Have you no backbone at all? If you would learn to assert yourself more, your relatives would stop treating you like an unpaid servant."

It was fortunate that there was little traffic, because he sent his horses along at far too brisk a pace for safety.

"But I quite enjoy supervising the household," Miss Jolliffe replied, not the least bit put off either by his wrath or by the reckless way the carriage was presently careening through the streets. Either she had no nerves, or she was too stupid to recognize the dangerous situation she found herself in.

"I find it much more interesting than paying social calls and gossiping with visitors," she said as calmly as if she were serving tea to the vicar's wife. "I especially like reading books on housewifery and collecting recipes and instructions, although some of the older ones are quite impractical."

He was about to explain to her that it mattered not whether she enjoyed being a drudge, because other people would only see that she was being ill-used. If she acted as if she were nothing more than a poor relation, everyone would treat her as such.

But just as he was about to begin his lecture, it occurred to him that her activities were actually an ideal preparation for marriage. After all, did he want a wife who slept until noon and had no idea how to write out a menu or how to instruct the housekeeper? Indeed he did not.

If Miss Jolliffe found enjoyment in managing her sister's household, he would be a fool to complain, especially since she did not seem to feel any compulsion to bore him with tips on the proper way to dress a roast or the easiest way to remove wine spots from carpets.

His temper considerably cooled, he slowed his horses to a more reasonable pace and drove in silence the rest of the way to the river. Crossing Westminster Bridge, he turned to the right and followed the road that bordered the Thames.

Although Miss Jolliffe did not pester him with questions about why he had chosen such an odd destination— or perhaps because she did not ask—he told her. "I have always had an affinity for the water," he said. "Doubtless from the thirteen years I spent in the merchant marines."

For a time he was content to watch the barges moving slowly past, then he felt compelled to explain himself more fully. "I was fortunate, I suppose. Some sailors come to hate the sea, but I came to love its vastness and beauty even while I learned to respect its power. The first thing a sailor learns—or in some cases the last—is that the ocean does not forgive mistakes. Even knowing that, when I arrived at the age of one-and-twenty and came into an inheritance, I used the money to buy the first of my ships."

Miss Jolliffe made a slight sound, and looking down, he saw pain in her eyes.

"But then—surely you do not mean to say that you were only eight when you went to sea?" she asked with dismay.

"It is not unheard of for midshipmen to be that young," he said harshly, "and it could have been worse, after all. I could have gone to sea as a common sailor. As it was, I received a good education in mathematics, navigation, accounting, and other such subjects required of ship's officers. To be sure, I am singularly lacking in Latin and Greek and have only read the classics in translation. But that deficiency has caused me no particular problems, so you may save your pity for someone else."

"I was not pitying the man you are now," she said quietly, "but I cannot help but feel compassion for the boy you once were, and likewise for all the other children who are sent to sea at such a tender age. Surely, after what you yourself must have experienced, you do not advocate such practices?"

His mind filled with so many painful memories that it took him a moment before he could answer. "No, I do not allow boys younger than twelve on any of my ships, not even as cabin boys."

"But I do not understand. If you were heir to an earldom, why on earth did your father put you in the merchant marines instead of the Royal Navy? And why at such a young age? Why were you not sent to Eaton or Harrow and then to Oxford or Cambridge first?"

When he did not immediately reply, she sighed and said, "I am sorry, I did not mean to pry into such personal matters."

Staring out at the water flowing past, never stopping, eternally changing yet staying forever the same, he began to speak once more, his voice calm and dispassionate, and yet it seemed as if the words were being forced up out of the darkest reaches of his soul.

"My father—or I should say, the man who was married to my mother—did not consider me to be his heir. She played him false, you see, and no one knows who her lover was. I suspect her husband would have been happy if I had not returned from my first voyage—if I had died at sea. He had an older son, so I was totally superfluous. The earl hated me so much, even when my half brother died three years ago of the fever, he did not send for me."

Beside them the river flowed onward, never pausing in its journey toward the sea, and beside him Miss Jolliffe sat silent and still for what seemed to him an eternity.

# 6

GABRIEL EXPECTED Miss Jolliffe to recoil from him in disgust, as any properly brought up young lady might be expected to do upon learning that her escort was in essence a bastard, but instead she linked her arm through his and asked, "Which of the countries that you have traveled to did you like the best?"

"England," he replied without hesitation.

She tilted her head and smiled up at him, and he felt some of the tension drain out of his body. Reaching the place where the road curved away from the river's edge, he turned the carriage around, and they started back toward the bridge.

"You say you love the water—do you miss being at sea?" she asked.

"There are times when I do, and I have considered purchasing a yacht for my own enjoyment, but for the most part life on board a warship or merchant ship is too brutal for any person of sense to wish to subject himself to it. But still, I find it soothing to go to the river or to the seashore, and I feel much more at home on the docks than I do in the drawing rooms in London."

"I have never been on board ship," she commented, "and doubtless I would find it a very strange and alien place."

"And now you have made me curious to know where you feel most at home."

"I used to feel at home when I was in my grandmother's room in Oakwood Manor, but she has been dead five years now, and everything has changed. It is odd—

78

even though I have lived with my sister for eight years, I cannot say that I truly feel at home in her house."

Gabriel started to reply, but before he could utter a word, her expression changed and she snapped out, "And no more than you do, do I want your pity." She was glaring up at him with the first sign of temper that he had ever seen her display.

"I do not pity you, Miss Jolliffe. I save my pity for people who are weak. You, however, are quite a strong person, although you do your best to disguise it."

"Indeed I am not," she replied tartly. "As you have pointed out to me not an hour ago, I am a spineless creature—a poor relation who delights in being used as a doormat."

He laughed. "On the contrary, it is your relatives who are weak. Only people who know themselves to be powerless have a need to browbeat someone else."

"And the person who allows herself to be browbeaten? She is not weak? You will excuse me for contradicting you, Lord Sherington, but your logic is faulty."

"I do not mind if you contradict me," he said, "but you will find I am seldom wrong, and certainly not in this case. It is only common sense to realize when one is not in a position to fight back. But it is inner strength that keeps a person from being broken in spirit, and you have that strength, Miss Jolliffe, despite what you may think."

She was a fraud, Verity realized. The man sitting beside her quite misunderstood the situation. It was just like that day in Nicholay's Fur & Feather Manufactory—all the strength she felt, all the fortitude he thought he saw in her—it all came from him.

Before Lord Sherington decided it amused him to befriend her, she had been so weak, her relatives had used her as they wished—ignoring her, ordering her around, criticizing her, humiliating her in front of others—and she had been too much a pudding-heart to object. Only when he was with her did she feel strong.

And after he lost interest in her? How well would she manage after he became bored with her and sought out someone new to entertain him?

Even worse, how could she suffer the pain of losing him without dying herself of a broken heart?

Linking her fingers tightly together in her lap, she tried to hide her agitation of spirit, wishing desperately that she could think of something innocuous to say that would get her mind off the coming pain. But she had never been able to chatter on about nothing in particular the way her sister and her niece did.

When Lord Sherington finally deposited her on her doorstep, it seemed but a foretaste of what was to come. He had revealed to her something of his past, and now she understood the reasons for the hunger she had seen in his eyes. Unfortunately, despite his insistence that she was a strong person, she knew she was not woman enough to fill the empty places in his heart.

Now, watching him drive away, she felt as if he had stolen the very soul from her body, but she doubted if he was even thinking about her.

And as always when he left her, her first thought was to wonder if she would ever see him again. This time the pain was already starting, because even though she had waited, hoping he would suggest another morning drive, he had made no mention of any future meeting between the two of them.


"He is quite taken with me, you know," Petronella confided in her best friend, Harriet Coupland. "I am sure that if I gave him a sign that I would welcome his advances, he would ask me to be his mistress."

Verity almost choked on her tea, but Harriet merely giggled and said, "Oh, Petronella, you would not dare be so bold."

"Certainly not, but I must tell you, it quite pains me to know I must someday break his heart. I believe, actually, that with a little effort, I can push him in Antoinette's direction. She is quite like me when I was a young girl, you know."

How she could utter such a tarradiddle was beyond all understanding, but as Petronella rattled on, Verity gradually realized that her sister was not consciously lying—she actually believed what she was saying.

"And he is quite grateful that Ralph is willing to give him advice on the political issues facing this country. Ralph says that he has almost persuaded Lord Sherington to take his seat in the House of Lords. That will be quite a feather in Ralph's cap."

There was a tap at the door, and Otterwall entered, bearing a letter on a salver.

Petronella snatched it off the tray, gave a shriek of delight when she saw the seal, then waved it triumphantly in Harriet's face. "There, what did I tell you, he has sent us another invitation."

"Who?" Harriet asked, craning her neck to try to see the letter more closely.

"Who? Need you ask? Lord Sherington, of course."

At her sister's words, Verity's heart missed a beat and then began to pound at double its normal speed. Lord Sherington had not yet grown tired of her company. Impatiently she leaned forward, wishing she could snatch the letter out of her sister's hands.

Well knowing she was the center of attention, Petronella broke the seal and carefully unfolded the heavy vellum, then read aloud, " 'I hope you will forgive the lateness of this invitation, but I would appreciate it if you and your family would join me in my box at the opera this evening.' There—what did I tell you. Two nights ago he took dinner with us, last night he escorted us to Lady Finzel's musical evening, and today he has invited us to the opera. Why, the man positively dotes on me, and cannot endure to let a single day go by without seeking out my company."

Harriet snatched the missive out of Petronella's hand and inspected it. "The invitation is addressed to Lord and Lady Wasteneys and Miss Jolliffe. I do not see that he has signaled you out for any special attention."

"Well, of course not, silly. That would be indiscreet. But it is me he is besotted with, of that you may be sure, even though he is forced to include my husband in the party for propriety's sake."

Leaving the two women arguing about the significance of the wording of the invitation, Verity hurried up to her room and began to search in her clothespress for a gown suitable for an evening at the opera.

But it was soon clear to her that she had allowed her wardrobe to become shockingly neglected. Since she had rarely gone out the last several years, all her evening gowns were old and out of style, and the colors were likewise quite drab. Nothing she owned was elegant enough to dazzle Lord Sherington, and she found that she very much wanted to impress him.

In a daring move, she went to her sister's room, hoping to find some discarded dress that could be made over. They were of the same height, so that would be no problem, and even though Petronella was possessed of a much fuller figure, taking in a garment was always possible, where letting it out would not have been.

At the very back of Petronella's wardrobe Verity found an absolutely stunning gold gown trimmed with bronze, which her sister had not worn in two years, but which with a few simple alterations would not look too dated. Carrying it back to her own room, she quickly tried it on.

The neckline gaped open, but a few tucks should fix that. When she looked at herself in the cheval glass, however, Verity knew that she could never wear such a gown, no matter how high or low the neckline.

The dress was indeed elegant, but all it did was make her appear even more colorless and insignificant than usual. She looked, in a word, like a sparrow trying to wear a peacock's tail.

Unable to look at her reflection any longer, Verity changed back into her regular dress. She had really no choice but to wear her gray silk, but perhaps she could at least persuade one of the maids to help her change the ribbons? And she could wear her grandmother's pearls, which would bring her comfort even if they did not turn her into a ravishing beauty.

That evening, while they were waiting for Lord Sherington to arrive, Verity caught sight of herself and her sister in the mirror. The contrast between the two of them was so great that no one would have ever taken them for sisters.

Decked out with the Wasteney emeralds, Petronella was more eye-catching than ever before, whereas Verity had to admit that she herself looked exactly like what Lord Sherington had accused her of being—a nondescript, easily overlooked, extraneous female. In other words, a poor relation.

But even while she was coming to that conclusion, Lord Sherington was announced, and Verity once again felt her self-confidence soar. Since she had no looks, he must find something to admire about her character. Or perhaps he, too, felt there was a bond between them?

At times like this, when he caught her eye from across the room, it seemed as if he did. And yet at other times it was obvious he was only trying to manipulate her.

Straightforward coercion she did not mind in the slightest. In general Lord Sherington made no effort to disguise the fact that he was not a man who concerned himself overly much with the wishes of the people around him, and she was perfectly content when he was snapping at her for something she had said or berating her for something she had done or simply ordering her to do his bidding.

But every now and then he seemed to be trying to disguise his true nature from her, although it seemed absurd of him to expect her to be taken in by a few token efforts to consider her wishes.

Indeed, absurd was the only word to describe his behavior. Since he was a man who was obviously accustomed to taking whatever he wanted from life, and since it was equally obvious that she was unable to tell him no, why on earth should he ever feel constrained to play the part of a proper English gentleman around her?

The singing was magnificent, but the attention they were receiving from the other boxes was making this evening an ordeal for Verity. Still, she was doing her best to emulate Lord Sherington and ignore the rude stares and pointing fingers of the other opera-goers, and she could only wish her relatives would do the same.

Antoinette had been left home with a sore throat, which had distressed her mother no end. But unfortunately Petronella's motherly concern did not demand that she stay home to nurse her only child. Seated between Lord Sherington and her husband, Petronella was obviously determined that not a soul in the theater should fail to notice in whose box she was sitting. To that end, she was smiling and waving at friends, acquaintances, and even those who Verity suspected were total strangers.

Bevis and Cedric, who had simply appeared and without the slightest by-your-leave made themselves at home in Lord Sherington's box, were even worse. They were openly ogling the opera dancers and carrying on a heated discussion as to the relative merits and reputations of the less than respectable ladies in the other boxes.

As for Ralph, Verity could wish her brother-in-law did not snore quite so loudly. He woke up only when the curtain came down at the end of the first act, and hoards of people, most of them barely acquainted with the Wasteneys, began squeezing into the box, all coyly soliciting introductions to Lord Sherington, whose frosty manner only encouraged them rather than discouraged them.

Petronella was in alt, gushing out welcomes, kissing the ladies' cheeks, and simpering when the gentlemen lavished compliments on her.

For once Verity was thankful she was so easy to overlook that no one appeared to notice her on the other side of Lord Sherington, who was large enough to make an effective shield.

By the time the curtain went up on the second act and the last of the intruders straggled out of the box, Verity could only wish her relatives might follow after them.

As if able to read her thoughts, Lord Sherington turned to Bevis and Cedric and said, "Might I ask you gentlemen a favor?"

Receiving an enthusiastically affirmative response, he continued. "My hunt master writes to inform me my hunters have been growing fat and sluggish from lack of sufficient exercise, but I fear my business is too pressing for me to ride to hounds this season. Might I persuade you both to stay at my hunting box in Gloucestershire and make use of them? It is rather indifferent hunting country, not at all what I am sure you are accustomed to, but perhaps you can contrive to amuse yourselves tolerably."

Verity thought her brother-in-law's nephews were going to expire on the spot with delight—either that or they were going to knock Lord Sherington head over heels into the pit, so enthusiastically were they clapping him on the back and telling him what a capital fellow he was.

"One of my grooms is driving up there tomorrow quite early," Lord Sherington managed to interrupt them long enough to say. "If you could be ready by eight, perhaps?"

Although they assured him they could be, neither young man made any move to leave the box. Verity was amused to see that Lord Sherington was up to this additional challenge.

"It is indeed a shame, but I suppose if you are to be packed on time, you will have to miss the rest of the opera."

How he managed to keep a straight face while Bevis and Cedric stumbled all over each other in their haste to leave the box, Verity would never know. Fortunately she was able to hide her amusement behind her fan.

Without the two of them the box was considerably quieter. Even Petronella finally seemed satisfied that she had attracted enough attention, and left off her waving, although she still directed her attention everywhere but to the stage.

Leaning over, Verity murmured in Lord Sherington's ear, "That was excellently done."

"I am glad you approve," he said in a voice meant only for her ears. "Tell me, Miss Jolliffe, does your brother-in-law hunt?"

"I am afraid he does not even ride," she answered.

"Then has he ever expressed an urge to see Jamaica? Or perhaps India? A long sea voyage would be quite easy to arrange."

"He dislikes traveling, and considers even Hampstead beyond the bounds of civilization, which to him decreases in direct proportion to the miles one travels from Whitehall."

"Pity," Lord Sherington said, turning his attention back to the singers.

The real pity was that Verity had never had a chance to travel and given her circumstances doubtless never would. Since she was a small child and her grandmother had read stories to her about distant countries and the strange customs prevailing there, Verity had always wanted to travel.

On the other hand, were she forced to choose between sitting beside Lord Sherington in a crowded theater and sailing up the Nile, she knew she would not hesitate to remain where she was.

Despite the best intentions, Gabriel could not bring himself to remain in the box during the second intermission. He would have liked to escort Miss Jolliffe out into the salon for some simple refreshments, but he knew too well that her sister would hang on his other arm if he even suggested such a possibility.

Having heard this particular opera before, he could tell when the second act was almost over, and before the intermission actually began, he rose to his feet and informed his guests that he was going to procure refreshments for them all.

As anticipated, Lady Wasteney leaped to her feet and reached for his arm, but by stepping back quickly, he managed to avoid her clutching hands.

"Ah, but only consider, my dear Lady Wasteney, that it will be a sad crush, not at all a suitable place for a lady. I could not wish you to be knocked about by all and sundry. It is better that you remain here, where it is safe."

She began to protest, of course, but he was out the door and away.

"Well, and as if I am not quite able to handle myself in a crowd," Petronella said huffily, sitting back down in her seat. "More than likely Lord Sherington is only slipping away for an assignation with his mistress."

"His mistress?" Verity said, hoping her face did not betray her emotions, which were in desperate turmoil.

"Eleanor Lowndes. She has been sitting opposite us all evening. Surely you have noticed her? The fourth box from the left and the next row up? Her red hair is quite unmistakable. She uses a henna rinse, or so I have been told."

"I am afraid I have not paid much attention to the people in any of the other boxes," Verity confessed.

"Then what have you been doing all evening, pray?" Petronella asked in astonishment.

A black-haired woman opened the door to the box and peered in.

"Lord Sherington is not here at the moment," Verity said, and the woman withdrew immediately. Turning back to her sister, Verity explained, "I have been listening to the singing, of course."

"The singing? Really, you are a hopeless case. Since an evening at the opera is obviously quite wasted on you, we would have done better to have left you at home." Petronella snapped open her fan and began waving it briskly in front of her face.

"Who is she?" Verity asked faintly.

"I am sure I have never seen her before in my life."

For a moment Verity was confused. "Oh, I did not mean the woman at the door just now. I meant Miss Lowndes."

"Mrs., not Miss. She is a widow with a rather dubious reputation. She was a McIntyre from the north of Ireland before she married a rich cit with one foot in the grave. Luckily for her, he did not last two years after the wedding, but unfortunately he was not quite as blind to her indiscretions as she thought he was. He left the bulk of his fortune to his grandnephew, and she got only as much as the law provides for a widow."

"Does he—that is Lord Sherington—does he intend to marry her?" Verity asked faintly.

"Marry? Honestly, sometimes you ask such stupid questions, you positively amaze me. I am sure Mrs.

Lowndes is convinced he will marry her in the end, but she is deluding herself. As beautiful as she is, you may count on it that when Lord Sherington decides it is time to acquire an heir, he will pick as his wife some pretty little thing fresh out of the schoolroom, not a widow who is already long in the tooth."

"How old is she, do you suppose?" Verity managed to ask.

"Six-and-twenty is what I have heard," Petronella answered promptly. "Now look at that woman in the third box over who is wearing all those rubies? Do you see which one I mean? That is Harriet Wilson, the most famous courtesan in London. And that is Lord Bathwell kissing her hand. Lady Bathwell must be absolutely livid. Really, he is an old fool to have visited that woman's box when his wife is also here at the theater with her cicisbeo."

Verity paid no attention to the people her sister was pointing out. The evening was ruined for her. Not only had she learned that Lord Sherington had a beautiful mistress, but she had also discovered some disquieting facts about herself.

Pictures of Lord Sherington holding another woman in his arms kept appearing in Verity's mind, no matter how desperately she tried not to think about such things, and the pain cut so deep, she felt as if she could no longer breathe.

Despite her assertions to Lord Sherington that one should never try to change the person one loved, she found herself now quite unable to control her jealousy. If any action on her part, no matter how low or mean, could have removed Mrs. Lowndes permanently from his presence, she would not have hesitated to do it. And even worse, she, who had never before hated another person, was now ready to hate a woman she had never met.

Verity was thoroughly ashamed of herself, but obviously she was beyond redemption, for despite everything, she could not keep from wondering what it would be like to live under Lord Sherington's protection.

\*　　\*　　\*

In no mood to associate with his fellow man, Gabriel was standing half hidden behind a pillar when a familiar voice spoke to him.

"Gabriel, my love, however did you come to share your box with a pair of nobodies like Lord and Lady Wasteney? Did they perhaps blackmail you, or have you lost a foolish wager?"

Eleanor Lowndes gave a low, throaty chuckle, but Gabriel was not amused. He had never had much tolerance for people who questioned his decisions, and he found nothing humorous in his mistress's remarks.

"Good evening, my dear," he said, barely glancing at her. "I was not aware that you were fond of the opera."

"You know what it is that I am most fond of," she said, her voice husky with desire . . . or at least with what he was apparently supposed to assume was desire.

Looking at her now, it seemed to him that she was rather garishly dressed, and it was odd how much she reminded him of Lady Wasteney. To be sure, Eleanor was years younger, but already she was beginning to look a trifle overblown, like a rose that was decidedly past its prime.

"Are you still angry with me, my love?" she said, batting her eyelashes at him. She moved closer, pressing herself against him, but he stepped away, finding her heavy scent too cloying.

As if she had not noticed his withdrawal, she laid her hand on his arm and gave it a squeeze. "Perhaps we could meet later this evening, after you have disposed of your guests?"

Looking down at her fingers, which were curled like claws around his arm, and also thoroughly irritated by the possessive expression in her eyes when she smiled up at him, Gabriel knew their relationship was over. "The house in Somers Town has another two months left on the lease," he said coldly. "Feel free to make whatever use of it you wish since I will not be needing it."

Her mouth gaped open, and for a moment she looked remarkably ugly. But she recovered herself quickly and said, "Surely you do not mean that you—that I—" Her eyes filled with tears, which spilled over and ran down her cheeks, but he made no move to offer her his handkerchief.

"Have I not made myself clear?" he asked. "Our relationship is over—finished—ended. Now do you understand?"

He could almost see the thoughts running through her head as she frantically tried to figure out some way to hang on to him, but something about his expression must have convinced her that she would only be wasting her time.

"You are heartless," she said, no longer troubling to keep the spite out of her voice. "And you have used me shamelessly."

He laughed at that. "Need I remind you that you were the one who shamelessly threw yourself at me? I needed only to open my bedroom door to you and you could not wait to rush inside."

She looked angry enough to claw his eyes out—not that she would have been able to do so if she had tried. "Everyone told me you were ruthless, but I was sure that you could not be as cruel as they made you out to be."

"Ah, then that is where you made your mistake. You should have listened to what everyone was saying." He turned to go, but again she caught at his sleeve.

"It is not Lord and Lady Wasteney you are interested in, is it, Gabriel," she said. "If you are giving me my congé, then you must already have your eye on my replacement. You intend to seduce the younger sister—that Miss Jolliffe, do you not! Such a pathetic little nobody, she will give you no real sport. Why she has no more figure than a boy." The widow's eyes narrowed. "Have your tastes become so perverted that you can prefer her to me?"

"My dear, do you have any idea how boring you have become?"

"You may think you can make any woman in London jump to do your bidding, but in this case you will rue the day you treated me so shabbily. I shall have a pleasant chat with Miss Jolliffe, and afterward you will be lucky if she will give you the time of day."

Gabriel smiled. "I had not realized until this evening how positively vulgar you are, Mrs. Lowndes. In fact, I would say that despite your pretense of being a lady, you have the soul of a tart."

She stepped back, her cheeks as red as if he had slapped her. "And you may be an earl, but it is clear to me that you are no gentleman."

"The difference between us is that I do not pretend to be what I am not, which you would do well to keep in mind. A gentleman would never kiss and tell, but I give you fair warning that if you so much as say good afternoon to Miss Jolliffe, or start a single innocuous rumor about her, you will find that all the *gentlemen* in the clubs will hear every detail of your behavior in bed."

"You—you—"

"Good-bye, Mrs. Lowndes. We shall not, I am sure, have occasion to speak together again."

Leaving his former mistress looking quite stricken, Gabriel worked his way through the rapidly thinning crowd, procured four glasses of champagne, and returned to his box just as the curtain was rising.

Miss Jolliffe thanked him for the beverage in her calm way, and he realized that while she lacked beauty, she did have countenance. In his wildest fantasies he could not imagine her indulging in such a vulgar scene as the one Mrs. Lowndes had just enacted for his benefit.

While her eyes were on the singers, Gabriel studied Miss Jolliffe's profile and realized that the lines of her forehead, nose, and chin were remarkably good. Moreover, as slender as she was, she was doubtless one of those lucky women who would age well—who would look much the same at fifty-six as she did at twenty-six.

She lacked the beauty of a rose, or even a daisy, but like a good wine, he rather thought she would only improve with age.

As if she could sense his attention, she turned to look at him, and he noticed that her eyes were also remarkably well shaped. They were indeed one of her better features, and he was surprised that he had not noticed before how pretty they were.

# 7

IT DID NOT matter that Lord Sherington had left her alone in the box while he went to meet with his mistress, Verity realized. Now that he was sitting beside her again, she admitted to herself that he could have a dozen mistresses and parade around with them in public—and she would willingly bear any disgrace just to be with him.

Leaning over, he murmured in her ear, "Do you wish to drive out again tomorrow morning?"

Too overcome with emotion to speak, she simply nodded her head.

"Nine o'clock?"

Again she nodded, and he turned his attention back to the stage, but she continued to gaze at him. More than likely Petronella was right. When the time came that Lord Sherington decided to provide for the succession, he would undoubtedly want a wife fresh out of the schoolroom, and it was understandable that until then he would prefer to have a racy widow for his mistress.

On the other hand, here and now it was Verity who was sitting by his side, and tomorrow she would be the one driving out with him. It was quite inexplicable, but she was not about to complain.

"Did you enjoy the opera last night?" Lord Sherington asked.

They were again heading down Pall Mall in the direction of the Thames, Verity realized, and she was so filled with joy, she wanted to throw her arms around Lord Sherington and give him a tremendous hug. Instead she contented herself with tucking her arm through his.

"I enjoyed the music very much," she said calmly.

"But?" he asked.

"But?"

"There was a hesitation in your voice, as if not everything was to your liking."

"You will think me foolish, but I dislike being stared at. I would have preferred to listen to the music without all the other people. Would it not be wonderful if one could enjoy such things in the privacy of one's home?"

He did not laugh at her silly fantasy, for which she was grateful, and when they again crossed Westminster Bridge and turned along the drive that bordered the river, she felt secure enough to question him about his years at sea.

The life he described to her was appalling, and she was amazed he had lived to tell about it, and so she told him.

"The first thing I learned at sea, even before I learned what a mizzenmast was, was that the strong survive and the weak do not. The second captain I sailed under taught me a lesson about power that I have never forgotten. He made me the man that I am today, and if I could be granted one wish, it would be to meet him again."

"He must have been a most admirable man to have won the respect of a child."

Lord Sherington turned to look down at her, and his eyes were colder than the wind that was whipping the water of the river into whitecaps.

"You misunderstand," he said in an emotionless voice. "When I say I would like to meet him again, it is only because I would like to pay him back for the torment I suffered at his hands. He was a bully of the worst sort, and I was the person on the ship least able to protect myself. The other officers were too afraid of him to lift a finger to help me. I still bear marks upon my back from the floggings he gave me, and he killed two sailors while I was on his ship."

Warmly wrapped though she was in the fur-lined cloak he had given her, Verity still shivered. Lord Sherington sounded so bleak she knew he must be reliving those days, and she regretted having called back those memories—not that she was reluctant to hear about them, but she could not bear to see him suffer again remembering them.

Gazing into the distance, he said, "Before the ship even rounded Cape Horn, I made a vow to myself that I would do whatever I had to do to survive. I was ten at the time, but I knew that someday I would have even more power than the captain had. It took me years to achieve my goal, of course, and I received inestimable help when I reached my twenty-first birthday. As I mentioned before, a distant relative left me a modest fortune, which gave me a financial base to build upon."

He turned to look at her again, and she was relieved to see that his eyes had lost some of their coldness. "Money is the source of great power, Miss Jolliffe, and you would do well to remember that. With money you can buy other people, body and soul. Since my twenty-first birthday I have never again allowed myself to be at the mercy of another human being."

He paused, as if waiting for her to contradict him, then went on, his voice still harsh. "Well before that time I learned that knowledge is almost as powerful as money. Books are more potent weapons than swords, Miss Jolliffe, but if you know other people's secrets, or even just their weaknesses, you will be able to control them.

"There are some who believe power lies in physical prowess, but it is vastly overrated, because muscles and a strong back can always be hired. Even the most decrepit old man, if he has sufficient money and knowledge of how to use it properly, can be equal to the strongest bruiser or the most accomplished swordsman."

Gabriel did not stop to question why it was so important to explain to Miss Jolliffe about power; he only knew it was vital for her to understand.

"You have to develop a forceful personality also—a strong will that can bend other people to your purpose. If you lack the determination to use the power you have acquired, other people will take advantage of you. If you hear people say that I am ruthless, then you should believe them, for only by being ruthless have I survived this long."

Looking into her eyes, he could see quite clearly that she lacked the capacity to wield power effectively, but he also realized it did not matter. He was strong enough to take care of her, to protect her from the sharks who fed upon the smaller fishes. Anyone who dared to hurt her would learn what true suffering was.

"And what about love?" she asked, her gray-green eyes turned trustingly up to meet his. "Is not love a powerful force?"

Gabriel found himself totally unable to answer. What could he tell her? If he told her the truth, that love only makes you weak—that if you love another person, you give that person power over you—then he would be defeating his own purpose, which was to make her fall in love with him.

But on the other hand, he found himself strangely reluctant to utter the usual fatuous drivel—to tell her what he knew to be an outright lie, namely that love is wonderful and all powerful.

"I cannot tell you about love," he said finally. "Although many women have professed to love me, I have never encountered true love before I met you. The love you bear for your family is unique."

Given such a golden opportunity, she should have told him she loved him also, but she did not. Instead she said, "It is quite possible that some of the women you have known actually did love you."

Angry that she had not declared her love, he said, "It was lust they felt, no matter how they tried to disguise it with pretty phrases. I understand that even if you do not, Miss Jolliffe."

Verity again felt jealousy twist her insides into a painful knot. She wanted to tell him that she was different from all those other women—that she did truly love him with all her heart—but she could not say the words that she knew he would never believe.

Nor could she remain silent. Smiling to hide the pain, she said, "I suppose now you are waiting for me to confess that I have been lusting after you since I met you."

Lord Sherington obviously was not interested in learning that a plain spinster of advancing years desired him.

"I am not in the mood for jokes," he snapped out, and jerking his arm free of hers, he turned the horses around and set them going at a rapid pace toward Curzon Street.

Verity silently cursed her wayward tongue, for it was obvious she had disgusted him by her vulgar remark. He did not speak on the way back, and when they finally arrived at her sister's house, he made no move to help her climb down from the carriage.

Why, oh why, had she let her jealousy get the better of her common sense?

By the time he reached his house in Grosvenor Square, Gabriel was still in a towering rage. Entering his study, he slammed the door behind him, then threw himself down in his chair and stared into the fire.

Miss Jolliffe should be in love with him. After all, he had been courting her night and day for nearly a week, and he knew himself to be not unattractive to women.

Doubtless every chit preparing for the upcoming Season would fancy herself in love with him if he even deigned to dance with her twice—and any number of more seasoned ladies had already made it quite clear that they would be more than happy to agree to any proposal he might make, whether honorable or dishonorable.

So why was Miss Jolliffe so resistant to his charms when no other woman was?

Thinking about it, he was compelled to admit that he was not actually handsome, and his manners were not polished, but he had never deluded himself. He was willing to admit that his attraction for women lay primarily in his title, his fortune, his place in society, and most of all in the power he could wield when it suited him.

To be sure, there were dozens—perhaps even hundreds—of women who would be quick to overlook the flaws in his character and to swear eternal love and devotion, but only so that they could control him.

What he had been forgetting when he considered his problem with Miss Jolliffe was that professing love for someone was not at all the same as truly loving that person. Giving most women a diamond bracelet or even a flowery compliment could produce an avowal of love, but such women were not capable of real love.

It was therefore not to be wondered at that it was taking him longer to win Miss Jolliffe's love than he had anticipated. On the other hand, although he was still waiting to hear those all-important words, she definitely did not seem to hold him in aversion, and she made no effort to avoid his company. Moreover, even when he had told her the shameful secret of his birth, she had not recoiled from him in disgust, as other so-called ladies would undoubtedly have done.

In fact, when he remembered the things she had on occasion discussed with him, he was inclined to think she trusted him. She had, after all, told him about her grandmother, and he did not think she was in the habit of exposing her inner feelings to other people any more than he was.

All in all, considering how much progress he had already made in such a short time, he could not doubt that in another week or two he would achieve his goal. Therefore it behooved him to begin putting his affairs in order for his forthcoming nuptials.

Rising from his chair, he went to his desk and wrote a brief note to Mr. Parkins, his man of affairs, instructing him to pay off the mortgages on Sherington Close.

And tomorrow he would also arrange to purchase a special license, so that he would not encounter any delays once Miss Jolliffe fell in love with him.

Gabriel had become such a familiar figure at the Wasteneys' residence that Otterwall, the butler, had quite lost his nervousness. He was, however, still properly deferential, and he announced Gabriel with all due formality. Gabriel could only wish his host and hostess would likewise refrain from displaying undue familiarity.

"Ah, my dear Sherington, welcome, welcome," Lord Wasteney said, crossing the room to shake his hand. Then with an arm draped around Gabriel's shoulders, the baron led Gabriel back to the baroness, who coyly indicated he should sit beside her.

Pretending not to notice, Gabriel deliberately sat down

in a small chair opposite her. The tea tray had already
been brought in, so he hoped that Miss Jolliffe would
soon put in an appearance—and that the daughter of the
house would remain in the schoolroom for a change.

"We were just discussing the dinner party tonight at
Porterlane House," Lord Wasteney said, puffing out his
chest. "All the most important Whigs will be there, and
we are invited every year. It has become quite a tradition
in the party, you know."

"Do you plan to attend, my lord?" Lady Wasteney
looked at Gabriel with such arch coyness, he had trouble
resisting the impulse to walk out the door without a backward glance.

"I had not quite made up my mind," he said, and was
rewarded for his perseverance when Miss Jolliffe appeared, followed, to his regret, by Miss Wasteney. Upon
catching sight of him, the annoying chit immediately
stopped walking in a normal manner and began to mince
into the room as if her legs were tied together at the
knees.

With a smile for Miss Jolliffe, Gabriel turned back to
Lord Wasteney. "These political functions are so awk-
ward, you see, when one knows virtually nobody."

Lord Wasteney immediate seized the bait. "I should
be more than happy to introduce you around, my dear
fellow. I do not flatter myself when I say I know everyone who is anyone in both parties. Not that you will see
a single Tory face this evening. No, no, you may be sure
there will be no cockeyed reformists in attendance at
Porterlane House spouting their radical nonsense to ruin
your enjoyment."

Lord Wasteney prosed on and on about who would
doubtless be there, giving thumbnail sketches of each
personality, but Gabriel paid only superficial attention.

Miss Jolliffe, he decided, was looking remarkably fine
this afternoon, and he deliberately stared at her until the
color rose in her cheeks. Then he winked at her and was
rewarded with the merest smile. Yes, indeed, he was
making quite satisfactory progress. Another week should
surely do the trick.

"So shall we count on you this evening, Sherington?"

Lord Wasteney said, and everyone looked at Gabriel in hushed expectancy.

Why not? he thought. An evening among politicians might well serve as an object lesson for Miss Jolliffe, who still did not understand all the intricacies of power.

"Do you know, Wasteney, you have thoroughly allayed my anxieties on the matter," Gabriel said, rising to his feet. "My mind is quite made up to attend this evening."

"Excellent, excellent," Lord Wasteney said, likewise rising to his feet.

"Then I shall pick the three of you up this evening at half past seven," Gabriel said, before he took his leave, well-satisfied with himself.

Miss Jolliffe had proved to be a remarkably intelligent woman. Tonight would be a test of just how fast a learner she was, and he would derive considerable enjoyment from watching to see how she comported herself.

How had it happened? Verity wondered after Lord Sherington departed. It seemed as if she could do nothing but offend him time and again, and yet he always returned, his anger gone as if it had never existed. Would she ever understand him?

"The three of us? Merciful heavens, what are we to do?" Ralph tottered back to his seat and collapsed beside his wife.

"Do?" she asked.

"He obviously expects your sister to accompany us this evening," he explained, "and her name was not on the invitation."

"Well, that is no matter," Petronella said, and Verity wanted to cry out that it was indeed a matter of life and death.

"Have you lost your wits, woman?" he said, leaping to his feet and looking quite apoplectic. "Do you wish to risk offending Lord Sherington now that I have finally succeeded where others have failed?"

"Sit down, my dear, and do compose yourself. I am sure Lord Porterlane is equally anxious for Lord Sherington to attend. We shall simply send a little note around explaining the situation, and I am sure he will correct what was undoubtedly a simple oversight."

Since Lord Porterlane had never given any indication that he was even aware of Verity's existence, she was certain that he had never had any intention of inviting her to his dinner party.

On the other hand, she was equally sure that once Lord Porterlane understood that he had a chance to persuade Lord Sherington to take his seat in the House of Lords, Lord Porterlane would find a place for her at his table.

Rising to her feet, she excused herself and went up to her room, where she could dream about Lord Sherington without distracting interruptions.

After the carriage deposited them at Porterlane House, Lord Sherington held Verity back slightly, allowing her sister and brother-in-law to get a little ahead of them.

"This evening I want you to pay particular attention and see if you are able to differentiate between those who wield real power and those who only suffer from the illusion that they do," he said in a low voice. Then without waiting for her reply, he tucked her hand firmly in the crook of his arm and together they walked up the steps and were admitted.

As soon as the butler announced them—"Lord Sherington and Miss Jolliffe"—a dead hush fell over the room where the other guests were assembled, and a veritable sea of amazed eyes were turned in their direction.

To be sure, the greatest part of their astonishment undoubtedly came from seeing Lord Sherington at a political function of any kind. But it was equally obvious that some of the curious stares were directed at her, and when a low murmur arose from the crowd, Verity knew beyond a shadow of a doubt that many of them were asking who Miss Jolliffe was and why Lord Sherington was escorting a little nobody like her.

Mindful of Lord Sherington's instructions, she paid close attention and therefore noticed when a few of the curious looks changed to calculating ones. Although she was sure she would never be able to remember who was who, much less give Lord Sherington an account of who held power and who did not, she did her best to note those faces in particular.

Quite early in the evening she realized that this dinner party was not precisely what it purported to be. Her brother-in-law had bragged so much about his position in the party that she had never thought to question his own assessment of his importance.

But it soon became clear to her that he had not been invited so that the party leaders could consult with him on matters of policy; he and the majority of the others were merely being paid back for their loyal support.

In an odd twist on what she was used to seeing in more social settings, the important people were the ones moving methodically through the crowd flattering first one peer and then the other, rather than the reverse.

She rather suspected that the more a person was fawned over—and Ralph received an inordinate share of the compliments being tossed about, which made him quite puffed up with his own consequence—the less actual importance that person had.

It was so easy to see, she was surprised that so many people appeared to be taken in by it. Were they so blind that they could not recognize when they were being used? Or were they simply so desperate to achieve the illusion of power that they deliberately pretended not to see what was so obvious?

She glanced across the room and found Lord Sherington watching her, and she recognized in herself the same folly she was scoffing at in these others.

Unlike a man, a woman derived whatever power she had from her beauty, her family, her fortune, or in rare cases her wit. Unfortunately, as much as Verity might prefer it to be otherwise, she was plain, her family was not particularly notable, her fortune was insignificant, and she was quite unable to drop bons mots into the conversation the way Lady Porterlane was doing. In short, Verity had to admit she had absolutely no power in society.

Which made it all the more strange that Lord

Sherington was deliberately seeking out her company since he was—by his own admission—driven by a desire for power. She could not delude herself that he was an altruistic man, which meant her intuition was right: he wanted something from her.

She knew she would have to make a greater effort to discover what his ulterior motive was, even though it was plain that she would doubtless be much happier—at least for the time being—if she continued to shut her eyes to reality, the way Ralph and the other aspiring politicians around her were doing.

The next morning Verity paced the hall, impatient for Lord Sherington to arrive. Although he had mentioned nothing about driving out, she had no worry that he would fail to show up. Whatever game he was playing with her, it was not yet over. And when the end came, she now had enough confidence in herself to be sure she would recognize it.

The clock in the hallway chimed nine, and she opened the front door and peered out. Lord Sherington's carriage was just turning the corner onto Curzon Street, and dark morning seemed instantly to brighten.

Pulling the door shut behind her, she hurried down the steps to the street, and as soon as he reined his horses to a stop, she was ready to climb into the carriage and take her seat beside him.

He said nothing during the drive to Hyde Park, and once they were through the gates, he took the road that lay on the north side of the Serpentine. Slowing the horses to a walk, he began to quiz her about the previous evening.

Without hesitation she described what she had observed. "I am afraid I cannot tell you the names of all the people there who share the illusion that they have power," she began, "but I can tell you who has the actual power."

She listed several men and one woman, then went on to analyze which ones held more power and which ones less.

"Then you think Lord Darley was the most powerful

person there?" Lord Sherington asked when she was done with her recital.

"Not exactly," she said. "I noticed that even Lord Darley deferred to you."

He did not contradict her, nor did he compliment her on how well she had done, but instead he merely asked her how her sister and brother-in-law had enjoyed the evening.

"They had a marvelous time. They completely accepted the illusion for reality. My brother-in-law believes that he persuaded you to attend the dinner, and my sister—" Verity hesitated, then said daringly, "my sister believes that you are so smitten with her charms that you cannot keep away from her."

Lord Sherington did not laugh at her last remark, nor did he become angry at her. Instead he merely stared down at her for the longest time with the oddest expression on his face. Finally he said, "And you, Miss Jolliffe—what illusions do you harbor about me?"

"None, my lord. I am fully aware that you are deliberately trying to manipulate me, but I have not yet figured out what it is that you are trying to achieve—what it is you want from me."

Although his tone remained mild, she could now see a spark of anger in the back of his eyes. "Last night's little exercise in observation has proved that you are not lacking in intelligence. If you make an effort, I am sure you will discover exactly what I want from you."

"It would be easier if you would tell me," she said, keeping her own voice just as calm as his.

His temper flared up, and without warning he reined in the horses, grabbed her chin, and pulled it around so that he could stare directly down into her eyes. "I give no charity, Miss Jolliffe, and sooner or later you will discover that nothing worthwhile is ever given to you."

She could hardly hear what he was saying. The touch of his hand on her face made it impossible for her to think. Only by locking her hands together under the folds of her cloak was she able to resist the need to reach out and touch his face.

Every day her love for him grew stronger and deeper.

Every parting from him was like death—every time she saw him again was like rebirth. If she were given the power to change him in any way, she would not make use of it. He was ruthless, uncaring, harsh, often bad-tempered, but she loved him with every particle of her being.

"Well, Miss Jolliffe. Do you think you can discover what it is that I want from you? In case you have not noticed, I am not a patient man."

His horses began to fidget restlessly, and Verity started to tell him that she would do her best to be quick, but then she changed her mind. Let him have a taste of his own medicine, she decided. "Your impatience is not my problem, Lord Sherington. I am not the one who is wanting something from you."

For a moment she feared she had gone too far, but then he gave a bark of laughter and released her chin. Flicking the reins, he dropped the subject of power and he began instead to tell her fanciful tales of the exotic places he had visited on his travels around the world.

Listening to him, she could not be quite sure if what he was telling her was the simple truth or if he was fabricating the stories out of thin air, but it mattered not in the slightest, because every word he uttered was fascinating.

She felt quite let down when he returned her to her sister's house, and mounting the steps to the front door, she was strangely reluctant to open it and return to her normal life. But the day was too cold to remain standing outside, so she overcame her aversion and went in.

She had not been lying when she had told Lord Sherington she loved her family, and she could not imagine ever ceasing to love them. But up until this time she had not actually considered the question of whether or not she also liked them. Loving and liking, she had discovered, were a world apart.

Except where Lord Sherington was concerned. She not only loved him with a passion that frightened her by its intensity, but she also liked him better than anyone else she had ever met.

Both liking and loving seemed to be such rare commodities in the world, especially in London. Was it ambition that allowed a lady to compliment a friend to her face even while decrying that friend's lack of fashion behind her back? Was it fear of being hurt that made the ladies of the *ton* kiss one another's cheeks while still managing somehow to hold each other at arm's length?

All Verity knew was that even while her hours spent with Lord Sherington were becoming more and more enjoyable, her hours spent in the Wasteney residence were becoming more and more difficult to endure.

# 8

"LADY OTTILLIA has been awaiting your return for over an hour," Kirkson said, taking Gabriel's coat. "I have put her in the rose salon."

"Calling before noon again," Gabriel said mockingly when he joined his aunt. "Have you come about yet another unbreakable family tradition that I have broken?"

"I will not have it, Sherington," she said, her jowls shaking with rage. "I will not have it, do you hear?"

"I hear, but I confess I haven't the slightest idea what you are talking about this time."

"It is scandalous—*scandalous*—and you must put a stop to it at once. It is unsupportable."

"Have you been nipping at my brandy again, Aunt Cudmore?" Gabriel held the decanter up to eye level, as if estimating the amount remaining.

"As if a Rainsford would ally himself with such a nobody. Why her father is only a knight, and I doubt if her dowry is above a thousand pounds."

Gabriel now understood the nature of his aunt's errand, and he no longer felt the slightest urge to tease her. "You are speaking of Miss Jolliffe, I presume?"

"It is so utterly preposterous—everyone is linking her name with yours. Really, Sherington, it is up to you to squelch such malicious rumors. Though doubtless if the truth were known, one would discover the gossip is all your fault. I should not be at all surprised if such scurrilous stories were started by some irate husband whom you have cuckolded."

"The rumors are not unfounded," he said calmly, and

at first he was not sure she had heard him, for she continued to rant and rave for some time.

Then suddenly she fell silent, as if her brain had finally caught up with what her ears had heard. "You are—you are—" she gasped out, shaking her head as if still unable to believe what he was saying. "No, it cannot be true!"

"I am indeed courting Miss Jolliffe," he said simply.

Rising to her feet, she glowered up at him. "I shall not allow it, do you hear me, Sherington? I shall not allow it!"

"If you or any of the other Rainsfords make any attempt to interfere in my life, you will discover what it feels like to be the target of scurrilous gossip. You will find that I myself am capable of an astounding degree of maliciousness. In short, Aunt Cudmore, you will find not only yourself and your husband ostracized from society, but also everyone you care about. I will allow you Bath and Tunbridge Wells, but not even your children's children will ever dare show their faces in London again by the time I am done."

"You could not be so ruthless," she said weakly, collapsing back into her chair. "I begin to think you are the Devil himself."

"But of course, Aunt Cudmore. You yourself have already pointed out that I am a fallen angel," Gabriel replied.

For the first time in his memory, his aunt was reduced to utter silence. On the way down to his study, he instructed Kirkson to assist his aunt to her carriage.

He had intended to drop in on the Wasteneys that evening, in the hopes that he might see Miss Jolliffe, but now he reconsidered. Perhaps it might be better to go to his club instead, to see for himself what was being said.

Verity sat alone in her room, staring into the fire. Normally she was a very energetic person, but lately she had become quite a dreamer, and every one of her dreams was centered about Lord Sherington.

Hearing a commotion in the hall, she awoke from her reverie and realized that her sister and niece had returned from a round of morning calls. Verity had begged off, giving as an excuse that she had too many tasks to do around the house.

Actually, she had done none of the chores and now found it difficult even to remember what it was she had intended to do.

There was a light tap at the door, and Verity assumed it was one of the maids, wishing to consult with her. But it was her sister who opened the door, her cheeks flushed and her eyes feverishly bright.

"Ah, Verity, might I have a word with you?" Without waiting for an invitation, Petronella entered the room and pulled a chair over to where Verity was sitting.

Verity did her best to hide her astonishment at her sister's unaccustomed behavior. As a general rule, Petronella did not go traipsing about the house seeking people out. When she wanted a word with Verity or her daughter or even her husband, she invariably sent a maid to fetch the desired person.

"It has been so long since we have had a chance for a comfortable coze, dearest Verity," Petronella continued.

Verity was tempted to point out that they had never had a comfortable coze—that Petronella rarely seemed to notice her except to issue orders, which Verity then did her best to carry out. But instead of baiting Petronella, Verity merely nodded her head and waited to hear what was on her sister's mind.

"Oh, dearest Sister, I think you are the only one in the world who can understand how desperately I want my beloved daughter to make a good match, for you are the only one who knows how unfairly I have been treated all my life—how I have suffered."

Verity was so astounded by her sister's words, she leaned forward slightly to smell her sister's breath, because the immediate explanation was that Petronella must be bosky. But there was no indication that she had been drinking anything but tea.

"All the time I was growing up, Mama and Papa treated me quite shabbily, as I am sure you know from your own experiences. It did not matter how hard I tried, I could never please them. The only one they ever cared about was our dear brother Francis. As the only son and heir, he could do nothing wrong. There was always money enough to buy him a new horse or a new gun or a new jacket, but they resented every penny they had to spend on me. I cannot tell you how many nights I cried myself to sleep."

Verity was surprised that Petronella was expressing her feelings so freely. Due to the large difference in their ages, the two of them had never shared confidences. But perhaps now that Verity was older, things were going to change? Perhaps Petronella truly wanted them to develop a closer relationship?

"You were so much younger, I suppose you were unaware of all that was going on. Then, too, you were always Grandmother's favorite," Petronella said, a momentary note of bitterness creeping into her voice. "All those miserable years I yearned to escape from Oakwood Manor—to find someone who would love *me* the best. I dreamed of the man I would marry, who would adore me and do everything in his power to please me."

Suddenly she began to sniffle. Confused by the sudden change of mood, Verity handed her a handkerchief, and Petronella wiped her eyes, blew her nose, and with no apparent effort regained her composure. "Archibald was so wonderful. You never met him, so you could not possibly imagine how handsome he was."

Archibald? Verity had never heard of anyone by that name who was connected in any way with her sister.

Petronella smiled sweetly, and her eyes took on a distant look. "His father was a viscount, and Archibald was considered to be quite a catch, you know. All the other girls envied me, and everyone said he was sure to come up to scratch."

Her lower lip began to quiver, and Verity quickly got up and fetched another clean handkerchief from her drawer.

"But then his father took ill, and he had to leave London, and I could not wait for him to come back because I knew Papa would never allow me to have a second Season. He told me before I left for London that if I came home I would have to settle for Squire Millard's son. So—so—"

Tears welling up in her eyes, she wailed, "So I had to marry Ralph. Oh-h-h—" She burst into tears, and Verity hurried to her sister's side. Dropping to her knees, she put her arms around Petronella and began crooning and rocking her back and forth.

"But now it does not matter anymore," Petronella said, her sobs stopping abruptly. Grabbing Verity by the shoulders and holding her at arm's length, she enunciated each word very carefully. "Because now I have a beautiful daughter, and I vowed when she was born that she would have everything I was never able to have. She is going to make such a good marriage that years from now people will still be talking about it. You will help me, will you not, Verity? Of course you will. You are my sister, so it is your duty to help me." Petronella smiled coyly.

"Of course I shall help you," Verity said soothingly.

"It will be the marriage of the Season," Petronella said, rising to her feet. "Once people see the way the wind is blowing, I shall be invited everywhere." Without a backward glance, she sailed majestically out of the room.

Verity let out her breath, which she had not even been aware she was holding. So much for a comfortable, sisterly coze. It was now no longer a mystery why Petronella had sought her out. She wanted Verity to use her influence with Lord Sherington to facilitate Antoinette's entrance into society.

Unfortunately, Verity's understanding of the situation had come a bit late. Even though she felt a deep aversion to manipulating Lord Sherington for her own end—or for her sister's purpose, which was essentially the same thing—she rather thought she had just promised to do precisely that.

But on the other hand, how could Verity refuse her own sister? All these years Petronella had had so much resentment bottled up inside of her—it was no wonder she was so difficult to live with.

And she had been right about one thing—Verity had been exceedingly lucky to have had their grandmother's love. Without her influence, Verity knew she would have grown up to be a far different person.

The only thing to do was to be honest with Lord Sherington rather than deceitful. If she explained the situation to him without any attempt at roundaboutation, surely he would be willing to dance occasionally with Antoinette once the Season started, and perhaps even take her up for an occasional turn around the park?

Knowing how strong-minded he was, Verity was quite certain that if he did not wish to be obliging, he would not hesitate to refuse point-blank. He was not, after all, a man who allowed social customs and polite manners to dictate to him what he might and might not do.

Gabriel was not pleased to discover that the betting book at Brooke's corroborated his aunt's story. The majority of the bets entered in it during the last week concerned him and his intentions vis-à-vis Miss Jolliffe. As much as he would have liked to put a stop to such wagers, he was enough of a realist to know that any action he might take would only make matters worse.

Cousin Phillip was the one betting most heavily that Gabriel would not come up to scratch. It would appear that Phillip had not only inherited the Rainsford jaw, but also the Rainsford propensity to gamble with money that he did not actually possess.

Well, if he thought he could rely on Gabriel to keep him out of debtor's prison, he would soon discover that he had made a serious error in judgment.

"Sherington, just the man I was looking for."

Gabriel turned to see Ibbetson approaching him.

"Thought you might like to play another hand or two of piquet," the round little man suggested.

Amused at his persistence, Gabriel said, "And how are your lovely daughters?"

"Oh, they are quite well pleased with their father. I managed to catch me two sons-in-law at Christmas, and another one is hooked but not yet reeled in," Ibbetson said, puffing himself up with pride. "M'third daughter wants to have a Season before she ties the knot, but the marriage contracts have already been signed, so there's nothing to worry about there."

"I begin to believe I should have enjoyed spending the holidays with you after all. It sounds as if you provided quite lively entertainment for your guests."

"Livelier for some than for others," Ibbetson said, winking and nudging Gabriel with his elbow. "Now about that hand of piquet?"

"If it is your fourth daughter you have in mind—" Gabriel began, but Ibbetson interrupted him.

"No, no, the chit ain't actually going to be out for another year. Still in the schoolroom, you know." He eyed Gabriel speculatively, then grinned. "Devil take it, I might have known you'd be suspicious. Thing is, I thought you might be persuaded to give me a hint—just a clue as to which way you was meaning to jump? I'd be happy to give you a cut of my winnings."

Amused by the man's candor, Gabriel shook his head with mock regret. "I am afraid if we played, all I would do is take your money again, leaving you considerably poorer and none the wiser."

"Ah, well, no harm in trying. Buy you a drink?" Ibbetson said with all the expansive good humor of a man newly freed from the burden of having four unmarried daughters.

Why not? Gabriel thought. Ibbetson obviously kept up with the gossip, and after a drink or two, he would probably not even notice that Gabriel was pumping him for information rather than vice versa.

Following the little dandy into the card room, Gabriel came face to face with his cousin, who was accompanied by two cronies. As unsteady as they were on their feet, it was readily apparent that all three had been drinking for some time.

Phillip glared at Gabriel with loathing. "You bastard," he said, slurring his words. Then with no warning he swung his fist right at Gabriel's face.

The swing was glaringly abroad, and sidestepping it easily, Gabriel caught Phillip's arm and twisted it behind his back.

"If you will excuse us," Gabriel said to Ibbetson and

the other two men, who were all three gaping at him in astonishment, "my cousin and I wish to have a private discussion." Shoving Phillip ahead of him, Gabriel headed for the door.

Phillip's two friends were obviously too foxed to understand what was happening, but Ibbetson trotted along behind. "Does this have anything to do with Miss—" he started to ask, but a single look from Gabriel was sufficient to halt the little dandy in his tracks and convince him that it was not in his best interest to speculate on such matters.

There were, unfortunately, several other members present, and Gabriel knew the story of this little contretemps would be all over town before morning. He therefore made no effort to be gentle when he forced his cousin out of Brooke's and into a hackney coach. Giving the driver instructions to take them to the Albany, where Phillip had rooms, Gabriel climbed in and took the seat opposite his cousin.

"You hurt my arm," Phillip said sulkily, rubbing the injured limb.

"Consider yourself lucky," Gabriel said. "The next time you accost me in public you shall not get off so lightly."

Obviously Phillip was not properly repentant, because he answered with a string of curses, ending with, "How dare you! How dare you!"

Gabriel sighed. Dealing with obnoxious drunkards was not one of his favorite pastimes, and under normal circumstances, he would simply have walked away and allowed his cousin to vent his spleen—and make an ass of himself—in public. But Gabriel wanted no scandal attached to Miss Jolliffe's name, and he rather thought she was involved in whatever burr was under Phillip's saddle.

"How dare I what?" Gabriel asked, wishing all his relatives did not suffer from an inability to speak concisely and to the point.

"I shall never forgive you for this—never! Do you hear?"

"Perhaps you might tell me what it is that I have done

to offend you?" Gabriel asked. Clearly it was the wrong thing to say.

"Your very presence in London offends me—nay, your very existence upon this earth must be offensive to all men of good breeding," Phillip said, his tone becoming surly.

"Yes, yes, I will grant you that my failure to expire is a great inconvenience to you, but since I have done nothing to cause you to think that my demise was imminent, I find that insufficient reason for you to screech at me this way."

"Insufficient reason? You paid off the mortgages on Sherington Close—do you not call that sufficient reason? You blackguard!"

Even knowing it would only enrage his cousin all the more, Gabriel could not completely repress a smile. "It is less than a month since you berated me for not paying off the mortgages, and now you are angry at me for doing so. Really, my dear cousin, you should strive to be a bit more consistent, else you can hardly blame me for failing to act in accordance with your wishes."

"You don't care tuppence about my wishes," Phillip said with a snarl. "You only paid off the mortgages because you intend to marry that—that *female*."

There was a long silence, and Phillip was beginning to shift uneasily on the carriage seat by the time Gabriel finally spoke. "Do you know, I had not realized before how brave you are. I doubt there is another man in London with courage enough to speak so to me. Or perhaps you are just too stupid to realize how dangerous an enemy I can be?"

"Bah, you would never lift a finger against me. Indeed you cannot, because I am your heir." Phillip's attempt to sound self-confident fell short of the mark.

"Before your tongue gets you into any more trouble," Gabriel said smoothly, "I had better explain some of the facts of life to you. To begin with, I am not a patient man. I have allowed you more liberties than most men because in the eyes of the world you are my cousin, even though the two of us know that our relationship exists only on paper. But tonight you have quite exhausted any credit you may have had with me. If you interfere in my life in the future, whether by word or deed, you will discover just how ruthless I can be. And do not expect the slightest mercy because of our supposed relationship."

"It doesn't matter what I do," Phillip said with a whine, "for you mean to destroy me in any case. If you marry that little nobody, you might as well put a bullet through my heart, for you will beggar me."

"No one forced you to make so many wagers on the length of my bachelorhood."

"It will be your fault if I lose all those bets, so you have an obligation to take care of things for me."

"I shall be more than happy to," Gabriel replied, and his companion sat up a little straighter.

"You will?"

"Indeed yes. And I shall even let you decide where you will be exiled—Calcutta or Jamaica."

Fortunately, they arrived at the Albany before Phillip had a chance to tell Gabriel exactly what he thought of that solution.

By the time Gabriel returned to his own house, his mood had not improved. He was, in fact, calling himself seven kinds of fool for having wasted an evening checking out the gossip in the clubs. He had accomplished nothing except to deprive himself of Miss Jolliffe's company.

Seeking what little consolation there was in a bottle of brandy, he sat alone by the fire in his study and tried to come up with a strategy for winning Miss Jolliffe's love. The trick, of course, was to figure out what it was that women wanted from men.

Actually Gabriel had figured that out years ago— women wanted power and control. The problem was that Miss Jolliffe was different from other females. She did not seem to have any desire to manipulate him for her own devious purposes.

By the time the bottle of brandy was half empty, it occurred to Gabriel that Miss Jolliffe might simply wish to be courted in a traditional way. Flowers, candy, and books of poetry were acceptable presents and might be the way to her heart.

To be sure, flowers were difficult to come by this time of year, and he had never seen any sign that Miss Jolliffe had a sweet tooth. But now that he thought about it, he did not doubt that if he searched through the hundreds of books he had inherited, he would find a volume of poetry suitable for a young lady.

Upon first entering the library, his task appeared daunting, but he soon realized he could skip the shelves that were laden with sets of large volumes bound in matching calfskin, and focus his attention on the bottom shelves where the smaller books were jammed together in a rather higgledy-piggledy fashion.

His ancestors—or rather, the Rainsford family— seemed to have had an inordinate fondness for improving sermons, he concluded after the first fifteen minutes. Although since most of the volumes did not even have their pages cut, it would seem that few of the Rainsfords had actually taken advantage of the opportunities available for improving themselves.

In the middle of the fourth shelf that he checked, he found a slender volume of Shakespeare's sonnets, which seemed exactly suited to his purpose. Next to it was a small, dusty book with a hand-tooled leather cover, and out of curiosity he pulled it from the shelf also.

Opening it, he discovered it was a journal containing recipes and instructions written in a variety of hands, some tiny and crabbed, others bold and flowing.

Remembering the glow in her eyes when she talked about running the household, he realized with glee that Miss Jolliffe would doubtless appreciate such a book more than she would a book of sonnets—or even a diamond necklace.

His immediate impulse was to take it to her at once, but a moment's proper reflection was enough to show him that would be foolish. Assuming he even found her at home—and given the number of invitations that were daily pouring into the Wasteney household, that was not at all a given—she would doubtless be surrounded by her relatives.

For such a gift to have the desired effect—namely to cause Miss Jolliffe to throw herself into his arms with avowals of eternal love—he needed to give it to her in private, which meant he would have to wait until their morning drive.

Taking his newfound treasure with him, he retired to his study, where he polished off the rest of the bottle of brandy and admired the insignificant-appearing volume that was destined to be the key to Miss Jolliffe's heart.

"Have you ever spent such an enjoyable evening?" Petronella gushed. "Such exalted company—such witty conversation."

"I thought the champagne rather inferior actually," Ralph said, "although the brandy was decent. Smuggled, no doubt, but no preventative would dare to inspect Lord Dalyrumple's cellars, of that you may be certain."

What was certain, Verity thought to herself, was that a party without Lord Sherington was decidedly flat, no matter how exalted the rest of the company. For despite the obvious expectations of the entire crowd assembled at Lord Dalyrumple's house for an evening of cards, Lord Sherington had not put in an appearance.

Fortunately her sister and brother-in-law were too obtuse to have noticed the looks of disgust and contempt that followed them out the door. Lord and Lady Dalyrumple obviously were of the opinion that they had been cheated—and that the Wasteneys were at fault.

Verity felt a niggling worry that Lord Sherington's absence that evening meant he had already lost interest in her, but then remembering her resolve, she firmly pushed such thoughts out of her mind and went to bed, there to dream about seeing him again in the morning.

Despite his absence tonight, he would come on the morrow, she reassured herself repeatedly. Whatever he wanted from her, he had not yet gotten it, so he would be in front of the house punctually at nine.

Then for an hour or so she would be able to look at his beloved face, hear his voice, and even touch his arm. For a short period of time she would feel herself truly alive, and the world would be a wondrous place.

*      *      *

In the morning Gabriel was halfway to the Wasteneys'
residence before he realized he had forgotten the little
volume of household instruction. He despised lack of
punctuality, and now he himself was going to be late.

For a moment he considered postponing giving Miss
Jolliffe the journal, but then he admitted he could not
wait another twenty-four hours, and with a curse, he
turned his horses around and headed back toward his
own house.

Just one street away from Grosvenor Square, he spot-
ted Fitch, his valet, climbing into a strange carriage . . .
except it was not actually a strange carriage. It belonged,
Gabriel realized, to his Aunt Cudmore, and instead of
driving away after his passenger climbed in, the coachman held the restless horses in check.

His suspicions immediately aroused, Gabriel turned off
on Chapel Street, where he quickly found a small boy to
walk his horses. Then approaching his aunt's coach on
foot, Gabriel positioned himself where he could observe
what transpired without himself being seen.

After about twenty minutes the door opened, Fitch
climbed out, and the coach drove away. The valet began
walking rapidly back in the direction of Sherington
House, with Gabriel stalking unobserved behind him.

Fitch entered by the servants' door, and after a discreet interval, Gabriel followed, luckily finding the door
unlocked. Voices were coming from the servants' hall,
and Gabriel recognized not only Fitch, but also the butler
and the housekeeper.

"So what does Lady Ottilia want us to do?"

"Yes, yes, what is the plan?"

"She is leaving it up to us how we do it, but one way
or another we must prevent *Lord* Sherington"—"There
was a sneer in Fitch's voice when he said the title "—from
marrying Miss Jolliffe or indeed any woman."

"It will not be easy," the cook said dubiously.

"Easy or not," the butler replied, "it is our only
choice. I have served the Rainsfords man and boy for
fifty-seven years, and it sticks in my craw that I have to
bend my knee to an impostor. One way or another, I'll

see a true Rainsford master of this house again before I go to my grave."

Clapping his hands slowly, Gabriel stepped into view. "Very prettily said." Looking around the hall, he saw what appeared to be every one of his servants, from butler to scullery maid, coachman to stable lad, and he felt an overwhelming rage that they had dared to conspire against him.

But he had learned as a young boy how to hide his anger, and his voice was quite cool and impassive when he continued, "You have one hour to pack your things, and then each and every one of you will leave these premises forever."

Jaws that had dropped open upon his unexpected appearance now snapped shut, and eyes that had goggled in surprise now narrowed in bitterness.

If he had seen any remorse, he might have relented . . . perhaps. But the question was moot, because all he saw in the circle of faces looking at him was resentment and hatred.

Pulling his watch out, he looked at it, then said, "You now have fifty-eight minutes." Nobody got up from his seat, but watching them glance at each other in growing consternation, Gabriel could see that the enormity of what they had done was finally beginning to sink in.

Finally the parlor maid timidly raised her hand and asked, "Please, m'lord, what about references?"

"I suggest you apply to Lady Ottilia, for you'll get none from me," he replied, again looking pointedly at his watch.

One of the footmen was the first to stand up and head for his room, and as if he were the signal the others had been waiting for, there was a general exodus. Fitch lingered behind, as if wishing to say something privately to Gabriel, but in the end he could not bring himself to offer up any excuses.

It took longer than an hour, because Gabriel inspected each of their bags before he allowed them to depart. Seeing what he was doing, one of the footmen and one of the upstairs maids quietly turned around and retreated to their rooms, reappearing a few minutes later with looks of total innocence on their faces.

The butler and the housekeeper were the last to leave, and they turned over their keys to Gabriel with obvious reluctance. He did not feel any particular sympathy for them, even though the mournful look on the butler's face when he paused in the door and gazed around the servants' hall for the last time would have won the man a place in any company of actors.

# 9

BY THE TIME Verity admitted Lord Sherington was not coming, her jaw ached from clenching it, and the pain in her stomach was so great she was not sure she could straighten up. With trembling limbs, she rose from her seat by the front door, removed her cape and bonnet, and silently gave them to Otterwall. Then keeping her head bowed so that she would not have to witness the superior look the butler was undoubtedly giving her, she walked the length of the hall to the door leading to the back stairs.

She wanted nothing more than to retire to her room and remain in seclusion for the rest of her life, but instead she forced herself to descend to the kitchen. She had never thought of herself as prideful, but now she found she could not allow anyone else to know the depth of her pain.

No matter what it cost her, she had to act as if this were a normal morning, and so she went about her usual chores, feeling as if every one of the servants were whispering about her behind her back—snickering about her—gloating that she had fallen from favor.

Every movement she made felt jerky, as if her arms and legs were controlled by someone else, and her voice sounded strange to her own ears when she discussed the state of the linens with the housekeeper, who thankfully did not appear to notice that Verity's heart was broken.

Suddenly there was a commotion on the stairs, and one of the footmen came literally bounding into view. "Quick, quick, Miss Jolliffe, he's here—his lordship's here! You've got to come quick."

It seemed as if the very room uttered a sigh of relief, and when Verity looked around, she saw that all of the servants, who moments before had appeared to be busily engaged in their own tasks, were now smiling at her.

"Hurry, child," the housekeeper said, giving her a push in the direction of the stairs. "You mustn't keep his lordship waiting. He's not known for his patience."

Verity fought back the urge to run up the stairs and fling herself into Lord Sherington's arms. With all the dignity she could muster, she walked with careful decorum as befit a lady.

The minute she saw his face, she knew she should have hurried. Although he was not scowling, experience had taught her to recognize the anger now lurking in the back of his eyes—anger she could only hope was not directed at her for keeping him waiting.

He did not apologize for the fact that he himself was over an hour late, but then she did not think he was a man accustomed to explaining his actions to others.

She, however, was so happy to be with him again, she was ready to find excuses for his behavior. After all, he had never told her specifically that he was coming at nine . . . although it did seem to be understood that they would drive out together every morning, she thought, feeling a tiny bit of resentment that she could not entirely suppress.

Contrary to his usual custom, Lord Sherington did not wait until they were out of the bustle of traffic to begin a conversation.

"I fired every one of my servants this morning," he said without preamble. Then he turned and looked at her as if wanting to judge her reaction to such an outrageous statement.

"I assume you had cause," she said, doing the best she could to hide her shock.

Apparently she was not entirely successful, because now his anger became clearly visible—in a word, he scowled down at her as if she were also a servant who was about to be let go.

"By accident I discovered they were conspiring with one of my relatives to act in a way that was directly contrary to my best interests." In detail he related what had happened—with one very significant omission.

"In what way were they intending to act against your interests?" curiosity compelled Verity to ask once it became clear he was done with his recital.

Lord Sherington's scowl deepened, and for a moment she thought he was going to bite her head off. Deftly steering the carriage through the traffic around them, he said flatly, "That is none of your business."

He was right, of course. But she could not help wishing that it was her business. It amazed her how angry she felt at the unknown servants who had betrayed him. Being turned off was too light a punishment—they deserved to be flogged and cast into the darkest dungeon.

"Well, Miss Jolliffe?"

Pulling her thoughts away from assorted dire retributions, Verity looked up at Lord Sherington. "I beg your pardon?"

"You have told me you are experienced in managing a household. So advise me on the best way to obtain a new complement of servants." The scowl on his face faded, to be replaced by a self-mocking smile. "Unlike you, I have no interest in domestic matters, and I absolutely refuse to cook my own meals and iron my own cravats and make my own bed."

If he had not mentioned his bed, she could have answered with more aplomb, but as it was, the thought of him lying in his bed was so distracting, it took her a good minute or two before she was able to gather her wits and say, "You would do well to turn the matter over to Mrs. Wiggins. She runs what I consider to be one of the best employment agencies in London, and I have always been satisfied with the servants she has sent us."

"And her direction?"

Verity told him the way to the employment office in Cork Street, and to her surprise, Lord Sherington immediately turned his horses around and started heading east on Piccadilly, apparently intending to waste no time in arranging for new servants.

She knew she should feel indignant and sorely put upon that he was dragging her along without even asking her if she wished to accompany him or if she preferred to return home. But instead she could not completely suppress the tingle of excitement and pleasure that he was allowing her to . . . to assist him in this matter—to act in the capacity of his wife, as it were.

Did he know how improper it was for her to accompany him to an employment agency? Recommending Mrs. Wiggins was one thing, but actually visiting her in her offices in the company of an eligible bachelor was not at all the thing.

If someone discovered what Verity was doing, that person would doubtless assume she and Lord Sherington were betrothed. And if the betrothal announcement were not immediately forthcoming, that person would then be convinced that Verity was Lord Sherington's mistress.

Remembering his cavalier attitude when he bought her the green cloak, she rather thought that in this case he would likewise not particularly worry about what behavior was allowable and what was definitely forbidden.

More than likely it had never even occurred to him to consider her in the light of an eligible female. There was, after all, no reason he should think of her that way since she had been on the shelf for so many years.

But still . . . surely there was some significance in the fact that he was allowing her to have such intimate knowledge of his private affairs?

On the other hand, he was probably doing nothing more than what he had said he wished to do—making use of her knowledge of household matters. After all, she knew he thought of her as a drudge—a poor relation shamelessly used by her relatives. Why should he not also use her when and where it suited him?

Just as he pulled the carriage to a stop in front of the building that housed Mrs. Wiggins's office, however, Verity had a flash of inspiration. Suddenly everything became crystal clear, and she knew, beyond a shadow of a doubt, what Lord Sherington wanted from her.

He wanted a friend.

That explained each and every one of his actions since the day they had met. To be sure, just why he had chosen her to be his friend, she could not say, unless he had likewise felt they were in some way compatible.

She would never do anything to cause him to regret his choice, she decided. She would be the truest, most helpful friend he ever had.

He climbed out of the carriage and turned to help her down. At the first touch of his hands on her waist, she felt a sharp pain in her heart. Looking into his eyes, she could not hold back the regret that he did not want anything more from her than friendship. There was so much more she could give him if he only knew . . . and if he only wanted what she had to offer.

Resting her hand lightly on his arm, she allowed him to escort her into the building. Friends . . . that was all very well and good, but what would happen when he decided to marry? How long would his wife allow him to continue a friendship, even of the most platonic variety?

Thinking about that unknown wife, who was probably still an innocent girl in the schoolroom, Verity felt a hatred even more intense than she had felt for Lord Sherington's mistress.

Even knowing how disgusted he would be if he suspected her of such thoughts, Verity could not feel properly ashamed of herself. Nor, despite the best of intentions, could she think about his future wife with any degree of equanimity.

Once they were seated in comfortable chairs facing Mrs. Wiggins, Gabriel informed the woman bluntly that he had dismissed all his servants and wished to hire new ones.

Mrs. Wiggins did not look at all pleased that he had brought her so much business, and when she finally spoke, her tone was cold. "I do not think that you represent the kind of client I wish to encourage, Lord Sherington."

The snub was calculated, and Gabriel felt his temper flare, but before he could rise to his feet or utter even a single curse, Miss Jolliffe laid her hand on his arm, and he felt the tension drain out of him, and his anger gave way to curiosity. If the meek and self-effacing Miss

Jolliffe thought she could handle this disobliging and insolent female, then he would enjoy watching her efforts.

And if Mrs. Wiggins decided to be equally insulting when she dealt with Miss Jolliffe, then she would quickly come to discover that his reputation for ruthlessness was well deserved.

"Lord Sherington's actions were not capricious or unprovoked, Mrs. Wiggins," Miss Jolliffe said in her calm, clear voice. "His lordship returned home unexpectedly and discovered his servants were holding a meeting in the servants' hall and discussing ways that they could deliberately act counter to his lordship's best interests. In fact, Lord Sherington overheard enough to discover that one of his relatives was conspiring with them to thwart his plans."

With every word she uttered, her voice became stronger, and she was speaking almost fiercely by the time she concluded, "And I do not think that Lord Sherington can be in any way blamed or held at fault for dismissing the lot of them. Indeed, I feel that he has shown remarkable forbearance in this matter."

There was a moment of silence when she finished, and Gabriel had the feeling that Mrs. Wiggins was every bit as astonished by Miss Jolliffe's show of spirit as he was. The older woman recovered quickly, however.

Turning to him, she asked, "So what kind of servants are you looking for?"

He knew very well that she expected him to enumerate butler, housekeeper, cook, and the required number of footmen and maids and grooms and so forth, but instead he replied, "I want servants who will be loyal to me at all times and on all occasions, and likewise ones who can keep their tongues from wagging about my affairs."

The corners of her mouth turned up slightly, and to his surprise, he discovered he was beginning to feel a measure of respect for Mrs. Wiggins.

"And what do you intend to offer them in return, my lord?" she asked, the insolence of the question offset by the expression on her face.

"I am quite prepared to pay double the prevailing wage," he answered promptly.

"I had heard that you are ruthless, my lord, but not that you are a fool," she replied.

Beside him Miss Jolliffe gasped, and her hand, which all this time had been resting lightly on his arm, tightened, as if to restrain him again from leaping to his feet.

His temper was not at all aroused, however, so he laid his other hand reassuringly over Miss Jolliffe's and answered Mrs. Wiggins calmly. "If you listen more closely to what the gossips are saying, you will discover that I reserve my ruthlessness for people who are cruel, greedy, selfish, or heartless. I do not direct it toward people who are doing their best, even when they make mistakes. I assume, of course, that you will be able to find me servants who are competent, and who will not attempt to shirk their duties."

To his surprise, Mrs. Wiggins did not look wholly convinced. "I am sure you mean every word you say, my lord, but people of your class seldom realize how easily they can hurt the feelings of their retainers—indeed, I think many people in the *ton* have never realized that the lower orders even have feelings that it is possible to hurt."

With scarcely a pause to weigh the possible consequences, Gabriel decided to trust this woman, who seemed more interested in protecting the servants she represented than in fawning over the employers who wished to hire those same domestics.

"I was sent to sea when I was eight," he said, unable to keep the harshness out of his voice. "There is nothing I do not know about the ways one person can degrade another, both openly and more subtly. I swore years ago that I would never make use of such practices, and to the best of my knowledge I never have, but for that you will have to take my word, which I do not give lightly."

Mrs. Wiggins studied him intently for a long time, as if debating a course of action. Finally she spoke. "What recommendations will you require, my lord? The reason I ask is that I have on my books a considerable number of servants who have been turned off on various trumped-up charges, and who therefore have no letters attesting to their good character."

Without hesitation, he replied, "Your recommendation is all that I need, Mrs. Wiggins."

"And do you wish to conduct the interviews yourself?"

"Do not be absurd," he said, standing up and assisting Miss Jolliffe to rise also. He handed Mrs. Wiggins a set of keys to his house. "The only thing I require is that my dinner be ready tonight by eight."

"You may leave everything to me, my lord," she said. Escorting them to the door, she added with a smile, "I believe you have made a wise choice, my lord."

It was only as he was helping Miss Jolliffe into the carriage that Gabriel began to wonder at Mrs. Wiggins's parting remark. Had she meant his choice of servants? Or had she been clear-eyed enough to see what his intentions were in regard to Miss Jolliffe?

He rather suspected the latter was true, and it only reaffirmed the wisdom of his decision to trust Mrs. Wiggins, who seemed to have remarkably good sense for a woman.

Halfway back to the Wasteney residence, Gabriel remembered the little book of household instructions and recipes in his pocket. He started to reach for it, but then it occurred to him that there was not enough time left to do the matter properly. Tomorrow morning would be soon enough.

He glanced down at Miss Jolliffe, and she lifted her gaze to meet his. Staring into her cool gray-green eyes, he had a premonition that he could give her dozens of presents without winning a declaration of love.

Feeling rather aggravated with her, he directed only half his attention to the traffic. But no matter how he pondered his predicament, by the time he pulled his horses to a stop in front of her brother-in-law's house, he had to admit he was still at an impasse—still no closer to understanding Miss Jolliffe than he had been in Northumberland.

No, that was not exactly correct. Over the last week or so, he had acquired a great deal more admiration and respect for her character than he'd had when he had first met her, which only strengthened his resolve to have her for his wife.

At the same time, that goal, which in the beginning

had seemed so easily obtainable, appeared with each passing day to be receding farther and farther from his reach. The only consolation he could think of was that since he was monopolizing her time, it was unlikely that any other man could succeed where he was failing.

Grasping her around the waist and lifting her down from the carriage, he felt his temper rising. Be damned if he would fail! He would make this woman his wife even if he had to throw her over his shoulder and carry her away.

With reluctance he released her, then said in what he hoped was a normal voice, "Tomorrow I shall endeavor to be here on time." It was not exactly an apology, but it was the closest he had come to one in years, and he wondered if she had the faintest understanding of how much he was humbling himself.

"I quite understand why you were delayed this morning," she said.

She smiled up at him, but no matter how he searched her eyes, he could see no hint of either elation or condescension. He could think of no other woman of his acquaintance who would have failed to recognize his momentary weakness and seek to take advantage of it.

Instead of driving away at once, he watched Miss Jolliffe mount the steps and be admitted into the house. Though he knew her to be six-and-twenty, at times like this she seemed as innocent and naive as a young girl fresh out of the schoolroom.

A rather dangerous state of affairs, he realized as he drove away. The world was too full of men—and women—who took a perverse delight in despoiling innocence and destroying naivety.

One way or another, he would have to marry Miss Jolliffe quite soon for her own protection.

Verity had no sooner stepped through the door than the butler virtually ripped her cloak away from her shoulders and snatched her bonnet off her head.

"Quickly, quickly, miss. She's been asking for you for the last half hour, and we had to tell her you'd gone to speak to the butcher." Shoving her toward the stairway,

Otterwall added, "She's in her boudoir, and if you make haste, she'll never suspect you've been driving out with his lordship."

With a hurried "Thank you, Otterwall," Verity dashed up the stairs like an out-and-out hoyden, then had to pause outside her sister's room to regain her breath.

Tapping lightly, she entered to find her sister reclining gracefully on the chaise lounge. "You asked to see me?"

"Where have you been?" Petronella asked crossly. "You know how I detest waiting. I vow, you have quite ruined my day."

"There was a problem with the butcher's account, but I have discussed it with him and found the error. He had inadvertently charged us twice for the same leg of mutton," Verity said, amazing herself by her ability to fabricate a plausible lie.

"Really, Verity, must you prattle on about such tedious matters when I have other things on my mind? I have the headache," Petronella said, pressing the back of her hand to her forehead. "As much as I might wish to, I simply cannot accompany Antoinette to her fitting this afternoon at Mademoiselle Beaufrère's."

Verity had no doubt but that five minutes after her departure with Antoinette in tow, Petronella would rise from her sick bed, miraculously recovered and quite well enough, thank you, to entertain callers.

But Verity dutifully agreed that it would be no trouble at all for her to take her niece to the modiste, and a few minutes later she was safely back in her own room, where she savored her few minutes of solitude while waiting for Antoinette to finish dressing and join her.

Thinking back, Verity realized it had been a most unusual morning, and the most astonishing part had been the behavior of the servants in this very house.

She had always assumed that they looked down on her because she was—despite her efforts not to admit it to herself—nothing more than a poor relation, treated with no respect by her relatives and shamelessly used by them as a household drudge.

When she reviewed the events of the morning, however, she realized that the servants had seemed to be almost as downcast as she was when Lord Sherington failed to put in a timely appearance, and the excitement when he had finally arrived had obviously been shared by all of them. That alone was enough to make her think the servants actually liked her—that they felt some affection for her.

But even more astounding, they had lied to protect her from her sister's displeasure, and the only reason she could think of for them to have done that was that they felt a certain . . . loyalty toward her.

Loyalty—the single requirement Lord Sherington had had for the servants he wished to hire. Unlike him, she was not paying the servants here double the prevailing wages—indeed, she herself was not paying them a single farthing—and yet they appeared to be loyal to her rather than to her sister.

Restless, Verity wandered around her room, unable to sit quietly. It was not that the servants' behavior displeased her, but . . . it was all very unsettling.

She stopped in front of the cheval glass and stared at her reflection. She had thought she knew herself, but although the image she saw in the mirror was the same one she had seen before she set out for Northumberland a few short weeks ago, somehow her perception of herself was different—indeed, it seemed as if she was changing more and more every day.

Who was she? What kind of a person was she?

She no longer felt qualified to answer those questions.

What did she want out of life?

That question she could answer with no hesitation, with no vacillations, with no self-doubts.

She wanted to be with Lord Sherington every minute of the day . . . and every hour of the night. Everything else she would part with willingly, even her immortal soul, if she could only be with him—as his wife or as his mistress or as his friend or even only as his housekeeper—for the rest of her natural life.

When Gabriel returned home at half past five, the door was opened to him by an unfamiliar man dressed in exceedingly shabby clothes.

"Good evening, my lord. I am Exeter, your new butler."

"Assemble the other servants, Exeter. I wish to meet them all," Gabriel said before stalking into his study and shutting the door. Then he cast himself down into his favorite chair before the fire and turned his mind once more to the problem of Miss Jolliffe, who was not supposed to be a problem.

Less than ten minutes later there was a tapping at the door, and Exeter entered and informed him the servants were ready for his inspection.

They were in truth a motley crew, ill-clothed and obviously ill-fed. So gaunt were they, in fact, that he felt as if he were back on board a ship that had not put in to port for a good three months.

One by one they were introduced to him, and they bowed or curtseyed, and he repeated their names, committing them to memory.

When he reached the end of the line, he did not dismiss them, rather he returned to his study, taking with him Mrs. Filbert, the new cook, who looked as if she were about to faint at his feet, but whether from hunger or fear he could not tell.

"Mrs. Filbert, I shall give you two weeks—" She became even paler if that were possible. "—and at the end of that time, I expect you to have fattened up everyone in this household. I am not interested in economy or frugality. You are to purchase sufficient meat and vegetables, and whatever fruit you can find in the market, and you are to stuff everyone until they are too full to get out of their chairs. Is that clear?"

To his great embarrassment, she began to cry. In between sobs, she told him he was a saint and other words to that effect.

He did his best to calm her, but she was still crying when he led her out of the room. Too late he realized that he had made a serious error in judgment, because the row of servants standing in the hall were staring at him in horror, as if he were some vile monster who had lured them into this house for some dreadful, unspeakable purpose.

Aggravated beyond measure, Gabriel scowled back at them. If he had stopped to think, he would have realized he was only compounding his mistake. To his disgust, some of the younger maids now looked so horrorstruck, he would not have been surprised if they had run screaming into the street.

The situation was deteriorating rapidly and positively demanded Miss Jolliffe's presence. If she were here, he had no doubt she would know exactly how to put these poor people at ease. He cursed the rules and restrictions of society that insisted a lady could not visit a bachelor in his residence without forever destroying her reputation, no matter what her purpose there.

But lacking her assistance, there was nothing he could do but tell the housekeeper he wished to speak with her privately. She, at least, did not look as if she would turn into a watering pot. Once they were alone in his study, she stood in front of him, her back ramrod straight, as if she were a gunnery sergeant reporting for duty.

"Certain conditions here are not to my liking, Mrs. Richards," he began, but to his amazement, she interrupted him before he could explain his wishes.

"Indeed, I can well understand that, my lord. I have no wish to cast aspersions on your previous housekeeper," she said, then immediately began to do just that. "But it is shocking the way things have been allowed to go to rack and ruin around here."

He was surprised at her accusations, which seemed a little extreme, but since he infinitely preferred her militant style to the emotional outburst of the cook, he allowed her to continue.

"The linens have been allowed to become quite yellowed, and it appears that no mending has been done for months, and if any of the furniture has had more than a nodding acquaintance with beeswax in the last year, then my name is not Mrs. Richards. The amount of dust in the draperies and the dirt under the carpet is scandalous, and furthermore, my lord—"

But Gabriel stopped her before she could continue her recital. "I am pleased that you are eager to start polishing the furniture and darning the sheets," he said mildly, "but for the moment such things are not at the top of my list of priorities."

The housekeeper looked at him reprovingly, and for a moment he almost thought she was going to tell him "A stitch in time saves nine," or some aphorism like that.

"I wish to know the condition of the servants' quarters. Are the rooms comfortable and well fitted out?"

For the first time since she entered the study, she did not meet his eye. "They are . . . adequate, my lord."

"Does this mean they are ready for inspection?" he said, giving in to the impulse to bait her.

She looked at him in horror. "Indeed, my lord—that would—but surely you do not intend—I had not—perhaps . . ." Her voice trailed off.

Pleased that he had at last reduced her to speechlessness, he began with the orders he had intended to give her in the beginning, before she had interrupted him.

"The first task I wish you to undertake, Mrs. Richards, if you have no objections"—he looked at her questioningly, but she merely pressed her lips firmly together—"is to see to it that all the servants in this household are properly attired. They are each to receive two sets of clothing, and I am counting on you to see that the fabric is of good quality. If there are not sufficient maids who are proficient with needle and thread, then you may temporarily hire additional seamstresses for however many days it takes. I trust it will not take too many days?"

"No, my lord, I mean, yes, my lord, I can arrange that, and no, my lord, it will not take too long."

"Once that project is underway, I wish you to purchase sufficient feather ticks, muslin sheets, and wool blankets for each of the servants' beds." He paused, to see if she was going to raise any more objections, but she merely pressed her lips more tightly together.

"You also have my permission to scavenge in the lumber rooms for any discarded furniture that may be useful in the servants' hall."

To his astonishment, the redoubtable Mrs. Richards also burst into tears and fell to her knees in front of him, clutching his hand and babbling something totally incoherent.

# 10

As UNFAIR as it was, Gabriel felt an immense anger at Miss Jolliffe for leaving him to handle such matters by himself.

Grasping the housekeeper's elbow and helping her to her feet, Gabriel decided while escorting the woman out that it was not totally unjust to blame Miss Jolliffe for his present difficulties. She had, after all, had sufficient opportunity to fall in love with him, and it was beyond his comprehension that she had not done so.

On the other hand, considering that he had just—quite unintentionally—reduced both his new cook and his new housekeeper to tears, the basic problem could be that his understanding of the female mind was deficient.

Knowing he was being unreasonable did not, however, stop him from feeling cross with Miss Jolliffe.

He could, he realized too late, have saved himself a great deal of trouble by using his new butler as a go-between, rather than speaking directly to the two women. Signaling the man that he wished to speak to him, Gabriel retreated once again into his study.

"I warn you, Exeter," he said as soon as the door was closed behind them, "that my patience is wearing exceedingly thin. If you feel compelled to interrupt my every sentence or to turn into a watering pot, I shall quite likely flog you with a cat-o'-nine-tails."

"I should not dream of behaving in such an unseemly way," Exeter said stiffly, his manner quite properly butlerish even if his clothes were so patched and mended as to make him look like a comical figure from a Covent Garden farce.

"In case you have not heard the gossip about me, I am a rich man—exceedingly rich—rich beyond your wildest imagination. Men as rich as I am frequently have our little whims, and I am no exception. That is only fair, do you not agree, Exeter?"

"Yes, my lord, indeed that is only proper," the butler said, keeping his eyes rigidly forward.

"Even if you think I am wasting my blunt, it is not for you to question my wishes, is that not so, Exeter?"

"Yes, my lord."

"Now that we have that clearly understood, it is my wish and desire that the fires in the study, the library, the morning room, and my bedroom be kept burning at all times."

The butler nodded his head.

"And furthermore, it is my wish—no, it is my direct order—that full coal scuttles are to be kept at all times in the servants' quarters, and that each of the servants is to be allowed to have a fire burning in his or her room whenever he or she desires, no matter what the season. Is that understood?"

The butler did not make a sound, and when Gabriel looked at him closely, he saw that tears were welling up in the man's eyes.

"Confound it, Exeter, I ordered you not to cry!"

"I am not crying, my lord," the butler said between clenched teeth.

Crossing to the little table where a decanter of brandy stood, Gabriel poured a healthy measure into a glass and offered it to the butler, who made no move to take it.

"With respect, my lord, I am a Methodist." His shoulders sagged, as if he expected Gabriel to dismiss him on the spot for being a nonconformist.

"Then at least I shall not have to worry about you making inroads in my cellars," Gabriel said before tossing off the brandy himself.

"I shall see that your wishes are carried out concerning the fires in the servants' rooms," Exeter said, once more in proper control of his shoulders and his emotions.

"There is one more thing." Walking around behind his desk and retrieving a bag of coins from one of the drawers, Gabriel tossed it to the butler, who caught it without blinking an eye.

"I know from experience what it is like to be penniless," Gabriel said. "Therefore I wish you to distribute one gold guinea to each of the upper servants and a silver crown to each of the lower servants. This is to be considered in the nature of a bonus, not an advance on wages."

Looking down at the bag of money in his hand, Exeter tried to speak, but it was obvious he was overcome by emotion.

"You may have heard it gossiped around town that I am ruthless," Gabriel said.

"Oh, my lord, I am sure you are not—" the butler said with a quavering voice.

"You would do well to believe it," Gabriel said, "for it is quite true."

Exeter looked at him with confusion written clearly on his face.

"I do not want anyone in this household to have any illusions about me. While I may in some ways be more compassionate than the average peer of the realm, I can also, when the situation warrants it, be completely and totally ruthless."

His words—or perhaps something in his tone of voice—made the proper impression on the butler. "I understand, my lord."

"I am glad that you do. It will be your responsibility to see that the other servants likewise understand. The punishment for dishonesty, disloyalty, or disobedience will be swift and merciless. And as Mrs. Wiggins may have told you, I shall not allow any gossip about my affairs. Do you think you can make that clear to the others?"

"I am sure I can convince them, my lord," the butler said, fear making his hands tremble and his voice quaver.

Gabriel sighed. This was all much more difficult than he had anticipated, but since Miss Jolliffe was not at hand, he would have to carry on as best he could.

"It will not be all that bad working for me," he said softly. "Despite my temper, which I am sure you have

also heard stories about, I am intelligent enough to recognize the difference between deliberate treachery and
an honest mistake. Anyone who is making a true effort
to serve me well and loyally will not need to fear that I
shall act capriciously and turn them off for an imagined
slight."

The butler did not look wholly reassured, but Gabriel
realized that he was walking a fine line—too much reassurance, and the man would doubtless fall to his knees
weeping in gratitude. Deciding it was more prudent to
leave the butler with a little anxiety, Gabriel stalked over
to the door, where he paused only long enough to say,
"Inform the cook that I have changed my mind and decided to dine at my club this evening."

Halfway to Brooke's Gabriel realized that he could not
stomach the thought of dining there. Not that the food
was not good, he just had no taste for the company. All
he wanted to do was spend a quiet evening with Miss
Jolliffe, who he was beginning to think was the only reasonable, rational person in all of London.

She would not burst into tears at the slightest thing.
Why, even stranded in Northumberland, she had remained cool and calm and completely in control of her
emotions.

Which was, he admitted to himself, undoubtedly the
reason he was having so much difficulty getting her to fall
in love with him. On the other hand, being a completely
emotionless, passionless female, she would certainly be
much easier to live with after they were married since
she would not have the hysterics at a moment's notice.

It was unfortunate that there was no entertainment
arranged for this evening. As frustrating as he found it
to have her relatives around, at least he could derive
some small pleasure from being near Miss Jolliffe.

Although he had not made a conscious decision to go
there, Gabriel realized his feet had followed his thoughts
and had led him directly to Curzon Street. Standing outside the Wasteney residence and looking up at the lighted
windows, he resolved to take his chances. The baron and
baroness were always so eager to toad-eat him, he rather
thought they would welcome him even if he came by at

four in the morning—or if, as in this case, he appeared unexpectedly just as they were preparing to go in to dinner.

And so it proved to be. The butler admitted him, took his hat, went to inform the master and mistress, and a few minutes later Lord and Lady Wasteney came hurrying out, their daughter trailing behind them, to assure him of his welcome.

"But of course you must dine with us," Lord Wasteney said effusively.

"It is only potluck, of course," Lady Wasteney said with a simper, "but we consider you almost one of the family."

Startled at her choice of words, Gabriel looked at her closely. Did she suspect what his intentions were toward her sister?

When Gabriel looked into Lady Wasteney's eyes, he saw a self-centered, calculating woman, who would stop at nothing to claw her way into the upper ranks of society. But on the other hand, he could not see enough intelligence there to make her a dangerous opponent.

Reassured, he allowed himself to be led into the drawing room, where he discovered to his vast displeasure that despite his lecturing her, Miss Jolliffe was still playing the role of poor relation—still sitting withdrawn from the others in her accustomed place in the corner. She cast him a guilty look, then responding to his frown, she put down her needlework and joined them all by the fire.

As he had expected, Lord and Lady Wasteney dominated the conversation, but Gabriel still took some measure of satisfaction in being near Miss Jolliffe, even though he had little opportunity to converse with her. After dinner, however, he began to think coming here had been a bad mistake. In his desire to see Miss Jolliffe, he had completely forgotten the dangers of dining *en famille* with the Wasteneys.

"Antoinette, my love, will you not entertain us on the pianoforte this evening?" Lady Wasteney said coyly.

Before Gabriel could gather his wits enough to think of a way to squash this revolting suggestion, Miss Jolliffe spoke up. "Perhaps Lord Sherington would prefer to play a hand or two of whist?"

"I am sure—" Lady Wasteney began, but her husband interrupted her.

"Capital idea, capital. You do play whist, do you not, Sherington?"

Gabriel hastened to reassure him. "I positively dote on the game. Nothing I like better."

"Splendid, splendid. My daughter hasn't a head for cards, so we are always eager for a fourth."

A table, chairs, and a new deck of cards were quickly produced by one of the footmen, but to Gabriel's dismay, he was skillfully outmaneuvered by the baron, who managed to take the seat opposite Miss Jolliffe.

With the first hand, it became quite clear that like her daughter, Lady Wasteney did not have a head for cards. Chattering away while she laid her cards down seemingly at random, she managed to lose not only the first hand, but also the next one, both of which Gabriel would have sworn were unbeatable.

Lord Wasteney, who could not refrain from smiling rather gloatingly every time his wife led the wrong card or trumped one of Gabriel's winning cards, was an average player. Miss Jolliffe, on the contrary, was not only quite skilled, but she also had a superb memory for what had been played. "I believe this two of hearts is good," she said serenely at the end of the third hand, taking the setting trick.

She smiled at Gabriel, and her eyes seemed to say, "If you are tired of losing, there is always Antoinette and the pianoforte."

He scowled at Miss Jolliffe, but instead of being put out of countenance, she trumped in on the fourth trick of the next hand and then proceeded to destroy—with the help of Lady Wasteney's incompetence, to be sure— all of Gabriel's carefully thought out strategy.

Nor did she show the least sign of proper repentance. Gleeful was the only word to describe her expression when time after time she ruined what could have been a rubber for Gabriel, whose good luck at being dealt most of the high cards was totally offset by his partner's lack of skill.

Given his reputation in London, Miss Jolliffe should have been more leery of incurring his wrath, but she clearly delighted in teasing him. On two occasions he realized she had deliberately held back the winning card until the last possible moment just to let him think he had a chance to win the hand.

Oddly enough, Gabriel had no trouble controlling his temper, despite how badly he was losing, because half-way through the evening he realized that he was actually deriving enjoyment from Miss Jolliffe's pleasure in beating him soundly.

That thought gave him a moment's pause, since considered logically, there was no reason why he should care if she was happy or not. The only explanation, he finally decided, was that the happier he made her, the more likely she was to fall in love with him.

As obvious as that was, he could not quite convince himself that it was the sole and only reason he wanted her to have a little joy in her life. He had a niggling feeling that there was more involved than just his scheme to win her love.

Walking home later, Gabriel had a second disconcerting thought. At the whist table Miss Jolliffe had proved herself to be a thoroughly skilled tactician. Was she perhaps equally skilled in other areas? While he was endeavoring to win her love, was it possible she was playing some deep game with him?

Would he marry her, only to discover that she was not the person he had thought she was? Would she, for example, reveal herself as a shrew? A chatterbox? A bore? A spendthrift? A snob?

But then he remembered her promise never to lie to him. In his financial dealings around the world, he had always trusted to his instincts as to whether or not a man was telling him a falsehood, and so far, his instincts had seldom failed him.

Right now his instincts were insisting that Miss Jolliffe had told him the truth, not only when she had made that promise, but on all other occasions likewise. It followed, therefore, that he had nothing to worry about—at least so long as he managed to secure her as his partner for future games of whist.

Entering his own house, he discovered he could already feel a difference in the atmosphere. Exeter and the other new servants were still shabbily dressed, and the furniture still needed dusting, and doubtless the linens were still yellow. But in some indefinable way the house seemed to exude a welcome instead of the hostility he had felt ever since he had taken possession of it.

Gabriel had a small glass of brandy in the study before going up to his room, where Mackley, his new valet, helped him prepare for bed. Retiring for the night, Gabriel felt quite content with his life.

Unfortunately, just as he was about to doze off, he had a third disconcerting thought, which totally banished sleep.

Looking back, Gabriel realized that Miss Jolliffe had always seemed to be an emotionless person, calm at all times and completely lacking the capability for passion. Yet this evening she had taken such delight in besting him at cards.

Almost a sensual delight . . .

He remembered the way she had peeked at him out of the corner of her eye after a particularly ingenious play—almost as if she were taunting him—daring him to . . . to what?

Feeling suddenly overheated, Gabriel threw back the covers and walked over to the window and stared out into the night. But his thoughts of Miss Jolliffe followed, to plague and distract him.

He could not rid his mind of the memory of her hands, which he had never really noticed until this evening. They were slender, almost delicate, and thinking about them, he could not help wondering what it would feel like to have her touch him—to have those graceful hands softly caress him.

He remembered also the way the curve of her neck had seemed to beckon him. So smooth and enticing, it had positively demanded to be kissed, and the tiny wisps of hair curling innocently and seductively at the nape had not made it any easier to resist.

But standing here in the quiet darkness, it was the memory of her eyes that bothered him the most—her gray-green eyes, which had glistened with a silken delight that was not at all suitable for a properly brought-up spinster of advancing years.

Turning away from the window and beginning to pace the room, he tried to convince himself that he felt tempted by Miss Jolliffe's charms only because it was so long since he had lain with one of his mistresses. All he needed to do was slake his lust on some convenient woman . . .

But he could not even carry that thought to completion. Other women no longer had any attractions for him—he could not even call to mind the faces of his former mistresses.

The realization came to him suddenly, but he could not deny its truth. The only thing that would relax him and allow him to sleep was if Miss Jolliffe were here sharing his bed. What he wanted was to see her eyes become cloudy with desire for him—what he needed was to see her pleasure grow—to see her desire him as much as he now craved her.

How much pleasure could he derive from pleasuring her? She had teased him this evening, and now his hands began to tremble at the thought of teasing her in return—of touching her, caressing her, tormenting her until she burned for him.

Dear God, he had so readily, so easily, so carelessly dismissed her as an emotionless, passionless female of advancing years, but this evening it was as if she had opened the shutters of her soul and allowed him to see the fire that was burning inside her—a fire that was still carefully banked, for which he was intensely thankful.

After this evening he knew he had to be the one—the only one—who was allowed to explore the depth of passion within Miss Jolliffe.

He felt chilled with the realization of how easily he might never have known her. Suppose some other man had seen what lay behind her plain facade? Suppose she had married someone else before he had even returned to England?

Even worse, suppose he had not listened to her pleas in Northumberland and had driven off and left her stranded at the Crown and Thistle?

He felt ill at the thought of how easily he might have lived his entire life without her, and pulling on his dressing gown, he went down to his study and poured himself a hefty measure of brandy.

The house lay quiet, the servants apparently all sleeping soundly, but it was a long time before Gabriel gave up his vigil and again returned to his too empty bed, there to toss and turn for hours.

It seemed to Gabriel that no sooner had he shut his eyes than Mackley, his new valet, was opening the drapes to admit the feeble rays of the cold winter sun. Considering how long he had lain awake, Gabriel would have cheerfully paid out a thousand golden guineas for the chance to roll over and go back to sleep.

But being late two days in a row to pick up Miss Jolliffe was not only unthinkable, but also foolhardy. Once might be excusable, but twice would be insulting.

She would forgive him, of course, no matter how feeble his excuse. But, he realized as he dragged himself out of bed, now that he had discovered she was not at all the emotionless spinster he had thought her, it would be unconscionable for him to deliberately—or carelessly—hurt her feelings.

Besides which, he realized while Mackley was shaving him, he was curious to see what she would say when he gave her the little book of household instructions. As much as he wanted her to profess her love for him, he was willing to give good odds that she would not utter the same cloying, honeyed phrases that his mistresses had invariably used. Whatever Miss Jolliffe said, the words would be unexpected. That much he had learned in the few weeks he had known her.

Nevertheless, over a breakfast of beefsteak and ale, he played a game with himself, trying to reason out logically what she might say, but none of the possible responses that came to mind seemed to be in keeping with what he knew about her.

Which was odd, because looking back, he could hear quite clearly in his mind what any of his previous mistresses would have said if he had given her the little book, which had, as any of them would have recognized immediately, no intrinsic value, and which was likewise in no way romantic.

In a word, females were in his experience so totally predictable that all of them, after the briefest acquaintance, invariably became quite tedious and boring. Miss Jolliffe, on the other hand, managed in her modest and unassuming way to become more intriguing with each passing day.

She was, as always, quite punctual, likewise an uncommon trait for a female, and by the time he pulled his horses to a stop in front of her brother-in-law's house, she was already standing on the pavement waiting for him to reach down and assist her into the carriage.

Her cheeks were flushed from the cold, and her gray-green eyes sparkled in the early morning sun—no, they did not sparkle, they glowed, like priceless antique jade, and he had to look away before he was caught in their spell.

Although she settled in her seat with outward calm, he had seen enough to know that this morning it was not at all easy for her to remain silent until they were in the park and away from the traffic.

He was not, however, going to relieve the tension that was emanating from her in waves by congratulating her on her skill at card-playing, nor, despite the fact that she had just cause to revel in her power over him, was he going to confess the sleepless hours he had spent during the night thinking about what it would be like to bed her.

In the end, his patience paid off. "Tell me," she said as soon as he drove the carriage through the gates of Hyde Park, "did Mrs. Wiggins manage to find the proper servants for you? I was positively agog with curiosity last evening, and I could not keep from wishing we might have an opportunity to speak privately."

He could not hold back a bark of laughter. Did she have any idea how thoroughly she had just put him in his place? His thoughts had been all on seduction, whereas hers had been on proper household management. She had, as usual, caught him completely off-guard.

"So distracted were you, thinking about my servants, that you were quite unable to concentrate on the cards," he said.

To his delight her face took on a rosy tinge. "Do not tease me, my lord. I was scarcely able to sleep a wink last night, wondering if you were all right."

The image conjured up by her words—which he was sure she had uttered in all innocence—was so instantly arousing, that his arms involuntarily jerked on the reins, causing his horses to rear up. Gabriel quickly got them under control again, much more easily, in fact, than he was able to control his own pulse.

With outward calm, he said, "Although they are a lean and hungry lot, I believe the servants Mrs. Wiggins chose for me will serve the purpose. I could have used your help in dealing with them yesterday, however." He had not intended to mention that, but once the words were out, there was no way he could call them back.

"My help?"

She was blushing again, he realized with delight. Yesterday he would have assumed she was embarrassed at the thought of doing something so improper as to visit a gentleman in his residence, but after an evening playing cards with her, he was no longer positive her thoughts did not occasionally stray across the line of what was proper for a lady in her circumstances.

Unfortunately, Hyde Park was not a convenient place to pursue that line of inquiry, so he described instead the interviews he'd had with the three upper servants. "In short, Miss Jolliffe," he concluded, "I managed in the space of a few minutes to reduce each of them to tears."

Miss Jolliffe made no comment, and looking down at her, he saw that tears were also spilling out of her eyes and running down her cheeks. Reining in his horses, he took his handkerchief from his pocket and began to wipe her face, but she caught his hand in both of hers and held it to her cheek.

"You are so good," she said. "I cannot think of any other gentleman who would have done such a noble thing."

For a moment he was tempted to let her keep her delusions about his character, but something—perhaps her promise never to lie to him—prevented him from letting her continue to believe something that was patently false.

"What rubbish," he said, feeling quite embarrassed. He pulled his hand abruptly away and tucked his now rather damp handkerchief back into his pocket. Signaling his horses to proceed, he said acerbically, "I was merely doing what was necessary to insure their loyalty."

"You will pardon me, my lord, if I do not believe you," she said, and he felt her hand on his arm.

Given a second chance to take advantage of her naivety, he again chose instead to point out to her the errors in her thinking. "You are mistaking my motives," he said bluntly, "and seeing nobility of spirit where there is in truth only practicality. I learned years ago that well-fed and well-treated sailors do not jump ship at the first port they put in to."

"And I suppose because of that policy, the captains of your ships never have to worry about sailing without a full complement of men?" she asked, gazing up at him with a smile in her eyes.

"Almost never," he replied. "But before you make any further attempts to canonize me, may I point out that keeping the same crew for several voyages results in increased profits?"

"I am sure it does. And treating servants as if they are also people who have feelings does much to ensure that a household will be well run."

"As I said, Miss Jennings, it is practicality and nothing more." He glanced down at her and discovered she was still looking up at him with complete approval—no, it went far beyond approval. In her eyes he could almost see the reflection of a halo above his head, and under his coat his shoulders fairly itched with the wings that were trying to sprout.

"One always has a choice, you see," she said. "And you are correct in saying that it is wiser to choose kindness. But surely you are aware that no matter how short-sighted it is, the majority of people in this world choose to coerce rather than to cajole."

"The majority of people have no choices to make," he said harshly, "because they are powerless."

"There is always a choice," she repeated. "Even in my situation, where, as you have rightly pointed out, I am nothing but a poor relation who is used as a household drudge, I can choose to shirk or I can choose to do my tasks to the best of my ability. Likewise, you have chosen to deal with your servants kindly, and by doing so, you have shown that you are a good man."

Her logic was impeccable, and he had to admire her analysis of the situation. But despite her skillful reasoning, he knew himself to be a ruthless man rather than an altruistic one, because motive was everything.

At this very moment he had in his pocket a small, leather-bound volume, whose contents he knew would give her much pleasure. But his reason for giving it to her had nothing to do with kindness and everything to do with self-interest.

And it was a measure of just how ruthless he could be that he had no intention of abandoning his efforts to make her fall in love with him, nor did he feel the slightest compulsion to warn her about the trap he was luring her into.

Deviousness, dishonesty, deceit—he would use whatever was necessary to succeed, and he would feel not the slightest twinge of conscience. All was fair in love and war, as the saying went.

Not that he believed in such trite clichés. He had learned long ago that nothing was fair. Success went to those strong enough to seize power and ruthless enough to use it, and self-sacrifice was for fools and saints.

Without feeling the slightest guilt, he took the little book from his pocket and gave it to his companion, who opened it and began to peruse its contents.

"Oh," she said, as much rapture in her voice as if he had given her a king's ransom in jewels, "wherever did you find this?"

"I happened to come across it in the library at Sherington House," he said, once again finding himself in the unaccustomed position of deriving pleasure from her unfeigned enthusiasm for his present.

"Could I borrow it for a few days?" she asked. "I would dearly love to copy some of these recipes, and I promise I shall take the best care of it."

Gabriel was torn between anger and amusement—between wanting to shake her and wanting to embrace her—between wanting to curse her for her naivety and wanting to protect her from any disillusionment.

"I intended it as a gift," he said flatly.

As he had anticipated, she did not bat her eyelashes up at him and praise him for having chosen such a perfect gift . . . nor, of course, did she profess her undying love and devotion. But then he had known for quite some time that she was not cast in the same mold as other women.

Instead, she said with more emotion and passion than he had ever before heard in her voice, "Oh, how can you bear to part with it?"

Her remark was not, of course, even vaguely close to any of the responses he had thought it possible she might make.

# 11

GABRIEL LOOKED DOWN at the column of figures he had just added up. The total was impressively large, but he felt frustration rather than satisfaction.

This latest enterprise was turning out to be successful beyond his expectations. Like every business venture he had ever embarked upon, it was going to give him a good return on his investment.

Due to judicious assessment of the risks involved in his various projects, followed by careful planning—and, he had to admit, with more than his share of good luck— he had managed over the years to make his fortune while avoiding all the disasters and catastrophes that had destroyed many a man in his position.

So why was he having so much difficulty in the matter of Miss Jolliffe?

Although not at all ready to admit defeat where she was concerned, he had to acknowledge that he was, at least for the moment, completely stymied. In a word, he could not think of a single strategy that he had not already tried . . . and that had not already failed him.

One turn around the park with him and any other woman would be confiding in her friends that he was about to propose marriage. One dance with him and her friends would be congratulating her on her conquest.

And yet, even though he was practically sitting in Miss Jolliffe's pocket, she was still treating him as if . . . as if he were her brother.

No, he corrected himself, she readily professed to love her brother, which meant he could not even claim that much.

He was about to vent his spleen on a particularly ugly vase that had been irritating him ever since he had moved into Sherington House, when his butler tapped on the door and entered the study, bearing on a silver salver a letter from Mr. Parkins, who had started out long ago as his accountant, and who had over the years become in effect a trusted financial advisor.

Breaking the seal, Gabriel quickly scanned its contents. It was a simple request to meet with him at his earliest convenience. Simple, but not at all usual in the normal course of events.

"Will there be a reply?" Exeter asked.

"Yes, send a message to Mr. Parkins that I can see him at three o'clock this afternoon," Gabriel said, and his butler bowed briefly and departed.

Left alone once more, Gabriel wondered if perhaps his luck had, after all these years, finally deserted him. Why else would Mr. Parkins have requested an unscheduled meeting?

In the mood he was in, Gabriel did not particularly care if his accountant was bringing him news that he was bankrupt. Money was only money, but Miss Jolliffe . . .

He cursed, and the vase shattered when it hit the wall, cracking the plaster in the process.


"So you see, my lord," Mr. Parkins concluded, "although there is nothing specific that I can put my finger on, the rents and other income from your primary estate in Suffolk are considerably below what one might justifiably expect them to be."

Gabriel studied the papers his accountant had brought him, for the first time in his life finding it difficult to see meaning in the numbers.

"I must admit," Mr. Parkins continued, "that my field of expertise lies in trade rather than in agriculture, but I have made discreet inquiries, and I am forced to the unpalatable conclusion that your estate is being"—he cleared his throat—"grossly mismanaged, shall we say?"

"Or there is also the possibility that I am being robbed blind," Gabriel said, looking up and meeting his accountant's eye.

"That is also a possibility," Mr. Parkins admitted with a smile. "Although it is hard to imagine anyone having sufficient courage and resolution to cheat you."

"But Suffolk is a considerable distance from London, and it is possible that my reputation has not yet reached the provinces," Gabriel said. Sherington Close was not only many miles, but also many years away from him. He had never been back there since the day he had been sent to sea as a very small and helpless child.

Gabriel knew what Mr. Parkins was expecting him to say—that he would go himself to Suffolk and investigate matters. It was, after all, what he invariably insisted upon doing when trouble threatened any of his investments.

But in this case, it was not only his memories he would be forced to confront, but there was also Miss Jolliffe, whom he would of necessity have to leave behind.

"Tell me, Mr. Parkins, you are married, are you not?"

"Twenty-three years come July."

"And I believe you have a daughter, do you not?"

"I have three, as a matter of fact, and two sons," the accountant admitted with an undisguised look of pride.

"Which means you should have some understanding of females," Gabriel said.

"Well, they do say, my lord, as how absence makes the heart grow fonder," Mr. Parkins replied with a smile.

"And is that your advice, or are you merely trying to coerce me into going to Suffolk so that you will not be obliged to make a journey during January?"

"I should say, it is a little of both, my lord."

As much as Verity had anticipated it, the end, when it came, left her feeling numb, as if she were no longer completely alive. Sitting huddled in her chair in the corner of the drawing room, she inspected the innocent-seeming piece of vellum that Otterwall had just carried in to her.

"I have been called away on business," she managed to decipher. That was all the note said—except, of course, for a scrawl at the bottom of the sheet that was apparently Lord Sherington's signature.

No indication where he was going—no hint as to when he would return.

He would not come back to her, of course. She was amazed that she had held his interest for as long as she had, but she had no delusions about the future.

Folding the note carefully, she tucked it between the pages of the leather-bound book he had given her. The little volume had been a farewell present, but fool that she was, she had not recognized its significance.

"Ah, there you are," her sister's voice sounded behind her, and Verity quickly slipped the little book under the pillowcase that she was supposed to be embroidering.

"Antoinette's new sprigged muslin is not at all satisfactory," Petronella said crossly, "And I want you to return it to Mademoiselle Beaufrère and inform her that we shall not be paying for it."

"In what way is it unsatisfactory?" Verity said, her voice sounding very weak and tinny to her own ears. "Perhaps it could be altered?"

"Altered? That is out of the question. The wretched gown is totally out of style, and I shall not be giving that incompetent woman any more of our business. With our standing in society, we can certainly do better than a wretched little émigré who pretends to have some mysterious connection to the French nobility. Bah! She calls herself a modiste, but she is a barely adequate seamstress. I would not be at all surprised to discover she is nothing more than some wealthy merchant's by-blow."

Verity knew she should inform Petronella of the social disaster that was bound to overtake them now that Lord Sherington had withdrawn his sponsorship, but she could not say a word.

"Well, why are you sitting there?" Petronella said even more crossly. "You shall have to hurry to be back in time to act as Antoinette's chaperone when the dancing master comes to give her instruction."

Verity laid aside her needlework, and keeping the leather-bound book carefully hidden in the folds of her skirt, she went upstairs as quickly as possible to change into a walking dress and half boots.

Once she was safely in her own room, however, she

made no more pretense of hurrying. Instead, she crossed to her dressing table and took out a sandalwood box that some long-forgotten sea captain had brought back from India years ago.

Taking a fine gold chain from her neck, Verity used the tiny key that was suspended from it to unlock the box. Inside lay a chamois pouch containing the string of pearls she had inherited from her grandmother.

On top of the pouch she carefully laid the book Lord Sherington had given her. Although she had not yet had time to read every word, she had looked through it and had identified seven different handwritings. Seven women had owned the book before her and had inscribed within it the things they had learned from their own experiences.

And she would be the eighth one.

That knowledge brought her the same comfort that she suspected Lord Sherington found when he was near a large body of water.

She did not doubt that the pain of his departure would be a long time in passing, nor that there would be untold nights when her pillow would be damp with her own tears. Likewise she knew there would be days when it would seem impossible for her to continue.

But life would go on, and she would survive, and someday, when she was an old woman, she would pass this little book on to another young woman, who would likewise write down her favorite recipes.

Touching it gently one last time, Verity closed the lid of the sandalwood box, locked it again with the little key, and then replaced the chain around her neck.

One other thing she knew: even if she never saw his face again or rode beside him in a carriage or heard the sound of his voice, she would never forget Lord Sherington, and she would love him to the end of her days and even, God willing, beyond the grave.

As a young lad on board ship, Gabriel had always dreamed of making his return to Suffolk in state, with coachman and groom, valet and luggage, and several liveried outriders to give him consequence.

But now that he was a man, he found such pretensions mattered to him not at all, which was fortunate considering the physical condition of his new servants and the state of their wardrobes.

Traveling alone in his phaeton, Gabriel found he felt no enthusiasm, no curiosity to see the place of his birth. He had expected to feel some satisfaction that he had, in the end, become the owner of the house and estate that his mother's husband had tried so hard to deprive him of.

His memories of the years he had spent within the walls of Sherington Close were so few and so nebulous that he felt not the slightest sense of homecoming when the Elizabethan mansion came into view.

Sherington Close. His home.

He reined in his team and sat there for a long time, looking at the edifice, which had been built on the site of a long ago monastery. It was, when all was said and done, only a pile of stones, artfully arranged, and as he had told Miss Jolliffe in Northumberland, he had little interest in or any affinity for such things.

A well-caulked hull or a properly sanded deck was, of course, an entirely different matter.

Having received word of his coming, the butler had the servants lined up in the great hall to welcome their new master to his ancestral home. The upper servants said all that was fitting, and the lower servants tugged at their forelocks with proper deference, but Gabriel could feel the same waves of hostility emanating from this group that he had encountered when he had taken possession of his London residence.

In time, they would come to accept him . . . or they would find themselves replaced. It mattered not to Gabriel which they chose, so long as Miss Jolliffe, when he brought her here as his wife, was not in any way distressed.

The following day Gabriel was inspecting the bailiff's account books and finding them much more complicated than the ones in Northumberland had been. Hardly surprising, considering the difference in the sizes of the two estates.

He did not lack a head for business, however, and he knew he would, in the end, have a clear grasp of what each entry signified. Unfortunately, it looked as if it would take him much longer than he had anticipated, which meant he would not be able to return to London as soon as he had hoped.

There was a tap at the door, and the butler entered to tell him the vicar had come to tea.

"I have taken the liberty of putting the Reverend Mr. Stephen Todd in the library, m'lord, if that meets with your approval," he said, "and I have instructed the cook to prepare a tea tray."

The servant's manner was properly deferential, but Gabriel was not deceived into thinking he had yet won the loyalty of this household, despite how calm things might seem on the surface.

The vicar was a younger man than Gabriel had expected, and in fact, did not appear to have yet reached the age of thirty. He was blond, well built, and were it not for the clerical collar he wore, Gabriel would have taken him for one of the Corinthian set. His was also the first face Gabriel had seen in Suffolk that bore a genuine smile.

"I should doubtless have waited until Sunday to see if you put in an appearance in church," the Reverend Mr. Todd said without preamble, "but my errand with you today has nothing to do with ecclesiastical business."

"Indeed?" Gabriel said. "Then may I offer you a chair and a glass of brandy, or do you prefer to wait for a cup of tea?"

"As the sacrificial goat, I think I would prefer spirits to cat-lap," the vicar replied, seating himself in a comfortable chair beside the fire.

"You intrigue me," Gabriel said, handing his visitor a drink and pouring one for himself. "Sacrificial goat?"

"As the person in this parish with the least to lose—I am unencumbered with wife and children, and my uncle is a bishop, so if you throw me out bag and baggage, he can doubtless procure another living for me—I have been chosen to sound you out on a number of topics," the vicar explained.

"I fear my reputation has preceded me," Gabriel said, taking the opposite seat.

"Actually, it has not, and therein lies the problem."

"How so?"

Swirling the brandy in his glass, the vicar gathered his thoughts, then raised his head and said with no trace of humor, "The good people of this parish, both the ones who reside on the estate and the ones who are independent of your direct control, have sent me to ascertain if you are cut from the same cloth as your father and older brother."

"I regret that I cannot tell you that," Gabriel said.

"Then I am wasting my time and your brandy," the vicar said, rising to his feet.

"You are too quick to concede defeat," Gabriel said. "Pray be seated and let us discuss this further." His visitor made no move to sit down, and Gabriel added, "I was not being facetious. Perhaps it might interest you to know that I cannot recall ever having met the late earl."

"And now," the vicar said, returning to his chair, "*you* begin to intrigue *me*. How is it possible for a son not to remember his own father? The earl died less than a year ago."

Familiar with the speed with which gossip could spread, Gabriel was not ready to answer that particular question. "Tell me first what kind of men the late earl and his elder son were."

"I would not wish to speak ill of the dead, especially in the presence of their nearest relatives," the vicar demurred, "although merely by saying that much I am sure you are clever enough to deduce what my general opinion of your father and brother must be."

"Do you play chess?" Gabriel asked.

Puzzled, the vicar nodded his head. "I am accounted a better than average player."

"Then you understand what the term stalemate refers to?"

Again a nod. "In this case I suspect it means you are not ready to tell me what I wish to know until after I tell you what *you* wish to know, and for my part I do not feel free to speak my piece until I have learned what kind of a man I am talking with."

"Precisely. I could not have said that better myself."

"And do you perchance play poker, my lord?" the vicar asked with another smile. "Do you know about bluffing?"

"The question at this time, my dear sir, is which one of us is bluffing and which of us holds the higher cards," Gabriel said.

"I see I shall soon be writing a begging letter to my uncle," the Reverend Mr. Todd said with a wry smile. "Where do you wish me to begin, my lord? Shall I first name for you one by one the assorted bastards your father and brother have begotten? Shall I list the young girls they have seduced and abandoned? Or would you rather I told you about servants who have been beaten half to death because they have aroused a drunkard's temper? Or shall I show you the cottages those two noble gentlemen ordered burned down out of spite because they took offense where none was intended?"

Gabriel could see in the vicar's face that he was speaking nothing but the truth. "I prefer that we start with financial matters," he said mildly. "I made this journey to Suffolk because my accountant informed me that the estate here was not producing as much revenue as it should."

"Revenue?" the vicar said, his voice rising. "Revenue? Your father has wrung every groat possible out of this land. He has beggared his tenants by raising the rents to impossible levels, and he never invested a single farthing in the estate, little caring that he was destroying the productivity of his own fields. And you ask about the revenue this land should be producing?"

In the silence that followed this outburst, the butler entered carrying a massive silver tea tray, which he set down on a table between Gabriel and his guest.

"Please inform the cook that Mr. Todd will be staying for dinner," Gabriel said.

"My God," the vicar said as soon as the butler had

left, "but you are the most cold-blooded bastard I have ever met."

Gabriel smiled. "Since you already have suspicions about the legitimacy of my birth—"

"I did not mean it literally," the vicar said somewhat shamefaced. "I am afraid I have a regrettable tendency to lose my temper, which my uncle has frequently informed me will keep me from ever being appointed to a bishopric."

"You asked why I was not well acquainted with the late earl, and the answer is quite simple. In the eyes of the law, he was my father, but in truth we did not share a drop of common blood. And his elder son was only my half brother. Do I need to explain any further?"

"I fear that if I attempt to comment, I shall once again be taking the name of our Lord in vain."

"Have some more brandy," Gabriel said. "And tell me what you know about my mother."

"I never met her personally," the vicar said. "She died before I came here. According to village gossip, she was quite standoffish and shunned local society. But my former housekeeper's sister worked for a short time as a maid in this house, and she—my housekeeper—used to hint that there was more to the story—that Lady Sherington had not been a voluntary recluse, but in actuality a prisoner. What you have told me makes me think that perhaps there is more than a little truth in the servant's story."

"Would you object if I questioned your housekeeper?" Gabriel asked.

"I am sorry, but that will not be possible. She married and went back to Ireland, and I am afraid I cannot even tell you in which county she now resides."

"It is no matter," Gabriel said. "I am sure some of the other servants have been in service here long enough to remember my mother."

"It will perhaps cause less gossip if you question your grandmother instead," the vicar said.

Feeling rather confused, Gabriel said, "My grandparents both died before I was born. Their stones are in the west wall of the church."

"No, no, I meant your mother's mother."

Something of Gabriel's shock must have showed on his face, because the vicar said, "But, my lord, you are looking quite pale. Have you been taken ill? Have I said something to upset you?"

Gabriel gave a shaky laugh. "Perhaps you would be so good as to pour me another brandy? It is not an everyday occurrence for me to discover I have a grandmother whose very existence I knew nothing about."

"And I must confess," the Reverend Mr. Stephen Todd said, handing Gabriel a glass filled to the brim with amber liquid, "that the interview with you this afternoon, which I thought I had prepared for so well, has not gone at all the way I expected it to."

"I should have known the moment I saw your jaw that you were not a proper Rainsford," the vicar said, stopping in front of a large painting of a man dressed in the clothing of the last century. "Behold, your predecessor, the sixth Earl of Sherington."

The gallery on the second floor of Sherington Close was lined with dozens of portraits, and although they all bore the same surname that Gabriel did, not a one of the people preserved on canvas was in fact related to him by blood.

Examining the picture the vicar was indicating, Gabriel said, "So this was my mother's husband. One wonders if the artist deliberately chose to portray his subject with reckless honesty or if he was simply not adept enough with the brush to disguise the earl's cruel nature."

"He was indeed a vicious man," the vicar said, "and much hated in the neighborhood."

"And the sins of the father, as it were, are to be visited upon the son who is not, in fact, actually a son."

"I sincerely doubt that, my lord."

"You mean you are willing to vouch for my good character?"

The vicar laughed. "A good word from me will not be needed once your tenants learn that you will be putting money into the estate rather than taking it out."

"And shall I be doing that?" Gabriel asked, finding

this man of the cloth to be quite an extraordinary fellow. Even though they had known each other only a few hours, it seemed somehow inevitable that they would become friends.

"As a matter of fact, some of us—I was instructed not to mention any specific names, lest the terrible wrath of my Lord Sherington descend upon certain unprotected heads—have prepared a completely detailed proposal for turning a rundown estate into the showcase of the county, which plan, coincidentally, I happen to have with me," the vicar said, pulling a sheaf of papers out of his jacket pocket.

Gabriel laughed and clapped his companion on the back. "Tell me, my dear sir, may I call you Stephen?"

"I would be honored if you would, my lord."

"Then you must call me Gabriel, and no I am not in my cups. But I find that so much weighty discussion has whetted my appetite. Shall we see if dinner is waiting for us?"

"And while we are dining, perhaps we could discuss the financial provisions you might be willing to make for the assorted baseborn children in this parish who so far have only been endowed with the Rainsford jaw."

"And perhaps, Stephen, if we spend the evening together, the subject of a new roof for the church might even come up, hmmm?"

"No, no, you have it all wrong. It is the vicarage that desperately needs a new roof. All the church requires is a new pipe organ."

The driver of the hackney coach was apparently accustomed to the eccentricities of the *ton*, because his face remained impassive when Verity told him where she wished to go. Perhaps he thought she had an early morning assignation with a lover?

What would he say if he knew that she was going to meet only a memory?

The drive down Pall Mall to the Thames should have been familiar, but she had never really noticed the drays loaded down with kegs and barrels, the peddlers pushing their hand carts, the shops with their shutters still closed.

She had crossed Westminster Bridge several times when she was driving out with Lord Sherington, but she had never really looked at its stones, or at the barges and boats and skiffs going under its arches.

The road along the water's edge went through a rather ramshackle district, but Verity had never before noticed.

But then, on her earlier visits here, she had been sitting beside Lord Sherington, and all her attention had been focused on him.

Reaching the place where the roadway left the river's edge, the driver turned his hack around and started back in the direction of the bridge.

Turning away from the window, Verity covered her face with her hands. She had hoped that returning to one of the places where they had been together might make her feel closer to Lord Sherington, but she had found nothing here but a vast emptiness.

She pulled the cloak he had given her more tightly around herself, but it availed little against the cold. The air outside was warmer than usual, but the chill she was feeling came from her heart.

On the afternoon of his eighth day in Suffolk, Gabriel explored the west wing of Sherington Close, which had been shut off and unused for many years. Starting in the cellars, which held nothing except cobwebs and beetles, he worked his way upward, giving the musty rooms only the most cursory inspection.

After an hour or so, he was rather grubby himself and quite ready to return to the main section of the house, until, that is, he opened the door of a tiny room in the attic and stepped through into his past.

The moment Gabriel entered the low-ceilinged chamber, his heart began to pound.

He remembered this room.

He had thought his unfamiliarity with the house and the grounds was because he had been too young for memories when he left . . . but he remembered this room in every detail.

Once this room had been his world. He had lived here, played here, slept here, eaten here. He had a vague recollection of assorted servants who had come and gone, tending to his physical needs, but they were shadowy figures, too indistinct for him to call back after all the intervening years.

Walking across the floor, he wiped the grime from the window and looked out. He knew this view. As a child he had memorized every tree, every distant cottage roof, every pathway below.

Too many memories came flooding back, and he realized that his life had been even more circumscribed here than on board ship, where he had lived and worked crowded shoulder to shoulder with other men and boys.

"You failed," he whispered to the dead man who had carelessly and callously littered the countryside with his bastards, yet who had adamantly refused to accept his wife's love child. "You could have destroyed me so easily. All you would have had to have done was keep me here, but instead you chose to send me away to sea, and in so doing, you gave me the entire world."

Turning back to the room, Gabriel looked around at the meager furnishings—the cot he had slept on, the few toys he had played with, the desk where he had done his lessons, and the fireplace . . .

Slowly he walked over to the fireplace and inspected it more closely. Without knowing why he was doing it, he knelt down and began to count. Four bricks over from the right, then three bricks up from the floor.

Still kneeling, he took hold of the brick, which looked no different from its neighbors, and began to wiggle it back and forth. Although his fingers were too large now for him to get a good grip on it at first, he was soon able to work the brick loose. Then he reached inside the hole and felt around.

With growing anticipation he pulled out a small tin box. Lifting the lid, he looked down at his childhood. Three glass marbles, a blue feather, and a miniature of his mother.

As soon as he saw her likeness, he heard again in his mind the soft whispery sound of her approaching footsteps.

She had come to him only during the dark hours of

the night, when no servants were about, and he wondered now if her husband had known of her nocturnal visits.

He remembered also the many nights he had listened in vain—straining his ears, but hearing nothing but the wind rattling the panes of his single window.

Every time she had come, she had held him in her arms and cried, but now, looking back through the long corridors of time, Gabriel had no idea who her tears had been for. Had she shed them for her son . . . or had she only been filled with pity for herself, that she had been caught out in an adulterous liaison, for which she had been imprisoned—and the truth of that allegation he had not yet determined—by a vengeful husband.

Had she come creeping through the darkness because she wished to see her son . . . or because she was hoping that somehow the physical evidence of her moral weakness might simply have vanished in the darkness? He was, after all, the blot on the family escutcheon.

He remembered the feel of her arms around him. He remembered the scent of roses that had come into the room with her. He remembered how soft her cheek had been when it was pressed against his. He remembered his own desperate longing to keep her there with him forever.

Beyond that, he could not remember, and the painted likeness of his mother that he held in his hand could not tell him what he needed to know.

# 12

WHEN THE MOON ROSE, Gabriel was still standing in the little room, which had grown quite cold. He rather suspected his servants were wondering what had become of him, and the cook was undoubtedly fretting that the dinner would be ruined. But still he made no move to leave the attic chamber.

Tomorrow would be time enough to go back to the light and the warmth and the people.

Tomorrow he would finish the most urgent business on the estate. The vicar, Gabriel had discovered, was a tireless taskmaster, but even Stephen must learn that Rome was not built in a day, nor a lifetime of mismanagement corrected in one week. And the day after tomorrow, Gabriel would leave for London . . . and Miss Jolliffe.

As difficult as it was for him to admit it even to himself, he missed her damnably.

All his life he had known himself to be a solitary person, but this week he had discovered there was a vast difference between being alone and being lonely.

Now that Stephen had put their fears to rest, the household servants were friendly and helpful. The tenants were enthusiastic about the new improvements he had agreed to. The squire had indicated his willingness to allow Gabriel to hunt with his pack.

But in the midst of all these people who wished him well, Gabriel still felt a loneliness that chilled him to the marrow.

What he had learned here in Suffolk had turned his world upside down, leaving him with the feeling that he

had built his life on sand rather than rock. Stephen would
undoubtedly enjoy that Biblical allusion, but there were
limits to what Gabriel was willing to discuss with his new
friend.

He needed Miss Jolliffe with her cool gray-green eyes
and frank way of speaking. He needed to tell her everything he had learned. He could discuss drainage and
thatching and the latest drill planters with a dozen men,
but there was no one else but Miss Jolliffe that he could
bear to talk with about his mother.

Perhaps if he shared his past with Miss Jolliffe, he
would be able to figure out who he really was. Too much
of what he had believed about his background—about
his family, his childhood, his home—had proved to be
merely illusion.

He wanted to have Miss Jolliffe beside him in his carriage where she belonged—he wanted to feel the light
touch of her hand resting on his arm—he wanted to be
sure she was dressed warmly enough.

He missed scolding her and lecturing her and arguing
with her, and he knew he was not going to be at all
patient with her when he returned to London.

But that would not be until the day after tomorrow,
which left tomorrow . . . and tonight.

The dark hours were a time for dealing with the ghosts
that haunted this room. A time for remembering . . .
and if he was lucky, forgetting . . . but not forgiving.


"It is not at all odd that he has dropped them. What
is passing strange is that he took up with them in the
first place."

Verity did not recognize the voice behind her, but she
could not doubt for a moment that the words were intended for her own ears—nor could she doubt that Lord
Sherington and her own family were the subject under
discussion.

"He is clearly deranged," a second person said. "I
have heard from a reputable source that he fired all his
servants with only an hour's notice, and then he hired
some riffraff off the streets to replace them."

They had chosen the wrong person to try to wound

with their spiteful words, Verity thought with an inward smile. If only they knew that she cared not one whit about their opinions of her and Lord Sherington.

Now, if they had expressed themselves within the hearing of Petronella . . . but no, that would have likewise been ineffectual. Verity's sister would not have even recognized that she was being talked about, much less insulted.

The Wasteneys' social standing had begun to slip the second evening Lord Sherington had failed to put in an appearance. As one day followed another without any sign of him, the slip had turned into a slide, and Verity rather thought that this evening, after more than a week of his absence, the slide was about to become a plummet.

The flood of invitations pouring into the Wasteney residence had, as Verity had expected it to, dried up almost immediately. But for the unfortunate few hostesses whose invitations had been sent out *before* Lord Sherington had abandoned the social scene, and whose events had been scheduled for *after* that fateful day, there was little that could be done short of barring the door when the Wasteneys arrived with Verity in tow.

Verity would have vastly preferred staying home these last several evenings, but how could she explain to her sister that they were no longer welcome? Petronella was so thick-skinned, she could be given the cut direct and not even notice.

That had actually happened once yesterday and twice this evening, and even as obtuse as Petronella was, sooner or later someone would make it so clear that the Wasteneys had fallen from grace, that even she would recognize that the very people who had welcomed her last week were now rejecting her.

Verity could, of course, have claimed a headache and thus had an excuse to stay home alone. But since she was the reason Lord Sherington had entered her sister's life, it would hardly be fair to abandon Petronella when the hour of her humiliation was approaching so quickly and so inevitably.

Family solidarity was rapidly losing its appeal, however, and Verity could not help but be thankful that this was the last evening they would have to go out. Tomorrow night Lady Thurmuncy was having a card party, but her guest list, for obvious reasons, did not include the name of Wasteney or Jolliffe.

By eleven o'clock, Verity's headache was real, and after much sotto voce pleading, she finally persuaded her sister to leave the party early, although Ralph decided to stay a little longer to discuss the political situation with a slightly inebriated member of Parliament.

"If you are sickening with something, Verity, I would prefer that you stay in your room tomorrow evening," Petronella said crossly when they arrived in Curzon Street, "for I have no intention of coming home early.

"Tomorrow? But we have nothing scheduled for tomorrow," Verity said, tiredly climbing the steps and waiting for the butler to admit them.

"Do not be silly," Petronella said with a trill of laughter. "Surely you know that Lady Thurmuncy is having a card party tomorrow? This evening I dropped her a little hint that our invitation must have gone astray, and I am confident she will send along another one in time, for she would not wish to exclude us, of that I am sure. We are quite the best of friends now."

Grateful that she had known nothing of this while they were still at the party, Verity followed her sister into the house. Otterwall relieved her of her cloak, and then to her surprise, he slipped a note into her hand, and all thoughts of her sister's foolishness were pushed out of Verity's mind.

Mounting the stairs to her room, Petronella chattered on, but Verity understood not a word that was said. The note in her hand had to be from Lord Sherington.

What would it say? Dare she hope? It was an impossible dream, and yet . . .

Once she was safely alone in her room, Verity was almost afraid to read the note for fear it held bad news, but in the end curiosity compelled her to unfold the piece of vellum.

"Nine o'clock," was all it said, with the oh, so familiar scrawl below.

After she had been so sure her life was over—that her

only joy would be in remembering Lord Sherington—it was such an unexpected reprieve, Verity scarcely knew whether she should laugh or cry. In the end she did both, holding her hands over her mouth lest someone hear.

That night she lay dreaming in bed for hours, but she slept hardly at all. Every time she dozed off, she awoke with a start, terrified that she had overslept and missed the rendezvous with Lord Sherington.

Even knowing she was being remarkably silly did nothing to slow the beating of her heart to a more normal rate.

All the way along South Audley Street Gabriel's anticipation rose, and by the time he finally turned the corner onto Curzon Street, his impatience to see Miss Jolliffe was so great, he was not in the mood to tolerate the slightest tardiness on her part. Fortunately for his temper, when he was a few houses away, the door of the Wasteney residence opened, and a figure emerged, enveloped in a familiar green cloak.

The face Miss Jolliffe turned up to him was positively radiant, and before she was even seated properly beside him, she blurted out, "Oh, how I have missed you! I am so glad you are back."

Gabriel had an abrupt urge to pull her into his arms and kiss her and tell her he had missed her also, but the words stuck in his throat, and he remained mute, acting as if all his attention was needed to handle his horses.

Miss Jolliffe did not seem upset by his silence. On the contrary, she tucked her arm through his, laid her head on his shoulders and he could not be sure, but he thought he heard her sigh.

Ever since he had seen his mother's picture, he had felt a deep restlessness that had made him irritable when he was awake and had kept him from sleeping well at night, and today he had felt a powerful need to drive along the Thames.

But somehow being near a large body of water no longer seemed as important as having an opportunity to talk with Miss Jolliffe as soon as possible. Consequently, he set his horses going at as brisk a pace as feasible toward Green Park.

"I have been at Sherington Close for the last week and a half," he said once they were out of traffic. "After the debacle with my London servants, I thought it might be a good idea to check out conditions on the estate. My agent here in London was not satisfied with the information he was receiving from the bailiff."

Looking down into Miss Jolliffe's eyes, Gabriel almost said that it had not actually been financial matters that had taken him to Suffolk—they could have been postponed until spring. What had mattered was being sure that the servants would treat Miss Jolliffe with respect when he took her there as his wife and as their new mistress.

"And what did you discover?" she prompted, and he wondered uneasily how long he had been staring into her eyes without speaking, like some besotted mooncalf.

"Oh, I found the most engaging scoundrel, who proceeded to fleece me unmercifully," he said lightly.

Miss Jolliffe looked suitably shocked. "Your bailiff is a crook?"

Gabriel laughed. "No, the bailiff is a rather stolid fellow and painfully honest. It is the vicar who is a shameless thief. In little more than a week, the Reverend Mr. Stephen Todd did his best to empty my purse. To begin with, he managed to coerce me into paying for a new roof for the vicarage and repairs on the church organ. But not limiting himself to ecclesiastical matters, he also talked me into building four new cottages and renovating eleven others for my tenants, and I think I have agreed to purchase any number of pieces of new farming equipment, although I am not sure he understands their purpose any better than I do.

"In addition, he has persuaded me to waive the rents for one year since my predecessor had previously raised them to unconscionable levels. And I have also provided pensions for the aged servants and annuities for all the Rainsford bastards that litter the countryside."

Gabriel's last remark was not at all suitable for the ears of a delicately bred single lady, but Miss Jolliffe—

being a superior sort of female—was in no way shocked by his revelations.

"I believe I should like to meet this Reverend Mr. Todd," she said with a smile.

Gabriel glanced down into her gray-green eyes, now gazing so artlessly up at him, and he was thoroughly appalled. Why had it never occurred to him what a perfect match Miss Jolliffe would be for Mr. Todd—and what a perfect vicar's wife she would make? He immediately regretted having ever mentioned the cursed fellow to her.

Unlike the fools who comprised most of the *ton*, the Reverend Mr. Todd was without doubt clear-sighted enough that he would not be misled for long by Miss Jolliffe's unprepossessing face and form. A brief acquaintance would be enough for him to recognize her sterling qualities, and then what chance would Gabriel have?

Not only was the vicar handsome and charming, intelligent and witty, invariably good-natured and even-tempered, but beneath the light and seemingly carefree exterior, Stephen was the most devout, the most truly *good* man Gabriel had ever known.

Given the choice between such a saint and a short-tempered, ruthless man like Gabriel, it was clear whom Miss Jolliffe would choose to wed.

To be sure, Gabriel was an earl, and the vicar, although connected to all the best families, was not himself a peer. Unfortunately, Miss Jolliffe did not seem to be at all impressed with nor the slightest bit awed by the members of the peerage with whom she had come into contact, so he doubted a mere title would influence her appreciably in his own favor.

After a moment's additional reflection, however, Gabriel realized he was worrying for naught. The Reverend Mr. Stephen Todd was not going to meet Miss Jolliffe until she was the Countess of Sherington—and once they were wed, Gabriel would see to it that she was not left alone in the company of charming rascals. And in the meantime, it would be wise to change the subject and in the future do his best to avoid all mention of the vicar.

"It appears the only thing the late earl ever did that

met with the approval of his neighbors and tenants was to fall off his horse and break his neck." Gabriel proceeded to describe his predecessor's transgressions and the resulting wretched condition of the estate in great detail, and Miss Jolliffe asked quite intelligent questions, proving her expertise went far beyond the sheep and wool industry.

"I suppose it comes naturally from being raised in the country," she explained when he questioned her broad knowledge of agriculture.

Gabriel was silent for a long time, his teeth clenched, his hands gripping the reins too tightly. Finally he managed to speak. "I, on the other hand, was apparently raised in a small room on the top floor of the west wing of Sherington Close."

Miss Jolliffe's eyes asked him a hundred questions, but she did not say a word, waiting for him to tell her as much or as little as he wished her to know.

He found himself wanting her to know everything.

"I do not remember ever being in any other room in that mansion, nor do I have any memory of the grounds around the house or the village nearby. My only memories are of being in that one room, looking out that one window."

He told her all that he remembered about his mother and all that he had learned about his mother's mother, Mrs. Everdon, which was very little. His maternal grandmother lived in London—in Marylebone—and the vicar received money for the poor of the parish from her every year on the anniversary of her daughter's death.

But more important, Gabriel told Miss Jolliffe what he could not remember and what he had not been able to learn. As he talked, he felt the ghosts one by one release their hold on him and vanish back into the ether.

Finishing his account, he reined in the horses, reached in the pocket of his waistcoat, and pulled out the miniature. Handing it to Miss Jolliffe, he said simply, "My mother."

"She is quite pretty, and her eyes are kind."

"Or so the artist painted her. I have no way of knowing what she was really like. There are only a few servants left who remember her, and although they were quite forthcoming, what they were able to tell me was rather vague, and their descriptions of her character were too conflicting for me to trust any of them."

"Doubtless your grandmother will be able to tell you more when you speak to her."

"I have no intention of seeing her," Gabriel said flatly, flicking the reins and sending the horses along the path again at a brisk trot.

"But if she lives here in London, surely it would not be too much trouble?" Miss Jolliffe began, but Gabriel cut her off.

"I despise all my relatives—every last one of them—and have no desire to add to their number. My grandmother has ignored me for years, and I see no need to bring myself to her attention. More than likely, as soon as I acknowledge the connection, she will jump at the chance to batten on my sleeve and expect me to pay her debts the way dear Cousin Phillip does. No, as far as I am concerned, the past has no hold on me."

"But, on the other hand," Miss Jolliffe pointed out in her usual calm and reasonable voice, "when one stops and considers it, you have never actually met any of your relatives, have you? Other than your mother, of course, and that was years ago."

Gabriel was momentarily stunned by her reply, but then he realized she was quite correct. None of the thoroughly obnoxious members of the Rainsford family were related to him in the slightest degree—except, of course, in the eyes of the law.

He had, in his entire life, never actually seen or spoken with a person related to him by blood except his mother.

"Why should you assume your grandmother is like the Rainsfords?" Miss Jolliffe asked politely but persistently.

But Gabriel did not need any more urging. Even before she finished pointing out the obvious—that since he did not resemble the Rainsfords in any way there was no reason to assume that his grandmother would either—he was turning the horses' heads north, toward Marylebone.

"Very well, since you are so keen on it, we shall go see her, but I warn you, if she makes any attempt to loosen my purse strings, we shall walk out the door with no ceremony, is that quite clear?''

"We?" Miss Jolliffe asked. "Surely you do not wish an outsider to be present at your first meeting?"

"Developing cold feet, are you? This is all your idea, so of course you are going to accompany me. That way if things fall out the way I fully expect them to, I shall have you right at hand, ready to accept the blame.''

"Oh," she said rather faintly.

"And perhaps when Mrs. Everdon does not turn out to be the sweet, loving grandmother of your imagination— which I suspect has been colored by memories of your own grandmother—then perhaps, Miss Jolliffe, you will learn not to give unasked-for advice.''

"Perhaps," she said, smiling up at him in a way that made it very hard for him to stay annoyed with her.

Gabriel drove right by his grandmother's house the first time, not noticing the narrow green building squeezed in between two wider buildings. "An auspicious beginning," he said after backtracking and finally finding the correct number.

Descending from the carriage, he helped Miss Jolliffe alight, then signaled a street urchin and for a silver coin hired the lad to lead the horses back and forth on the street to keep them from becoming chilled.

He would never admit it to Miss Jolliffe, but a part of him could not keep from wondering what he would find behind the yellow door. The more sane part of him wanted to abandon this foolish venture forthwith.

Lifting the knocker, he let it drop a single time. Perhaps, if he was lucky, his grandmother would not be home, and he could postpone this confrontation. . . .

As much as it pained him to acknowledge it, even to himself, without Miss Jolliffe's support he would not have had the courage to face the unknown. Given the slightest excuse, he, who had faced razor-sharp swords and loaded guns without a qualm, was ready to turn tail and run like an abject coward.

But Miss Jolliffe was standing beside him, all eagerness to meet this unknown grandmother of his.

If the old lady was a social-climbing mushroom or a conniving schemer, he could handle that.

But suppose his only living relative—at least the only one that he knew of—was not completely without virtue? What if she made him feel he had some sort of obligation toward her?

That was what he could not face . . . at least not alone.

Footsteps could be heard, and slowly the door was opened to reveal an old woman wearing such an odd assortment of clothes, one on top of the other, that she looked like a ragpicker. "What do you want?" she said in a querulous voice.

"We wish to speak to Mrs. Everdon," Gabriel said, praying this old crone would not turn out to be his grandmother.

"Then come in and shut the door before you let in all the cold air." Muttering to herself, the frightful old woman shuffled down the narrow hallway toward the back of the house, then raising her voice, she added, "You can wait in the sitting room while I fetch her."

Gabriel looked at Miss Jolliffe without saying a word, but she could obviously tell what he was thinking, because she said with a smile in her voice, "It is still a bit too early to turn tail and run."

Before he could suggest that they reconsider this whole thing, she entered the house, and he was obliged to follow, albeit reluctantly.

Inside was only moderately warmer than outside. Two doors led off the hallway, the one at back through which the servant had vanished, and the one at the front, which apparently led to the sitting room.

Opening it, Gabriel found a small room which though sparsely furnished, showed signs of frequent use—two chairs were pulled up close to the fire, which smoldered sullenly.

Even he could see the signs of poverty—the broken springs poking up from the cushion of the settee, the chair leg mended inexpertly with wire, the holes worn through the carpet, the frayed edges of the curtains over the front window.

"What odds, Miss Jolliffe," he murmured, "that the

prodigal grandson and his overflowing purse will be welcomed with open arms?"

Behind him the door opened, and his mother's voice said, "You wished to see me?"

For a moment Gabriel was frozen in place, unable to move a muscle. Then with great effort he turned, fully expecting to see his mother's familiar face.

But the woman in the doorway was far too old and wrinkled to be his mother. And his mother had been in her grave for more than a quarter of a century.

This, then, must be his grandmother. She was whitehaired and shrunken, her face ravaged by time, but her eyes were still bright with intelligence. Considering the condition of the fire, it was not difficult to understand why she was dressed in the same extravagant number of clothes as the maid had been.

"May I ask your name, sir?" she said with all the dignity of a duchess. Then she lost her composure completely—her eyes widened, her face turned white, and her voice trembled when she said, "Gabriel! Is it really you? Or am I only dreaming again?"

Approaching him, she touched his arm, as if to reassure herself that she was awake. "Oh, my dear boy, welcome home!"

Now there were tears filling her eyes, and they spilled over and ran down her faded cheeks.

Feminine wiles, Gabriel told himself. Very well done, to be sure, but nothing more than an attempt to manipulate him. Unfortunately, she had betrayed herself by recognizing him. Doubtless she had been spying on him ever since he'd returned to England, wondering how she might contrive an introduction.

He shot Miss Jolliffe a look of censure, but her expression remained bland.

"Oh, dear," the old lady said, producing a handkerchief from her sleeve and wiping her eyes, "my wits have surely gone begging. I have not even asked you to sit down."

She indicated the settee, and Gabriel offered Miss Jolliffe the cushion that was intact, taking for himself the one with the broken spring, which turned out to be every bit as uncomfortable as it looked.

"I am surprised that you recognized me," he said, "since I do not believe we have ever met."

The old lady was not discomposed to be caught out so easily. "Oh, but you look exactly like my late husband, God rest his soul. I have his portrait over the mantel if you would like to see for yourself?"

Gabriel rose and followed her to the fireplace, but away from the single window, the room was too dark to see the details of the painting. Taking a candelabra from the mantel, the old woman lit the candles, which were little more than stubs, and handed it over to him.

Holding it up so that he could see better, Gabriel looked at the portrait. Beneath the powdered wig of an earlier generation, he saw his own face looking back at him.

# 13

"WHEN I LEARNED that my daughter had named you after my husband, I knew for sure that you were not the son of that monster," Mrs. Everdon said, setting down her teacup.

Sitting beside Verity, Lord Sherington made no move to drink his own tea, nor to eat any of the meager collection of thin sandwiches Agnes, the old serving woman, had produced at Mrs. Everdon's request.

But then he had been singularly quiet ever since he had looked at the portrait of his grandfather. Even now, half an hour after he had stared up at it as if thunderstruck, tension fairly radiated from him, and Verity could not begin to guess the emotions he must be feeling. But as yet he had given her no indication that he wished to depart, and so she stayed by his side, hoping that she could be of some help.

"Why do you call the late earl a monster?" she asked when the pause in the conversation began to be uncomfortable.

"Because he was a wicked man—the most truly depraved man I have ever known," the old lady replied. "My husband was a merchant, and many called him a hard man. He may have been as ruthless as they said he was, but he was honest, his word was his bond, and no one could rightfully have accused him of being mean or cruel. My lord Sherington, on the other hand, was all manner of depravity disguised behind a charming mask. I have three letters—" She stood up and went to a tall secretary and opened a drawer, removing a thin packet of folded papers.

"My daughter wrote us the first letter after she had been married only a few months, begging us to save her from the vile man she had married. We were appalled to read what he was doing to her—his cruelty was unimaginable. My husband went to Grosvenor Square determined to fetch her home." Tears began to roll silently down Mrs. Everdon's cheeks.

"What happened?" Verity asked softly.

"The next day they found my husband's body on Finchley Common. The earl, of course, denied that Gabriel had been to Sherington House the night before, and though I protested, the magistrate ruled that death had been caused by a highwayman. There were several operating in that area, and my husband's body had been stripped of all valuables.

"But I have always known in my heart that the earl murdered my husband. I tried myself to see my daughter, but I was denied admittance to Sherington House, and when I tried to send messages to her with one of our footmen, the notes were all sent back unopened. Lacking any male relatives to assist me, there was nothing more I could do. Except that during the Season I would go every night to where I knew there was to be a large ball, and I would stand in the street and wait. If I was lucky, I would see my daughter going in on her husband's arm. I am sure she knew what I was doing, because she would always scan the crowd, as if looking for someone, but she never gave any sign that she had seen me."

The old woman paused, as if gathering her strength to go on. "The second letter I received from her arrived several months after you were born, Gabriel."

Lord Sherington stiffened beside Verity, and without thinking, she reached out to him. He immediately grasped her hand and clung to it tightly, still not speaking.

What anguish he must be feeling. It was difficult enough for her to keep from raging at the injustice of it all, and how much worse it must be for him. This was his mother and grandfather, after all, whose sufferings were being recounted.

"What did your daughter say in the second letter?"

Verity asked, her voice steady, betraying none of her emotions.

"She sent it from Suffolk. The servants there were kinder than the ones in London, although most of them were too terrified of the earl to risk helping her. But one of the maids had decided to return to her family in Yorkshire, and she used the opportunity to help my daughter. When the maid left, she managed to smuggle out my daughter's letter, which she posted to me when she was suitably distant from Sherington Close.

"My daughter wrote that she no longer even had the illusion of freedom she'd had in London—that there in Suffolk she was being held prisoner in her own home and was not even permitted to attend church on Sundays. She also told me that her husband had sworn an oath that she would never be allowed to leave her rooms until she agreed to send her misbegotten son away to a foundling home."

Lord Sherington's grip on Verity's hand tightened until it was painful, but she only clung to him all the more tightly.

"My daughter was not even permitted to see the babe, although sometimes in the middle of the night when her husband had passed out in a drunken stupor and was not likely to awaken, she would sneak up to the little room where the child was kept."

Verity remembered the pain in Lord Sherington's voice when he had said, "I was raised in a little room on the top floor of the west wing." He had wanted to know the truth about his mother, and now that truth was only causing him more pain.

"In the third and final letter," the old woman said, years of resignation evident in her voice, "my daughter told me that she had gone to your room and found it empty. Without informing her, that monster had sent you away to sea. When I read that, I confess I did not know whether to laugh or to cry. I had to rejoice that you were free from the earl's clutches—yet I knew not what dangers you might face. And I think even then I suspected that without you my daughter would have no will to live. In truth, I received word of her death not five months later."

The room they were sitting in was as still and cold as a tomb, and Verity was only glad she had not put off her cloak. Lord Sherington's face had a white and pinched look about it, but she rather doubted it was the temperature of the room that had chilled him since he was normally oblivious to all but the most biting wind.

But the old woman was not done yet. "From the day you were born, I have prayed to God to keep you safe from all harm. And I have prayed for myself also, asking that just once before I died, I would be able to see you with my own eyes and hold you in my arms and tell you how much I love you—how much I have always loved you."

Mrs. Everdon rose to her feet, and Lord Sherington did likewise, pulling Verity up with him. Dropping her hand, he stood stiff and unyielding while the old woman embraced him. Stepping back, she held out the letters. "I have saved these for you."

"Thank you," he said, and those were the first words he had spoken since he had seen his grandfather's portrait. And the last words, for he turned on his heels and walked out of the room without saying anything more. A few moments later, they heard the outer door shut.

"I know he must seem cold and heartless," Verity said, "but I assure you, he cares deeply about his mother."

Mrs. Everdon said, "He is just like his grandfather. My husband was never one to wear his feelings on his sleeve. Indeed, he considered it a sign of weakness for a man to display any emotions, except, of course in the bedroom. I think I may have made a grave mistake. Perhaps it would have been kinder if I had not told my grandson the whole story today, so that he would have time to adjust gradually? I have had years to reconcile myself to what happened, and even so I cannot think about my daughter without weeping. But I have waited so long to see him and tell him about his mother."

She turned sad eyes toward Verity. "Now I suspect he will not come back to see me a second time. I have followed his career with great interest, and from what I have learned about his character, I am afraid he will not allow himself the weakness of loving an old grandmother who proved to be of no use to his mother and who can be of no use to him."

Verity wished she could reassure Mrs. Everdon that Lord Sherington would return, but she could not even convince herself. "I know he is ruthless and bad-tempered and quite set on getting his own way," she said, "but I do not believe he has ever done anything cruel or mean or dishonest. So I think it is possible he may some day wish to see you again."

"Anything is possible, but in this case it is not likely," the old woman said, making an effort to smile. "But I cannot complain, because God has, at long last, granted my prayers, and it would be greedy of me to ask for more. But you must not pity me, child, for this has been a most memorable day for me."

A look of puzzlement crossed her face. "Do you know, it has just occurred to me that I do not even know your name. I am sure that if Gabriel had married, I would have heard of it, but are you perhaps his betrothed?"

"I am Miss Jolliffe," Verity said, "and we are not betrothed. I am just his friend."

Mrs. Everdon raised her eyebrows, and Verity hurried to correct her misconception. "No, no, I did not mean that as a polite way of saying that I am living under his protection. I am truly just his friend—just someone he seems to enjoy talking with."

"But you, I think, would like to be more? I am not wrong, am I, when I think you love him."

"With all my heart," Verity confessed after a brief hesitation. "And doubtless you will think I am totally depraved, but if he asked me to be his mistress, I would not—I could not—tell him no. I rather suspect, in fact, that I shall never be able to deny him anything he wants from me. But he asks for nothing more than companion-ship, and I can only pray that he will not soon grow bored with me."

"And I shall add you to my prayers also, child," the old woman said.

Verity started for the door, then turned back. "Would

you like me to come visit you occasionally? I could not, of course, repeat anything Lord Sherington told me in confidence, but I could at least reassure you that he is well and in good spirits."

"Oh, bless you, my child, I should like that above all things," the old woman said with tears in her eyes.

To her surprise, Verity found that Lord Sherington was still waiting for her, and when she emerged, he signaled the boy walking the horses that they were ready to go.

Tossing her up into the carriage and then climbing in himself, Gabriel took the reins, then asked in a harsh voice, "What were you doing in there after I left?"

For the briefest moment Verity hesitated, not wishing to betray his grandmother, but then she remembered she had promised never to lie to Lord Sherington. Knowing she owed him her first loyalty, she confessed, "We were talking about you." She hoped that he would not ask for more information, but of course, he did.

"And what did she say?"

"She is convinced that you will never come to visit her again."

"More than likely she is correct in that assumption," he said, staring straight ahead.

"But she is your grandmother—your own flesh and blood!" Verity burst out without meaning to.

"An accident of birth, nothing more."

"Well, you will have to admit that you were wrong about one thing. She made no attempt to loosen your purse strings."

"But I suspect she has persuaded you to champion her cause, has she not?"

"She made no mention of money," Verity said, which was the truth if not the whole truth, because his grandmother had been willing to accept Verity's assistance when it came to learning more about her grandson's activities. "And even you must have noticed that she is living in dire straits."

Beside her Lord Sherington made a sound of disbelief, and they covered the remaining distance back to Curzon Street in silence.

Verity was about to climb down out of the carriage when she was struck by the most astounding thought. So astonishing was it, in fact, that she was momentarily rendered speechless.

When she made no effort to get out by herself, as was her habit, Lord Sherington climbed out, walked around the carriage, and grasping her firmly around the waist, lifted her down.

Looking up into his eyes, which were still bright with anger, she found her voice. "Who gave you your inheritance on your twenty-first birthday?"

Her question had obviously caught him off-guard, and before he could recover, she went on. "Since the earl and your half brother were both still alive then, it is obvious that none of the Rainsford family would have given you a penny. Your mother's father died before you were born, and your grandmother said she had no male relatives to help her. So who was the unknown relative who provided you with the means to make your fortune?"

She watched the anger drain out of his eyes, and finally he said, "I have no idea, but I intend to find out without delay." Without bidding her good-bye, he climbed back into his carriage and drove off.

Mounting the steps, Verity suspected she knew already. Given what Lord Sherington had told her about the late earl, he would not have married a merchant's daughter—unless, of course, she had provided him with a handsome dowry. It would appear that the Everdon family had, at one time, been prosperous. To be sure, they could have suffered financial reverses.

But there was another possible explanation for Mrs. Everdon's present poverty, and Verity rather thought it would prove to be the correct one.

What Lord Sherington's reaction would be when he discovered the truth, she had no way of predicting.

Otterwall opened the door, and his eyes were wide with fear. Before he could utter a word of warning, he was shoved aside, and Petronella stood there. It was obvious she was in a towering rage, and from the way she was glaring, it was equally obvious that Verity was the target of her anger.

To her dismay, Verity realized she had stayed out much too long. It was now grown so late in the day that Petronella had risen from her bed and discovered Verity was not tending to her chores. But that still did not explain her sister's present hysteria, which seemed excessive for such a minor offense as taking a couple of hours off from the duties of the household.

"Traitor! Liar! Deceitful little tramp!" Petronella screeched.

Verity decided it would not be a good idea to let the neighbors and interested passers-by hear the rest of this angry tirade, so she pushed past her sister and firmly shut the door behind them.

"You knew—all the time, you knew!" Petronella screeched, "and yet you have been shamelessly betraying me, your own sister! I have nursed a viper to my bosom—an ungrateful viper!"

"But—" Verity tried to say, not at all sure what she was supposed to have known.

"Antoinette is the one who is going to marry Lord Sherington—I told you that myself, and you agreed to help me!"

Perhaps it was due to the emotional scene she had just taken part in, but Verity lost control of herself for a brief—and disastrous—moment. In a word, she laughed in her sister's face.

The idea of Lord Sherington ever offering for Antoinette was so preposterous, even when her sister's face became redder and redder, Verity could not stop laughing.

She regained control of herself only when Petronella slapped her across the face so hard that Verity was knocked off balance. She would have fallen had Otterwall not caught her and set her back on her feet.

Stunned, Verity stared at her sister, whose face was so contorted with hatred, she seemed a veritable stranger.

"You shameless hussy," Petronella said, her tone low and menacing. "Sneaking around behind my back, having illicit assignations with his lordship. I'll not have it, do you hear? I'll not allow such goings-on in my house. I forbid you ever to drive out with him again or see him or speak to him, do you understand me?"

Verity did not hesitate, nor did she pause to consider the rash step she was taking. "I understand. Now you must understand that I will see Lord Sherington whenever he wishes to see me. I will drive out with him when he invites me, and I will receive him when he comes to call—"

"Not in this house you shall not! I will not allow you to carry on a degrading affair for all the world to see while you are living under our protection. I have my daughter to think about, and I will not have her reputation besmirched by your shameless behavior. You promise me now that you will never see his lordship again, or you shall not spend another night under this roof! Promise me this instant!"

"I shall never promise that," Verity said, and Petronella lifted her hand as if to strike her again. Raising her own hands but not her voice, Verity said, "But I will promise you this. If you strike me again, I will not turn the other cheek."

It was quite clear to Verity that she had been deluding herself for years, pretending that despite Petronella's sharp tongue and caustic manner, deep inside her she harbored at least some sisterly feelings for Verity.

But the animosity that was now evident in Petronella's eyes clearly was more than merely a momentary displeasure caused by a single event. Her anger was not a passing mood that would vanish once this particular misunderstanding was cleared up—once Verity explained that she had no claim to Lord Sherington's affections, nor any ambitions to wed him.

Which meant Verity had no real choice as to what she should do now that her sister's true feelings for her were out in the open. She could, to be sure, follow the safest course and agree to give up Lord Sherington. After which, if she groveled sufficiently, her sister would doubtless agree to allow Verity to continue in her assigned role of unpaid household drudge.

Verity was not proud of the fact that a short month

ago she would doubtless have begged for her sister's forgiveness, even knowing that she had done nothing for which she needed to be forgiven.

But now, after having been with Lord Sherington all these weeks, Verity knew if she chose to knuckle under to her sister's petty tyranny, he would despise her for being a coward—and she admitted he would have just cause. Indeed, she would not be able to forgive herself if she acted in such a spineless fashion.

With firm resolution, she turned her back on her sister and climbed the stairs to her room, where she began to pack her things.

Deprived of the freedom to express herself physically, Petronella followed, cursing Verity, taunting her, calling her every despicable name she knew. With only a slight effort, Verity discovered she could completely ignore every word her sister was saying.

A bare half hour later, Verity left the Wasteney residence and walked away without a backward glance, carrying all her worldly possessions in a portmanteau and two bandboxes. She felt not the slightest twinge of uncertainty, nor any particular regret that she was so completely severing the connection with her sister.

Gabriel did not waste time returning to his own home. Instead, he sought out Mr. Parkins in his office near the docks.

"I need you to ferret out some information for me," Gabriel said, staring out the window. Even though the office was on the second floor, they were not high enough to see the river itself. But he could see the tops of numerous masts rising above the neighboring warehouses. "It concerns a rather large sum of money I received fourteen years ago when I turned one-and-twenty. I was told it was an inheritance from a distant relative, whose name was not mentioned on any of the documents I was required to sign when I took control of the money. Now I wish to find out who actually gave me that money."

"Who was the solicitor handling the affair?" Mr. Parkins asked.

Gabriel told him.

"I have heard of him. He is a member of a reputable firm, and if he was instructed to keep your benefactor anonymous, you may be sure he will do just that."

"There has to be some way to find out," Gabriel said with a curse.

"It will not be easy. Fourteen years is in and of itself a severe handicap, and if at the time the documents were drawn up, sufficient effort was made to hide the identity of your benefactor, it may well be that we shall never uncover the truth despite our best attempts." Mr. Parkins was silent for a long time, mulling over the possible ways to approach the puzzle. "If only you had some additional information, it would greatly increase our chances of success."

Gabriel did not want to say what he suspected—did not want to put his conjectures into words.

"If you know anything more, no matter how trivial it might seem, you had better tell me," Mr. Parkins prompted.

Without turning to face him, Gabriel said, "It is quite possible that the money came—may have come—from my grandmother, Mrs. Gabriel Everdon."

The night was long, and sitting alone in his study, Gabriel had more than enough time to read his mother's letters over and over again.

He wanted very much to believe that he had at last uncovered the truth, but he could not dismiss the possibility that everything she had written had been the product of an unstable mind—that, in fact, the accusations she had made against her lawful husband had been the hysterical rantings of a mad woman.

Bothered by his inability to see the past clearly, he took a clean sheet of foolscap from his desk and began to set down the evidence, aligning it in two columns.

The servants in Suffolk had hated and feared the previous earl . . . but set against that, the servants in London, recently turned off, had been loyal to the earl even after his death.

The vicar had told tales of petty acts of meanness indulged in by the earl and his elder son . . . but even Stephen had had to admit that the evidence was primarily circumstantial—that he had not witnessed the misdeeds in person, and that not even in the most blatant cases had anyone felt sure enough to ask for a formal inquest into the events.

The earl had not been popular in Suffolk . . . but he had apparently been liked well enough in London.

Gabriel had his own memories . . . but they were the memories of a child. What he remembered was too little . . . what he had forgotten was too much. And even in adults, memories could play tricks—could deceive.

Today his grandmother had told him a dramatic tale, filled with villains and imprisoned ladies, quite like a novel from the Minerva Press . . . but he could hardly use his grandmother's account to validate the letters since she had admittedly gained all her knowledge of the events from the letters themselves.

In point of fact, he did not even have any proof that the letters he was reading had actually been written by his mother, because he had no other specimen of her handwriting.

Even if he were willing to concede that the old lady honestly believed that the events had transpired exactly as she had related them to him, that proved nothing.

And if she knew them to be false? Or perhaps merely exaggerated? Could she be hiding the fact that she knew her daughter had always been unstable?

That behavior would be quite in keeping with what he knew of females, who appeared to be born with a thorough knowledge of how to be cunning and devious.

Looking at the double list he had written, Gabriel cursed his lack of solid evidence, but everything he had discovered so far was pure hearsay.

Folding the piece of paper carefully, he tucked it into his pocket, and resolved that on the morrow he would show it to Miss Jolliffe. Perhaps she could see something that he was overlooking.

And if she was likewise unable to reason away his doubts, then he would arrange a comfortable annuity for his grandmother, and that would be the end of it.

Never would he let another man—or woman—control him, nor would he allow the dead to have any influence on him. The past was not important, only the present and the future.

Gabriel's mood was not improved in the morning, and he was not prepared to tolerate any laxness on Miss Jolliffe's part. When he arrived in front of Lord Wasteney's residence and she did not immediately appear, Gabriel did not sit patiently in his carriage waiting for her.

Climbing down, he tied the reins to a hitching post, took the steps two at a time, and pounded vigorously enough with the knocker to wake the dead—or in this case, every member of the household.

Otterwall opened the door, but instead of inviting Gabriel in, the butler stared at him goggle-eyed.

"Fetch Miss Jolliffe and be quick about it," Gabriel said, striding into the hallway.

The butler opened and shut his mouth as if trying to say something, but then he apparently thought better of it, for he scurried down the hallway and disappeared into the shadows.

Gabriel paced back and forth, and the house was so quiet, he could hear nothing except the sounds of his own footsteps. Where the deuce was Miss Jolliffe? He felt his temper rise. If he had any idea whether she was upstairs or down, he would go find her himself, but she could even be in the attics or cellars for all he knew.

Finally the butler reappeared, still looking completely discomposed. "I have been instructed to ask you to wait in the drawing room if you would be so kind, my lord."

Since it would not be fair to blame Otterwall for Miss Jolliffe's lack of punctuality, Gabriel bit back the curses he wanted to utter. "Tell her to be quick; I do not like to keep my horses standing in this weather," was all he vouchsafed to say, and the butler hastened to assure him that a groom would be fetched to walk them up and down.

Which did not augur well for the rapid appearance of Miss Jolliffe. And Gabriel was correct in that assumption. He was forced to wait a good half hour before the door to the drawing room opened to admit—

He cursed under his breath again. It was not Miss Jolliffe, but her brother-in-law, who entered.

"Now see here, Sherington, what is the meaning of this? You can't come barging in on a man at this hour of the morning—it's indecent."

Lord Wasteney spoke in the same demented way favored by the Rainsford family, and Gabriel began to think that half of London belonged in Bedlam, especially Otterwall, who apparently did not recognize the difference between Miss Jolliffe and the unctuous baron.

Grinding his teeth, Gabriel thought of suitable punishments for the hapless butler, who now stood hovering in the doorway wringing his hands. "I have no intention of depriving you of your beauty sleep, Wasteney. In fact, I have no interest in talking with you at all. I have come to fetch Miss Jolliffe, and if she is not produced forthwith, I shall be forced to seek her out myself."

Lord Wasteney puffed out his cheeks and turned an alarming shade of red. "I'll not have such talk in my house! It's disgraceful enough what you've done—indecent is what it is—and don't think you can foist her off on us after you are done with her, for sister-in-law though she may be, I'll not take her in again."

Striding over to the baron, Gabriel caught the little man by the front of his waistcoat. "What the devil are you talking about?"

Rolling his eyes wildly, Lord Wasteney looked around for help, but the butler had prudently vanished. The baron made an ineffectual effort to remove Gabriel's hands, and began to whimper.

Releasing him in disgust, Gabriel said, "Tell me where Miss Jolliffe is."

Lord Wasteney straightened his clothing, cleared his throat, and said, "Lady Wasteney gave me to understand that my sister-in-law chose to leave the protection of my roof to—er—that is—to—"

"Say what you mean to say!" Gabriel snapped out at him, and the baron took an involuntary step backward.

"My wife informed me that you have seduced Verity and set her up in that house of yours in Somers Town."

"And that is the truth," a shrill voice said, and Gabriel turned to see the aforementioned Lady Wasteney standing in the doorway.

With his wife there to stiffen his spine, Lord Wasteney found his courage again. "So we shall have to ask you not to come calling here again, and if you persist in doing so, be warned that I shall instruct my servants to deny you admittance. If you possessed a shred of decency, you would realize for yourself that you cannot possibly be welcome in this house after you have so callously enticed my wife's sister away and persuaded her to leave the protection of her own family. After all, there are limits to what can be tolerated, my Lord Sherington, even for a libertine like you."

# 14

LADY WASTENEY opened her mouth, but Gabriel forestalled whatever comment she had been going to make. His voice icy with disdain, he said, "I have neither seduced Miss Jolliffe nor enticed her into leaving. Moreover, I have not seen her nor heard from her since yesterday when I returned her safe and sound to this house after our morning drive, which was quite innocent and aboveboard."

"Innocent? Do not think to deceive me, my lord," the baroness said, a malevolent look on her face. "My sister is far from innocent, and you, of all men, must know that. Why, she has been brazenly parading around town these past several weeks in clothing provided by you. And do not try to deny it, for there is no way she could have bought that green cloak for herself. You paid for it, there is no doubt in my mind on that score, and what you have purchased with that gift is equally obvious."

"A gift? Who has received a gift?" the daughter of the house said, merrily entering the room in carefully studied déshabillé. "Oh dear," she squeaked in pretended surprise, "no one told me we had company." Clasping her hands over her breast in the manner of an ingenue on the stage in Covent Garden, she continued, "Oh, this is dreadful. Now that you have compromised me, my lord, I suppose you are honorbound to marry me."

To do him credit, Lord Wasteney looked utterly dumbfounded by his daughter's wanton manner, but for her part, Lady Wasteney looked positively rapacious—quite enraptured by the notion that her daughter had so cleverly ensnared a rich earl.

But Gabriel was not called ruthless for nothing. "My poor deluded child, you could promenade down Rotten Row stark naked and hanging on my arm, and I would not marry you."

"Well, of course not," she giggled, "for then my reputation would be in tatters like my aunt's, and you would only be willing to offer me a carte blanche."

Gabriel was strongly tempted to slap some sense into the silly chit, but instead he said, "I am not willing to offer you anything except advice, and my advice is that you would do better to retire to the schoolroom where you belong."

With a fulminating scowl, Antoinette flounced over to the settee and cast herself down on it, apparently under the impression that if she sat there pouting long enough Gabriel could be induced to change his mind.

Easily ignoring her, Gabriel asked Lord Wasteney point-blank, "Precisely when did Miss Jolliffe leave this house?"

The baron looked uneasy. Apparently he was at last beginning to understand that he had been grossly misinformed. "I was not actually here when she left. You will have to ask my wife."

Gabriel turned to the baroness, who was looking quite as sulky as her daughter. "She began packing as soon as she returned from her assignation with you and left before an hour was up. Such an ungrateful gel. After all we have done for her, to pay us back in such a fashion."

"What prompted her to leave?" Gabriel asked, but Lady Wasteney was not willing to answer that question.

"I am sure I could not say. You will have to ask her that."

"I shall be sure to do that as soon as I find her," Gabriel said. "But in case it has slipped your mind, your sister has now been missing almost a full day. So I ask you again, where did she go?"

He was met with blank looks.

"Perhaps—" Lord Wasteney started to say, but he was interrupted by a commotion in the hallway.

For a moment Gabriel's heart quickened, but even

while he was hoping that it might be Miss Jolliffe, Lord Wasteney's nephews came bounding into the room.

"Ah, Lord Sherington, just the man we were wanting to see," one of them said.

"That hunt master of yours is a most disobliging fellow," the other one said. "Quite fussy about the least little trifle, and every day we hunted, he became more disagreeable. Why just two days ago, he told Bevis and me that if we even came within fifty yards of one of his horses or hounds again, he'd take a horsewhip to us."

"I did my best to remain calm—simply told the insolent fellow that they were not, after all, his own personal horses and hounds, they were yours."

"And *I* merely pointed out that since *you'd* invited us to make use of them, it was not *his* place to deny us their use.

"Then the chap had the audacity—"

"Cursed impudence, I call it."

"—to fetch out his shotgun and threaten to pepper us with buckshot if we didn't clear out of Gloucestershire altogether."

Making a mental note to double the hunt master's wages, Gabriel tried once more to bring the attention of the imbeciles and dolts surrounding him back to the matter which was of primary concern. "I am not interested in discussing hunting," he said with exaggerated patience. "Miss Jolliffe has disappeared, and I am anxious to find where she has gone."

"Verity? Disappeared?" one of the two young men asked, a look of bovine bewilderment on his face. "How odd."

"Not the kind of girl to up and decamp," the other one said.

"Must have been abducted, although that doesn't seem much like Verity either."

"She left of her own free will," Lady Wasteney said with a sniff.

"And we have already determined that she did—um—er—*not* run off with Lord Sherington," Lord Wasteney explained further, glancing sideways at Gabriel.

"So if it is possible for you to pull your wits together

for a moment," Gabriel said, "perhaps you might help us reason out where she might have gone."

Logical reasoning did not come easily to the two brothers, but after a suitable interval of forehead creasing and chin rubbing, one of them finally said, "If it was Antoinette who was missing, I would look for her on the stage at Covent Garden."

Hearing her name mentioned, Antoinette piped up. "Lord Sherington has compromised me, but he has refused to marry me."

When neither of her two cousins appeared to be interested in defending her honor on the dueling field, she resumed her sulking.

"But Verity hasn't got the face or the figure to tread the boards. Doubt if she could even get herself hired on as an opera dancer."

"Probably gone home to Northumberland," his brother said, nodding his head as if pleased with his own cleverness. "Only place she ever does go."

Giving up his efforts to extract information from the Wasteneys, Gabriel persuaded them—at least he hoped he'd managed to drum it into their thick heads—that if anyone inquired about Miss Jolliffe or came to call on her, they were to say that she was laid down in bed with a sick headache.

After another half hour spent fruitlessly questioning the servants—whose level of intelligence was in general vastly superior to that of the various Wasteneys—Gabriel was forced to conclude that the information he needed was not to be found in this household.

On the way home he cursed the baron and baroness, their posturing offspring, and the two buffled-headed young men. The servants, at least, had expressed genuine concern for Miss Jolliffe, and had vowed to report to him anything they might happen to hear through the servants' grapevine, which rivaled the *haut ton* for speed of gossip.

Just as he reached Grosvenor Square it occurred to him that the logical place for Miss Jolliffe to have gone after she was thrown out by her sister—and Gabriel did not think for a minute that Lady Wasteney was innocent in this whole affair—was to Mrs. Wiggins's employment agency.

He stopped off at home only long enough to send all the grooms and footmen out to the various staging houses, with orders to concentrate first on the ones serving the north of England, but with instructions to ask questions at all of them.

Except for the green cloak, which according to Otterwall Miss Jolliffe had been wearing when she left home, the description of Miss Jolliffe was not going to be very helpful. She did not have the kind of looks that naturally drew masculine eyes toward her. But on the other hand, she would have no reason to travel under a false name, so if she was on a waybill, he would be able to pick up her trail.

Once the servants set off on their assignments, Gabriel drove himself to Cork Street, certain in his own mind that he would quickly discover where Miss Jolliffe had hidden herself.

"If she came to me seeking a position, I would have no difficulty placing her," Mrs. Wiggins said. "But I have not seen her since the day she accompanied you here. Do you wish me to inquire at some of the other agencies?"

"I do not wish all and sundry in London to know that Miss Jolliffe has left her sister's house," Gabriel replied.

"Perhaps if I approach them under the guise of looking for a housekeeper for a client. I can make the job specifications so narrow that no one except Miss Jolliffe will meet the criteria."

Frustrated that he could not take a more direct approach, Gabriel agreed that Mrs. Wiggins's proposal might be effective. Returning home, he felt as if he had aged ten years in one morning.

He retired to his study, there to wait impatiently for the grooms and footmen, who returned one by one, none of them bringing any news of Miss Jolliffe. The last one arrived after midnight, having ridden north along the Great-North Road for the first three stages, just to be positive she was not on her way to Northumberland.

But no one in any of the staging inns or posting houses had seen her. No one remembered hearing her name, no one had any information—or indeed any interest in—a rather plain spinster with mouse-brown hair and gray-green eyes, who may or may not have been wearing a green cloak lined with fur.

Females were a curse and a plague, Gabriel decided three days later. Made from man's rib, they were the source of considerable aggravation. And Miss Jolliffe, who had seemed to be superior to other women, was certainly proving to be most adept at driving him to distraction.

Despite his best efforts, which included hiring a Bow Street runner, Gabriel had not been able to find anyone who had seen Miss Jolliffe since she had packed her bags and left her sister's house.

His anxieties had grown with each passing day, and unable to think of anything better to do, he had himself spent hours driving through the streets of London, searching the crowds for a figure in a green cloak.

The nights had been worse. The nightmares he'd had as a child had returned, precisely the same in every detail except one: in the dreams that had tormented him these last three nights, it was Miss Jolliffe he was desperately trying to find rather than his mother.

As a boy of ten or eleven, he had sworn an oath that he would somehow acquire the power to control his own life, and by resolution and force of will, he had finally banished the nightmares.

Yet now all his wealth, all his knowledge, all his power availed him naught. He was as helpless as he had been when he was a child.

And it was a woman who had brought him to this sorry state. He cursed Miss Jolliffe for what she had done to him and vowed to himself that when he found her again, she would never leave his side, even if he had to chain her to his wrist.

He eyed the untouched bottle of brandy sitting on the table beside him. No amount of resolution could keep his imagination from producing visions of Miss Jolliffe in terrible danger, and he knew how easy it would be to find oblivion at the bottom of that bottle. But he could not drink himself into a stupor of forgetfulness when she was lost.

Lost. Dear God, he felt like a ship whose masts were down, and whose anchor chain had parted. Without Miss Jolliffe, he was drifting, floundering, with rocky reefs all around threatening to destroy him.

He had to find her—he had to.

The pain cut too deep—deeper even than when he had learned his mother was dead and lost to him forever.

Suppose in a fit of despair, Miss Jolliffe had thrown herself into the river?

But when he thought about it, that idea was too preposterous for him to believe for a minute. Miss Jolliffe was too sensible, too reasonable, too practical to do anything like that. She was not irrational and prone to hysterics, which meant that whatever she had done, there had to be logic behind her decision. Which meant all he had to do was figure out rationally what that logic was, and he would be able to find her.

With renewed hope, he began to consider everything he knew about her character—trying to remember every word she had ever spoken to him. But his thoughts were interrupted by a tapping at the door.

Exeter entered and announced that Mr. Parkins was there to see him.

"Show him in," Gabriel said.

After three days of everyone in the household walking around sunk in gloom, it was a shock to see someone smiling, but Mr. Parkins was positively beaming.

"My lord, you will be quite pleased with what I have discovered."

For a brief second Gabriel thought his accountant had found Miss Jolliffe, but then he recollected the task he had given Mr. Parkins. Somehow it no longer seemed important to Gabriel to discover the source of his inheritance, but mere courtesy demanded that he hear the other man out.

"It was as you suspected. Starting approximately a year before your birthday, Mrs. Everdon began liquidating her assets. To begin with, she auctioned off her horses and carriages and a rather fine collection of paintings. Next she disposed of a large estate in Hampshire and various smaller holdings in Surrey and Sussex. Following which, she sold her remaining shares in her late husband's company, and a considerable number of government consols. And when all that was done, she sold her house in Berkeley Square complete with furnishings.

"I have done my best to calculate the total amount she realized from the sales, although in some instances I was only able to estimate the value of what she sold. Shortly- before your birthday, she pensioned off all her servants except one, purchased the house she is now residing in, and bought herself a small annuity. As nearly as I can calculate, the sum of money she had left was so close to the amount that you inherited that I think there can be no doubt about who your benefactor was."

All the pieces of the puzzle fell into place, and the truth that Gabriel had been searching for was plain for him to see. Knowing that his grandmother had loved him enough to sacrifice all her wealth for his sake, he could no longer deny that his mother had loved him enough to sacrifice her freedom for him, and neither of them had ever asked anything of him in return.

Rubbing his forehead with his fingers, he admitted that he had been wrong. All those years he had been a short-sighted fool, who had thought he knew everything there was to know about power. But he had not understood the power of love.

In his arrogance he had told Miss Jolliffe that she was unique—that all other women were cut from the same cloth—that they were all selfish, self-centered, grasping, and incapable of anything more than lust. Yet compared to his mother and grandmother, he was the one who had been self-indulgent, self-seeking, egotistical.

He could almost believe that losing Miss Jolliffe was a just and fitting punishment for his pride and arrogance.

If he ever found her again, he would be a changed person. He would reform completely. Never again would he lose his temper. Never would he attempt to manipulate Miss Jolliffe or any other person for his own advantage. And he would accept all his responsibilities, even the ones that had been thrust upon him by circumstance, such as taking his seat in the House of Lords.

He was ready to promise anything—make any vow—if only he could find Miss Jolliffe.

Beside him Mr. Parkins cleared his throat. "Would you be wanting me to follow through on this information in any way?"

"No," Gabriel said, feeling very tired, "I shall go and see my grandmother myself."

The morning was already unseasonably warm, bringing promise of a day more suited to the beginning of April than the end of January. Londoners were going about their business with smiles on their faces and a bounce in their step. Gabriel found them all quite irritating.

Knocking on the door of the little house in Marylebone, he was admitted by the ancient serving woman, who ushered him into the same room as before. He found his grandmother already there, sitting before a fire that was giving off considerably more heat than the previous one.

"You did not tell me the entire story the other day," he said after declining an offer of tea.

"I told you the essential parts," she replied. "What I left out is unimportant."

"It is important to me. Despite your efforts to remain anonymous, I know that you beggared yourself in order to provide me with an inheritance on my twenty-first birthday. If you try to deny it, you will only be wasting your breath."

"The money was mine to dispose of as I saw fit. I could think of no better way to spend it. My solicitor tried to persuade me that I should leave my assets safely invested in government consols, but I considered you to be the better investment. And time has proved me correct. I am so proud of you. You have brought me happiness beyond measure, and my only regret is that I was unable to help you until you came of age."

"I wish to pay you back," Gabriel said. "With interest."

Standing up, the old woman approached him, and

reaching up, she cupped his face in her hands. "You have already paid me back a thousandfold. You are flesh of my flesh, and bone of my bone. I have loved you from the day you were born, and I shall never stop loving you even after death."

Tentatively he put his arms around her, almost afraid to touch her she appeared so tiny and frail. "How could you love me when you'd never even met me?"

"Oh, my dearest child," she said, "it was the easiest thing in the world."

Somewhere a door slammed, and instinctively Gabriel dropped his arms and stepped back.

"Oh, Mrs. Everdon," a familiar voice called out, "I have found a really meaty mutton bone, and I believe I shall make some Scotch broth for supper."

To Gabriel's total astonishment, a smiling Miss Jolliffe appeared in the doorway. Looking very pretty in her green cloak, she was carrying two market baskets that were filled with assorted produce. Her cheeks were red from being out in the wind, and they turned even rosier when she saw him—and her smile became even broader.

"What are you doing here?" he asked with what was truly incredible restraint.

Her smile began to falter, and she eyed him a bit warily, as if trying to think up a plausible story.

"I have already spoken to your sister and brother-in-law," he said, giving her no opportunity to concoct some Banbury tale. "So I know the circumstances under which you left their house."

"I am sorry if they said anything to embarrass you."

Gabriel realized he was beginning to grind his teeth, but he remembered his vow not to lose his temper, and he made a valiant effort to calm down. "Your cork-brained relatives are not the matter under discussion. What I want to know is what you are doing here—in this house."

"It is quite simple really," Miss Jolliffe said, setting down her baskets. "I was planning to return to Northumberland, but I wished to say good-bye to your grandmother, so I came here first. While we were talking about things, it occurred to me that with the income from the small trust fund my grandmother left me, plus the annuity your grandmother has, the two of us, by pooling our resources, could live quite comfortably together. Also Agnes, your grandmother's serving woman, is getting quite on in years, and it is difficult for her to manage things as well as she used to, and since I am quite capable of running such a small household with no help, that made it seem like an even more advantageous arrangement. And so your grandmother agreed, and here I am, and we are finding it is all working out quite well."

Gabriel stared at Miss Jolliffe in astonishment, unable to believe it was all so simple—and yet he had been unable to deduce it by himself.

"And do you know," she continued, once more smiling brightly, "the most amazing thing is that I discovered the little book of recipes you gave me used to belong to your grandmother. She got it from her own grandmother, and she gave it to your mother on her wedding day, and some of the notes in it were written by your mother. Is that not indeed almost miraculous?"

Miss Jolliffe seemed prepared to rattle on all day, but Gabriel was determined to return to the crux of the matter. "Why did you not send word to me that you were staying here?"

She hesitated, the smile once more fading from her face. "I am not sure. Perhaps it was a natural reluctance to admit that you were right and I was wrong. I realize now that I was a fool to give my love to people who are incapable of ever loving me back, and I have resolved that in the future . . ." Her eyes widened and whatever words she had been about to say died in her throat.

Gabriel had never been so angry in his life—a terrible rage swept through every vein in his body, and a red haze partially obscured his vision.

This could not be allowed! After all his efforts to win Miss Jolliffe's love, he was not going to allow her to elude him—to change her mind at this late date.

Taking three steps forward, he scooped Miss Jolliffe up in his arms and carried her out the door. She was clinging to his neck and saying something to him, but the roaring in his ears was too loud for him to hear a word.

Dumping her unceremoniously into his carriage, he turned around and almost fell over his grandmother, who had followed him out of the house. Mindful of her old bones, he was more careful when he picked her up and deposited her beside Miss Jolliffe.

Driving with almost reckless abandon to Hanover Square, he turned down George Street and pulled his horses to a stop in front of the imposing portico of St. George's Church. While he was helping his grandmother out of the carriage, Miss Jolliffe climbed out by herself, but before she could escape—or simply decide to wander off on her own—he caught her by the hand and virtually dragged her into the building, leaving his grandmother to follow.

He ordered the first person he met—a cleaning lady, as it turned out—to find the rector and inform him that his services were required immediately. Eyeing him askance, but not daring to contest his right to order her around, she scurried away to do his bidding.

"My lord," Miss Jolliffe said softly, but he did not allow her any protest.

"If you value your skin, do not say a word," he ordered. "I have a special license in my pocket, and when the rector comes, we are going to be married. Today. This hour. Do not even think about trying to dissuade me, because I have completely lost patience with you, and I am not prepared to be at all reasonable in this matter."

Miss Jolliffe's eyes grew round, and her cheeks whitened, but she made no further attempt to deflect him from his course.

The rector, when he appeared a few minutes later, apparently recognized that he was dealing with a man who had been pushed beyond his limits. He made no effort to protest the irregularity of the circumstances, at least not once Gabriel had shown him the special license.

The only recommendation the rector made was that his vicar be summoned to serve as the second witness since otherwise they would be forced to have the cleaning lady make her mark. Gabriel was agreeable to any suggestion, so long as the rector understood that no delays would be tolerated.

And as for Miss Jolliffe, he had a firm grip on her hand, and there was no way she could disappear on him again. Like the rector, she seemed at long last to have gotten it into her head that there would be no point in making the slightest attempt to thwart his wishes.

# 15

STANDING BESIDE Lord Sherington, her hand firmly held in his, Verity felt sure she must be dreaming. Unaccustomed to the church being empty, she found the silence deafening, and her ears strained to hear the first notes of the organist who was not there.

No candles had been lit, but the early morning sun burst exuberantly through the beautiful Venetian glass window above the altar, bathing their tiny wedding party in ethereal colors.

Tentatively she sneaked a peek at Lord Sherington's face, but his features were stern and unyielding. She felt guilty, knowing she had somehow—unwittingly, to be sure—made him feel he was obliged to marry her.

With all due pomp, the rector began intoning the words of the marriage service—words that would bind her henceforth to the man she had loved seemingly forever.

Lord Sherington doubtless felt constrained to marry her because he had been in a small part responsible, even if only obliquely, for her sister's decision to disown her. Knowing that, Verity admitted in her heart that she herself had a moral responsibility to release Lord Sherington from any obligation he might feel he had to her, which was undoubtedly what was behind this sudden determination to marry her.

"Marry in haste, repent in leisure," the old saying went. But what about marry in anger? For his lordship was indeed extremely angry with her and making no effort to hide it.

The preacher droned on, reading aloud familiar words

that seemed as incomprehensible as if they were in a foreign language, increasing Verity's feelings that this was all unreal.

But it was not. It was truly happening.

Lord Sherington could not be allowed to sacrifice himself in the name of honor. And she was the only one who could save him. All she had to do was simply refuse to give the proper response at the proper time. Because no matter how much she might desire it, this was a most improper marriage.

"Do you, Verity Anne Jolliffe, take this man to be your lawfully wedded husband?"

She tightened her lips, determined to remain silent and thereby do the right thing, but Lord Sherington hissed something at her, and turning to look up into his eyes, she knew she was every bit as wicked as her sister had accused her of being. She was shameless, and when all was said and done, she could not resist her own immodest desires.

Without meaning to, and fully intending not to, she blurted out, "I do," and with those two innocent seeming little words, she committed herself to Lord Sherington, for better and for worse . . . and for all time.

The rest of the ceremony continued without interruption, except when Lord Sherington was asked to produce the ring. He had not, it seemed, remembered to purchase one, but without a second's hesitation, he stripped the large signet ring from his own finger and placed it on hers. Then he curled her fingers around into her palm and held her fist tightly enclosed inside his own larger hand, as if determined to ensure that the ring would not slip from her finger and be lost.

"With this ring, I thee wed." His voice was deep, and the words were said with such vehemence, Verity imagined she felt the rafters of the church shaking from the force of his will . . . but perhaps it was merely her own heart skipping a beat.

A ridiculously short time later, the rector pronounced them man and wife, their signatures were recorded in the marriage register, Mrs. Everdon and the vicar signed as witnesses, and the deed was done.

Verity wanted very much to sit down. Her legs were shaking too much to support her properly, but Lord Sherington wrapped one arm around her shoulders and by leaning heavily on his strength, she managed to leave the church without disgracing herself.

Outside the business of the world went on as usual—servants hurried by on errands, peddlers called out their wares, horses trotted by pulling every kind of carriage and wagon. It seemed almost as if nothing earth-shattering had just occurred.

"Sherington, well met!" a round little dandy accosted them. "Ibbetson," Lord Sherbrooke said, his arm around Verity's shoulder beginning to lose some of its tension.

"And Miss Jolliffe, I believe." Lord Ibbetson tipped his hat to her.

"Not any longer," Lord Sherington corrected him. "May I present to you the Countess of Sherington?"

Verity looked at her new husband in astonishment. He was grinning broadly, all his earlier rage now completely vanished. He appeared, in fact, remarkably relaxed and at ease. He did not at all look like a man whose life had just been ruined by an intemperate marriage. If anything, he appeared to be rather pleased with himself.

"May I dare to hope," the little man began, his own smile now stretching from ear to ear, "that I have the honor—the truly inestimable, incalculable, *invaluable* honor—of being the first to wish you happy?"

"You are indeed the first," Lord Sherington said. "And it might interest you to know that I have not as yet gotten around to sending an announcement to the *Morning Post*."

"By Jove, but you are a true friend," Lord Ibbetson said, clapping Lord Sherington on the back. "And I promise my youngest daughter will remember you in her prayers from this day forth. I am forever in your debt, Sherington, and if ever I can repay the favor?" A sly look crossed his face. "I could, for example, easily ensure that your cousin will find the weather more to his liking on the Continent than in England. What say you?"

Lord Sherington nodded once, his expression enigmatic, and with a deep bow, the little dandy hurried away.

"Is that man a lunatic?," Mrs. Everdon asked. "Surely he should not be allowed to wander around loose with his mind so patently disordered."

"On the contrary, he is quite awake on all suits. The odds being currently offered in the clubs are three to one that I shall not, in the end, actually marry Miss Jolliffe. Now that my Lord Ibbetson has discovered I have already done the deed, he is on to a sure thing. Being no fool, he is undoubtedly hurrying to accept all bets before others learn of our nuptials. With very little effort on his part, he stands to double, perhaps even triple his modest fortune, thereby substantially increasing the amount he will be able to give his fourth daughter as a dowry."

Mrs. Everdon accepted his explanation with a nod, and allowed her grandson to assist her into his carriage—this time in a more decorous manner than earlier.

But Verity was staggered by the information Lord Sherington had casually tossed out. The gentlemen of the *ton* had been wagering that he would marry her? But if they—then that would mean—but how could—

His hands grasped her around the waist, and he started to assist her into the carriage, but she pulled back. "Did you intend to marry me, even before my sister—before—" Verity could not repeat the unkind and unjust accusations Petronella had made.

Looking down into her eyes, Lord Sherington smiled, and there was nothing of repentance in his smile. He more nearly resembled Lucifer, the fallen angel, than the archangel after whom he was named, and Verity could not completely repress a shiver.

"I have been carrying that special license around in my pocket for weeks, my dear, and since yours is the other name inscribed upon it, it would appear that I must have intended to marry you. If there have been any doubts on that score, there were none in my mind."

His logic appeared to be valid, but before she could formulate a reply, he began to move his hands on her waist, rubbing his thumbs against her ribs, caressing her back with his fingers. Awash in the sensations his hands were producing, Verity lost all ability to reason.

Bending over until his lips were almost touching hers, he said, "And do you know, my sweet, I have not the slightest interest in what your intentions were. We are married now, come what may, so I strongly advise you to study how best to please me."

His eyes gleamed so wickedly, Verity felt her bones melt, and she swayed toward him—wanting him so badly she was sure she would die if she could not hold him—touch him—kiss him—

But he resisted her efforts to get closer, and instead lifted her up and deposited her in his carriage. Climbing in beside her, he flicked the reins and drove to Grosvenor Square without, apparently, giving her another thought.

She had her wish—the wish she had scarcely dared to dream. She was now married to Lord Sherington. He was her husband, she was his wife, and they were bound to each other until the cold stillness of the grave should surround them.

But it all felt strange and unbelievable, because she *still* had not the slightest idea why he had wanted this . . . or if he had wanted this. . . .

Verity Rainsford, Lady Sherington. Even her new name sounded completely foreign to her ears and would take some getting used to.

But it was no more unfamiliar than the man sitting beside her. She had thought she knew Lord Sherington, but today's events had proven her wrong. He was a total stranger.

And he was her husband.

Now that Miss Jolliffe was firmly bound to him by the laws of God and the laws of man, Gabriel decided he did not need to rush matters any further. He had gained himself enough time to court his wife properly—to play the part of a gentleman and wait a week or two until she learned to love him before he made any effort to consummate their marriage.

Today he had, after all, quite deliberately not given

her any opportunity to refuse him, nor even time to collect her wits after he had rushed her off to the church. He felt not the slightest regret for what he had done, no matter that he knew full well he had acted disgracefully. But then he had never claimed to be a saint.

Besides, regrets were invariably futile, and he had every intention of being a good husband—patient, kind, and solicitous of his wife's feelings. She would have no cause to complain, even if she were the complaining sort, which thankfully she was not.

Their arrival at Sherington House in Grosvenor Square was enough to set the entire household in a tizzy. "You have found Miss Jolliffe, my lord," Exeter said, his face betraying quite unbutlerish emotion.

"The *former* Miss Jolliffe has indeed been found," Gabriel said, untying his wife's cloak and removing it from her shoulders. Handing it to the butler, he continued, "But as you can see from the ring that is about to fall off her finger, she is now the Countess of Sherington. We have just come from St. George's Church."

Servants appeared as if conjured up by magic, and the very house seemed to breathe a sigh of relief before Exeter remembered his duties and lined everyone up to welcome their new mistress.

She was going to make a superior countess, Gabriel decided, watching the former Miss Jolliffe win over his household staff. She had a regal bearing that would have done a duchess proud, while at the same time she was not the least bit high in the instep.

In a short space of time Mrs. Filbert had retreated to the nether regions to prepare a proper wedding breakfast, and Mrs. Richards had sent several of the maids up to see about preparing the countess's bedroom, which was separated from Gabriel's by a small sitting room.

"You will also need to prepare a bedroom for Mrs. Everdon, who is coming to live with us," he said, and his grandmother, who had been standing quietly beside him, began to protest rather vociferously.

"There is nothing you can say," he said flatly. "I have quite made up my mind, and I shall brook no arguments. I have no intention of letting my nearest relative starve in some little hovel in Marylebone. I shall naturally allow you to bring your serving woman with you if that is what is bothering you."

To his amazement, his grandmother got a mulish look about her eyes. Raising her voice, she snapped back at him, "I have run my own life since my husband died, and I do not intend to start obeying some man's orders at this late date."

"I will not tolerate such foolishness," he shouted, and everyone else in the entrance hall became so still, one could almost hear the dust motes in the air bumping against one another. "You are coming here to live, and that is that!" he bellowed, and the echo of his voice came back from somewhere far above.

"Not if you lock me in my room and feed me nothing but bread and water," his grandmother screeched up at him, her voice almost as loud as his had been.

Before he could do just that, a hand was laid on his arm, and a soft voice beside him said, "But of course you must live here. We have already discovered that we suit, you and I, and now that I am your granddaughter-in-law, it would be unconscionable of you to abandon me to the not-so-tender mercies of your grandson. I beg of you, Mrs. Everdon, do not desert me in my hour of need. It is quite obvious that if I am left alone with this ofttimes violent gentleman, he will bully me and boss me around without the slightest qualm. You would not wish such a fate on someone you have called friend, would you?"

By the time his wife finished her speech, his grandmother was chuckling, and even Gabriel was hard put not to smile. On impulse he kissed the top of his wife's head.

His grandmother met his glance, and for the first time he saw much of himself in her. He might have his features from his grandfather, but it was obvious some of his quick temper and stubbornness had come from this old woman. And perhaps also some of his same strength of will and determination to succeed.

"I will not even consider a room that does not receive the morning sun," she stipulated. "And if you have nothing that suits me, I shall return to my own home whether you wish it or not."

It was, of course, total capitulation, but his wife had the tact to pretend otherwise. In her usual calm voice, she said, "Mrs. Richards shall show us which rooms are available, and I do hope that one can be found that you will like."

As soon as the housekeeper led the two ladies away to settle the matter of bedrooms, Gabriel dispatched three of the footmen with several of the grooms to pack up his grandmother's possessions and transport everything, including her ancient serving woman, back to Grosvenor Square.

In a very short space of time, even if she remained obstinate, his grandmother would find herself settled under his roof. And he strongly doubted that she would be able to persuade any of his servants to go against his wishes and move her and her belongings back to her own house.

Feeling very satisfied with himself but a little uncomfortable that Miss Jolliffe—that is to say, the countess—was not by his side where she belonged, he went in search of his wife.

Verity did her best to suppress a smile. Her new grandmother-in-law was already instructing Mrs. Richards on the proper way to clean windows, and even though Mrs. Everdon had not yet agreed to stay, it was obvious to Verity that the old woman would, after a suitable interval, yield to her beloved grandson's wishes.

Some slight sound made Verity turn, and she saw Lord Sherington standing in the doorway motioning with his hand for her to follow him.

Thinking he wished to discover if his grandmother had agreed to stay, she silently tiptoed out of the room, leaving the other two women deep in their conversation.

"I am sure we will have no trouble persuading her to live here," she reassured him, but he appeared distracted, as if his mind were on other things. Catching her by the hand, he led her swiftly down the corridor and pulled her into a large room, shutting the door behind them.

Verity looked around and her heart gave a lurch. The bed was massive and seemed to dominate the room. Its furnishings were deep wine-colored satin, trimmed with black velvet, quite different from the light dimity ruffles she was used to.

Trying to avoid looking at the bed and all it implied, she glanced away and found herself looking instead at a red lacquered chiffonier with brass hinges and fastenings in the shape of dragons. It was exotic and in some way alarming, and Verity was both fascinated and repelled by it.

Above it on the wall hung a massive sword—a great curved blade with jewels embedded in the hilt. It was quite pagan-looking, not the least like the proper swords an Englishman carried, and she involuntarily caught her breath and jerked her eyes away.

Then she caught sight of a curious blue porcelain dog sitting on the floor by the window. He seemed to be laughing at her. Unlike the chest and the sword, she found the dog oddly comforting in a comical way.

And she needed all the reassurance she could get, because this was obviously Lord Sherington's bedroom . . . and Lord Sherington's bed . . . and he was her husband . . . and she had, less than an hour ago, given him the right to possess her body. . . .

He already possessed her soul.

As casually as if they had been married for years, Lord Sherington unbuttoned his jacket and tossed it carelessly onto a chair. "There are many things I am sure you are wishing to discuss with me in private."

Discuss? Seeing him in his shirt sleeves, Verity was so filled with longings to touch him, to hold him, to caress him, that she could not have carried on a rational conversation if her life had depended upon it.

He tugged at the knot in his cravat, but his neckcloth proved to be surprisingly recalcitrant. With an oath, he moved toward the bellpull, obviously intending to ring for his valet. Not wishing for anyone else to intrude on their privacy, Verity quickly forestalled him.

"Let me help you, my lord" she said, her voice so soft and breathless, she was not sure he could hear her.

But apparently he did, because after a moment's hesitation he changed direction and came over to where she was standing by the door. "Call me Gabriel," he said, catching her chin and tilting her face until she was forced to look into his eyes.

"Gabriel," she murmured obediently. The force of his will was overwhelming. Trapped by his glance, she was powerless to move. After what seemed an eternity, he released her chin and looked away. Raising her hands, she began struggling with nerveless fingers to undo his cravat.

Feeling her fingers delicately tugging at the cloth at his neck, Gabriel sucked in his breath, and all his good resolutions to leave her untouched dissolved into nothingness. Slowly and carefully so as not to startle her, he began to remove the pins from her hair, and soon the heavy weight of it fell down around her shoulders, and his hands of their own accord tangled themselves in the light brown curls.

Never before had he felt a woman's hair that was so soft. . . .

Intrigued, he felt his desire growing. What other secrets was she hiding? Reaching behind her, his hands deftly found and untied the ribbons holding her bodice together, and with a gentle whisper, her dress slid down the length of her body and settled itself on the floor.

Clad only in her chemise, she stood before him, her head slightly bowed and her cheeks tinted a delicate rose. Her skin was translucent, like the finest Chinese porcelain, and he could see the bluish veins beneath her skin.

His glance traveled the length of her graceful legs, then followed the sweet curves of her body, which were only partially concealed by her chemise, and he was shaken by the intensity of his desire to possess her.

With both hands, he cupped her face, then bent down and kissed her on her lips, which trembled sweetly beneath his.

Thoroughly bemused and captivated by the taste of her, he began to press kisses on her neck, and to slide his hands down her body. So drugged by desire was he, that it took him a moment to realize that she was whimpering.

Loosening his hold on her, he raised his head and looked into her eyes and saw that she was dazed, helpless before the strength of his passion. She reached out to him, as if to steady herself, and he realized the enormity of the wrong he had done her.

She had trusted him, and he had deliberately deceived her.

Her very submissiveness was a silent reproach, and unable to look at the trust in her eyes—the misplaced trust—he turned his back and said harshly, "You have nothing to fear from me. I realize I have forced you into this marriage."

Despite knowing he had wronged her unforgivably, he could not say the words that would undo what had been done. "If I were a gentleman, I would release you from your vows, but I am afraid I am not that altruistic. You are my wife now and forever, and I shall allow no man to come between us. I give you my word, however, that you will have time to accustom yourself to this marriage. I will not force you into my bed."

"Time?"

"As much time as you need."

"Always keeping in mind, of course, that you are not a patient man."

Her voice held laughter, which made his temper rise, and he could not keep the anger out of his own voice. "Do not push me, my dear wife, or I shall not be responsible for what happens. Leave this room at once, for you will not be offered a second chance."

There was a light touch on his shoulder. "And if I choose to stay?" she asked.

His shoulder burned beneath her hand, and he said, "You cannot wish to stay."

"I have promised never to lie to you," she pointed out simply, and her openness and honesty made him feel his own guilt all the more.

Thankful that she could not see his face, he said, "But I have deliberately and willfully misled you."

She did not make a reply, but he felt the room grow cold with her unhappiness—unhappiness that he had caused her.

"You asked once what I wanted from you, and I refused to tell you." His shame was too great for him to go on.

Her courage, however, was greater than his, and she asked a second time, "What is it you want from me?"

She was too close—it would have been so easy just to turn and wrap his arms around her and say something—anything—that would allow him to take what she was offering so willingly. But he could no longer deceive her, whether by his words or his silence.

"The day I picked you up at your father's house, I made up my mind that you had all the attributes I was looking for in a wife."

"You are mocking me, my lord."

He wanted very much for her to call him Gabriel again, but he had forfeited the right to demand anything from her. "I am quite serious. Hearing your views on love, I cold-heartedly decided to make you fall in love with me so that I could have a wife who would not try to change me."

"I will never try to change you—" she started to say, sliding her arms around his waist and pressing herself against his back.

Desperately Gabriel fought to resist the temptation to ignore his conscience—to simply take what he wanted. "But I wish to change—just tell me what kind of husband you want, and I will be that man. I will do anything in my power to make you love me."

"Make me? *Make* me?" she questioned, and the laughter was back in her voice.

He groaned. "Forgive me. I am . . . accustomed to having my own way." It was difficult, but he forced the words out. "It will not be easy for me to learn patience, but I am determined to give you the time you need. And I hope that . . . that someday you will find it in your heart to forgive me . . . and to love me."

"I forgive you now, and as for loving you, I am afraid I have not been completely honest, either," she said.

Without releasing him, she ducked under his arm and slid around until she was in front of him, hugging him with surprising strength. "There is something I neglected to tell you."

Without waiting for his brain to issue an order, his arms went around her, and he felt as if he had come home at last.

"I did not lie precisely," she said, her face buried shyly in his chest, "but I definitely did not tell you the whole truth. You see, I fell hopelessly in love with you the first day we met."

Overcome by emotion, he could not speak for a long while. Finally he managed to ask, "Why did you not tell me?"

"That would have been rather presumptuous of me, would it not?" she said, her voice betraying her own doubts. "After all, I am a rather plain spinster who did not take."

Gabriel laughed, and the sound filled the room. "You have been completely misinformed, my love. I have traveled the world around, and you are the most beautiful woman I have ever seen in my life."

Clearly astounded at his words, she left off hiding her face and looked up at him.

"And in case it has slipped your mind," he said, giving her a light kiss on the forehead, "you gave up being a spinster this very morning when you said the vows that made you my wife."

Scooping her up in his arms, he carried her over to the bed and gently laid her down. His eyes never leaving hers, he began to unbutton his shirt. "And as for thinking you did not take, I shall do my best to alleviate any doubts you may have on that score. You are quite thoroughly 'taken,' my love, so you had better accustom yourself to that idea."

The shadows were deepening in the room, and his wife lay sleeping in his arms. Gabriel had never in his life felt so deeply contented. He had searched the world over without knowing what he was looking for; he had hungered without knowing what would satisfy his craving.

And now, for the first time in his life, he felt replete. Completely and totally at peace with the world.

All his life he had struggled to be free of the control of other people. And now he had given this woman absolute, total power over his life—over himself.

And yet he felt no fear. Almost as if by making himself vulnerable, he had made himself even stronger.

Was this love? This desire to please rather than to be pleased? The emptiness when she was away from him and this feeling of completeness when she was beside him?

She would know. "Verity," he whispered, and she stirred in his arm, snuggling even closer to him.

Even her name meant truth. He would ask her, and she would tell him, and he could believe her, for she had promised never to lie to him. And he trusted her as he had never trusted anyone before.

He wished she would wake up, but she continued to sleep as one exhausted, which was hardly surprising considering that as innocent and inexperienced as she had been, her passion had matched his own.

She needed to rest; he needed to talk to her.

He was not a patient man.

Savoring every moment, he began kissing her awake, sliding his hands over her soft curves, stroking and caressing her, and delighting in the way she moved and stretched beneath his touch.

She was drowsy and only half awake at first, then looking up at him, her eyes widened and filled with joy, like a child who has received a most wondrous present.

As if he were the most wonderful man in the world.

She was the most wonderful, the most beautiful, the most perfect woman in the world. And she was his.

"I love you," he said.